I0645740

Masters of Haven

TOO CLOSE

LIIA ANN WHITE

Too Close
ISBN # 978-1-80250-553-5
©Copyright Liia Ann White 2023
Cover Art by Kelly Martin ©Copyright July 2023
Interior text design by Claire Siemaszkiewicz
Totally Bound Publishing

TOO CLOSE

Dedication

This one's for Dani. This book would literally not have happened without you.
Thank you for being my constant sounding board and guiding light. I cherish your friendship and wise advice more than you'll ever know.

Prologue

Everything hurts. God, it hurts so much.

Belle became more aware of her body, the agonising ache that pulsed through her every muscle, joint and nerve ending. Managing to open her eyes, her left one throbbing, she blinked and tried to clear her blurred vision. She stared at the white ceiling tiles, then looked down to a dark beige curtain that surrounded her bed…a hospital bed.

How the hell did I end up in hospital?

Searching her memory, she came up with nothing but darkness. Belle tried to sit up, letting out a pained groan as a shot of pure agony tore up her arm when she applied pressure to it. A wave of nausea washed over her, heating her chilled skin and causing a sheen of sweat to erupt over her exposed flesh. She had never felt this bad in her entire life, like she'd gone through a woodchipper.

Everything was battered and bruised, even her teeth.

Is that even possible?

Panic began to overwhelm Belle as she struggled to breathe through the pain. The walls closed in on her. The blanket around her legs was suddenly too heavy. At the right moment, an older woman pushed the curtain aside and entered Belle's vicinity. With a kind smile on her face, she looked Belle over and moved to stand at the head of the bed.

"You're awake," she said in a soothing hushed tone. "How are you feeling?"

Belle blinked, unable to form the words she wanted to say. *I'm in agony. What happened? Why am I here?*

The nurse reached beside Belle and placed a small device in Belle's hand before pressing the button on the top.

"This will help."

A sharp sting poked the back of Belle's hand and shot up her vein through her arm to her shoulder, where it radiated through her chest and began to heat her entire body. It resulted in an unfamiliar but not entirely unpleasant tingling sensation. Within seconds, the constant pulse of agony had begun to dull to a roar of pain. Sighing in relief, Belle clenched her hand around the painkiller pump.

"It's a fentanyl pump. Press it when you need to," the nurse said, flashing her another kind smile. "There's a limit to how much it will release, so you can't overdose. But you're in a bad way. You need the pain relief. No being brave on my watch."

In a bad way.

That was one way to put it. Pressing the button again, Belle noted the now-familiar sting as it ran its course through her body before she finally relaxed. The roaring pain turned into a dull ache that she could feel but no longer cared about. The pain receptors in her brain had been effectively turned off and Belle managed to gather her thoughts again and focus on her surroundings.

"I'll get the doctor. He wants to speak with you. Press the call button if you need anything." The nurse wrapped the cord for the remote around the frame of the bed so it was within her reach.

Belle's "Thanks" came out garbled and croaky, since she was unable to open her jaw properly. A shot of searing pain tore through her face and neck when she tried to speak again. Instead, she relaxed into the bed and waited. Lying there, she noted her vision was still blurred and her depth perception seemed to be off. Closing her left eye, she noted it was fine, but when she closed her right eye, she was unable to see a thing.

Thinking back, Belle tried to focus on what had happened, what had landed her in the hospital and left her in such a state. Then she remembered the incident with her boyfriend, Bryce. She'd discovered him fucking his secretary at his office. *Total cliché.* Belle had left in a fury and gone home...then he'd broken in when she'd refused to open the door for him. Filled with rage, he'd stalked towards her, backhanded her and grabbed her by the throat.

Fuck. He'd beaten her. *Did he do all this to me?*

Belle remembered their confrontation... The way his face had contorted into absolute rage as he tightened his hold on her throat, cutting off her air before he smashed her head against the wall.

"You think you can leave me? Who the fuck do you think you are?"

Face red, he'd sneered at her, his enormous, muscular body looming over her. She'd never seen him angry before and it was truly terrifying.

Without warning, one fist had hit her right in the diaphragm, forcing the air from her lungs in one painful blow. She'd gasped and tried to squirm out of his grasp, lashing out at him, scratching his arms. He'd called her names... *"Worthless, useless piece of shit, fucking bitch, fucking cunt..."* Then he had slammed her head against the wall again and... There was nothing. No more memories.

The memory of what had happened next was gone from her mind. It was terrifying.

She took a chance and looked at her body, wondering what injuries lay beneath the white hospital blanket. Her arm, draped over the blanket, was in a cast. The bastard had broken her fucking arm.

The curtain moved and a tall, broad man wearing a button-down shirt and white lab coat entered the vicinity and introduced himself. Belle instinctively recoiled at the sight of the large man and tried to bury herself in the bed. He stilled and offered her a smile. The expression in his eyes said she looked as bad as she felt.

"What happened?" she asked through her scratchy throat.

"We were hoping you could tell us. What do you remember?"

"My boyfriend... He attacked me, but...I don't remember much."

Why the hell couldn't she open her mouth properly? Could he even understand what she was saying?

"I understand this must be scary, but there are some police officers here to discuss the incident with you. They have a few questions."

Is that what they call a big man beating the living shit out of a woman? An incident?

"You have a concussion — memory loss is a common side effect. But I do believe your memories will return in due course." His kind eyes never left hers. "You've sustained some serious injuries, Miss Winters. You're going to be here for a few days. We've contacted your mother, as she was your emergency contact on our system. She's waiting outside."

Belle's heart sank. *Mother is here? Fuck.* She hadn't been in a hospital since she'd had surgery at sixteen. Of course her mother was still listed as her emergency contact despite their volatile and tense relationship.

"My phone," she rasped. "My friends are my emergency contacts."

The nurse reached for her phone from the cabinet beside the bed, handing it to Belle. She unlocked it and found both Larissa's and Amara's phone numbers and asked the nurse to call them.

"Is there anyone else we can call?"

Belle winced the second she shook her head. She had nobody else in her life. Not anymore.

"What are my injuries?" Her words slurred as a cloud of fatigue enveloped her brain, the adrenaline and shock beginning to wear off.

The doctor frowned at the chart. "I mentioned the concussion. You also have whiplash, a bruised larynx, a slight fracture in the left side of your jaw, both bones in your left forearm are broken, a couple of cracked ribs and a severely sprained ankle. You have an abundance of bruising on your ribs and abdomen as well as ten stitches in the back of your head that you need to remain mindful of."

Fuck. That was quite a list.

"It appears you put up quite the fight. A lot of your injuries are defensive."

"Good. I'd hate to think I wussed out and huddled in the corner."

He offered her one more sympathetic smile before leaving. "I'll send the officers in, then you get some rest."

A female officer entered, asking for a recount of the events. Belle gave her all the information she'd remembered so far, including Bryce's details and possible whereabouts. The coward had apparently called the ambulance for Belle then taken off, leaving her unconscious on her living room floor.

The nurse returned, ordering Belle to press the painkiller pump button again.

"Don't be a hero," she stated before leaving.

Finally alone and desperate to get some pressure off her lower back, Belle adjusted the bed and bent her right knee, digging her heel into the mattress to roll onto her side.

She moaned in pain just as her mother entered the room, looking as closed off as the last time Belle had seen her. There was not a single sign of worry on her pretty face. No love in her eyes. Not even any pity.

"What did you do?"

Everything in Belle froze and she forced herself to press the painkiller button again, desperate for anything to stop her from feeling the emotions that swirled inside her.

"Bryce beat the shit out of me," Belle said, her words garbled, her mouth not opening anywhere near enough for her to be properly understood.

"Bryce," was all Mother said before she pursed her lips.

Mother continued to stand at the end of the bed, not making a single move to comfort her only child who was in visible pain.

"I knew you had bad taste in men, but this takes the cake."

"Seriously?" Belle couldn't hide her hurt. "You're going to blame me for this?"

"If you choose to date the wrong type of man, you have to expect things like this will happen."

Who the fuck says something like that?

"I have offered time and time again to set you up with the right kind of man. A man who will take care of you financially, so you don't have to work in that menial job anymore."

Belle rolled her eyes despite the pain it elicited. That menial job was a very successful landscaping business that Belle had built from the ground up. Her parents had never approved of her landscaping career. Manual labour was beneath them, and Mother wanted nothing more than for Belle to retire and become a socialite like she was herself.

"Now is not the time to discuss this."

"Maybe now that this has happened, you'll listen to me," Mother said. "I only want what is best for you."

But she didn't. Mother wanted what was best for *her*. Belle couldn't have been any more different from her parents. She didn't want to live a shallow and empty life like they did. She wanted a life with meaning, a life with love.

"You need to give up on finding love, Belle," Mother all but sneered. "Love doesn't exist. You're a fool for thinking otherwise."

That was it. The line she'd been fed her entire life. And right now was not the time she needed to hear it.

"Get out."

"Excuse me?" Mother snapped, her elegantly shaped brows moving into a frown.

"Get out." Belle tried to yell but it came out a rasp. "I don't want you here."

"Here we go. Time to have another tantrum, is it?"

All her life, Belle's parents had referred to her shows of emotions as tantrums.

"I don't want to see you again." Belle kept her calm despite her heart breaking in two.

Her mother didn't love her. Neither did her father. They were incapable of it. All they'd ever done was criticise everything Belle had done with her life, and she was finished with it.

"Get out before I call for security."

Mother gave one last assessing gaze, looking down her nose at Belle. "You're pathetic," she snarled before turning to leave the room.

Numb, Belle sank against the bed and tried to allow her brain to process what had just happened. But she couldn't. Then her two best friends arrived. One look at each of them was all it took. Belle gave in to the tears burning her eyes and lost her shit, letting out a broken sob as she cried like a lost little girl. Her friends wrapped her up in warm hugs, allowing her to cry without asking questions.

All of her fear, frustration, anger and sadness came out in tears that stained her cheeks. Once finished, she felt nothing but pure disappointment. She'd been stupid. She'd trusted the wrong man and he'd hurt her. All because she was so desperate for love. She'd spent her entire life wanting to belong.

What a fucking idiot.

Chapter One

Two years later

Belle was in a rut. For weeks—months—she'd had bad scene after bad scene. Everything was lacklustre, awash in a dusting of grey No emotions were involved, and the bare minimum of sexual attraction was present with each scene. It wasn't enough for her to truly enjoy herself. And she couldn't seem to drag herself out of the pit she'd been sliding into. Right now, she was at the bottom, unable to see the light. It was grim.

Trying to concentrate on the Dom working on her, she focussed on the feeling of the light flogger working its way up and down her back. He was waking her skin, warming her up, but it wasn't having the desired effect on her. Her mind wandered. She wasn't present. It wasn't fair to either of them.

All she'd wanted for tonight was to disappear into that submissive headspace she craved. The one that helped her slip away from the real world and become enveloped in pure sensation, losing her worries. But the

Dom she'd chosen tonight wasn't hard enough. He was a soft Dom—despite him saying otherwise. He didn't command her submission, not like others had.

Belle had known she wasn't physically attracted to the man, despite him being attractive, but he'd said he was a firm and strict Dom. Perhaps he was to other women—women who didn't have a stubborn independent streak a mile long like she did. But for Belle, he wasn't hard enough. Now she couldn't understand why she'd agreed to play with him. She was probably self-sabotaging again. *My psych will be thrilled with this revelation*, Belle thought sarcastically.

Closing her eyes, she let out a slow, controlled breath through pursed lips. *Just focus,* she told herself. She tried to just feel. *Whack. Whack. Whack.* The strands of leather hit her bare skin, tempting, yet not capturing her attention. Shutting her mind off, Belle tried to lose herself, to concentrate on him, but…just couldn't… There was not a single sign of arousal or submission in her.

God dammit.

Moving to stand before her, the Dom shoved a hand into her hair and closed it in a fist, tilting her head back until she looked at him. Even that did nothing for her. Not a damn thing. Most of the time, a simple tug on her hair was enough to make Belle want to melt. But, with this man, it elicited nothing. He was too inexperienced.

His gaze softened when he caught the disappointment in her eyes.

"You're not into this at all, are you?" he asked, his own disappointment evident.

"I'm sorry," Belle mumbled.

Absolutely pathetic. Worthless.

Releasing her hair, he began to undo the restraints. Belle slipped on her top after he handed it to her and followed him out of the scene area.

"We'll try it again, another time," he offered before leaving.

Belle knew better. There would be no other time. She was running out of single Doms to play with, especially the hard-arses that she was usually attracted to. Her choice to play with a man once or twice before moving on was made out of necessity, but it wasn't one she enjoyed. Not anymore, at least.

Deep down, Belle wanted a man to call her own. A Dom to claim her. Someone to care for her, someone she could care for. Someone she could love. She wanted what her friends had. But to find that, she would have to open herself up. That wasn't her strong suit. She didn't know how to do it anymore. Belle was a closed book to men. A tome sealed shut.

And now she was failing as a submissive. She visited Haven, her favourite BDSM club, each week because it gave her a safe space to explore her kinks. Each member was vetted and had a mutual goal — exploration and pleasure. It was the one place she could find experienced Doms. They were very difficult to locate in the vanilla world.

Unfortunately, Haven's community was small and close-knit. Most of the members knew of the incident she'd had with Bryce. They had cut him out of the community as a whole and blacklisted him. They'd had her back. But a lot of them still looked at Belle as that broken woman who'd had a panic attack the first time that she had tried to scene afterwards. Even new members seemed to know of her and what had happened. It was humiliating. The BDSM community in Perth was too small sometimes.

Soon, word would get out that she could no longer perform as a submissive and her reputation would be ruined. Perhaps it was time for a break. Time to take a step back and focus on other aspects of her life for a while.

A familiar, deep voice called her name. She turned to find her friend and ex-Dom Ayden striding towards her in all his charming, handsome, powerful glory. The aura of dominance about him meant he never went unnoticed. The eyes of each available submissive nearby were drawn to him. The man was considered a commodity in the club. And Belle had always understood why.

Sighing, she forced a smile when she looked up at him, his large body towering over her. If only things had worked out between them, she wouldn't be in her current predicament. They'd seen each other for a couple of months last year, but their spark had flamed out. Since their mutual separation, Ayden had become one of her closest friends. It had happened slowly, but he had crawled beneath her skin and now she couldn't get rid of him. Not that she'd want to. Even if he did tease and irritate her from time to time.

"What happened to your scene?" he asked.

Belle shook her head, the pit in her gut becoming even deeper. "It wasn't happening. I'm going to say bye to the others and head home."

Ayden gave her a look. That irritating Dom look that said they would discuss her issues later, whether she liked it or not. He tugged at the silver-trimmed dungeon monitor vest he wore and looked around the room.

"I'm almost done with my DM shift. Go sit with the others and I'll be there in a few minutes."

She knew better than to argue with him when he was in Dom mode. Within the club's walls, she had to show him the same respect she would any other Dominant. Outside, she didn't listen to him. She taunted and teased him as she did her other friends. As a Master of Haven, Ayden had the right to hand her off to other Dominants for punishment or reprimand. He had the further right to order her around because Belle was considered under his protection. He had never once taken advantage of the power she'd given him. It was probably the reason she listened to him.

Heading for the bar with her head held high, Belle ordered herself a Dr Pepper and glanced around the main club room while waiting. Amara soon approached, looking quite the sight. Amusement bubbled inside Belle. Dark-brown hair messed, lips swollen, cheeks pink, eyes all glassy — Amara appeared to have been thoroughly used. Belle couldn't help but feel the pang of envy that struck her right in the chest.

Amara had met her Dom and fiancé Sullivan last year. The man had completed her in ways Belle couldn't fathom. Since then, Amara had returned to her old self. Positive, fun-loving and, above all else, happy. That was all Belle wanted out of life — happiness. She couldn't remember what it felt like to be happy anymore.

With both of her friends now partnered up, Belle was becoming sick of feeling like the third wheel when she visited one of their houses. She'd always been the odd one out. She should have been used to it. With her family, with the few friends she had growing up and now again. And it sucked.

Mentally shaking her head, Belle pushed away the negative thoughts and smiled at her friend and confidante. "Don't you look like you just got thoroughly fucked?"

"Sullivan used a damn spanking bench. I thought it was going to be a quick scene, but he ended up taking me right there in front of everyone."

Belle laughed. "And you loved every second of it."

"I really did." The other woman grinned.

She smiled at her friend, genuinely happy to see how far the other woman had come in recent months. Amara had had a rough go of it over the previous couple of years. Then she had met Sullivan and gained her confidence back. Last year she would never have partaken in a public scene—now she couldn't get enough of them.

"Are you doing anything else tonight?"

Everybody knew that Sullivan was insatiable when it came to Amara. The man practically walked around in a constant state of arousal around his fiancée.

"He threatened to take me upstairs once he's had a break." She shuddered. "I just want to go home. I'm wrecked. The bastard already beat on me at home earlier today."

"Oh, please, you love it."

Amara was a submissive and masochist. Having Sullivan "beat" her was one of her favourite things. While Belle used to enjoy a moderate amount of pain in her kink play, she could never endure what Amara did.

The other woman got that dreamy look in her eyes, the one caused by love. "I do."

That damn pang of envy returned. Belle took a sip of her Dr Pepper and allowed the fizz to calm her churning stomach.

"I thought you were playing," Amara said with the slightest hint of worry in her tone.

"I couldn't get into it," she replied, trying to ignore that familiar wave of shame and disappointment that threatened to take over and ruin her mood. "I don't know what's wrong with me."

"Oh, sweetie." Amara rested a gentle hand on Belle's arm. "There's nothing wrong with you. You're tired and depressed. Don't even try to deny it."

"You know you living with Sullivan has become a real pain in my ass, don't you? I used to be able to hide my depression and anxiety from you."

Sullivan lived with clinical depression. Belle had post-traumatic stress disorder which often resulted in bouts of depression and anxiety, even panic attacks. Two years after the incident, she was still trying to get used to the mood swings and panic attacks, still trying to recognise her triggers.

Before, she'd been able to hide her symptoms from her friends, plaster that fake smile on her face and pretend everything was okay while she was dying on the inside. But now that Amara lived with Sullivan, she recognised the signs far easier and pointed out whenever Belle was depressed or anxious. And Amara was right. Belle was depressed.

"Well, you can't hide anything from me now, so you just have to deal with it." Amara, the brat, stuck her tongue out and grabbed her drinks off the bar top. "Come on, let's join the others."

* * * *

Sitting on a black leather lounge by herself, Belle looked to the two happy couples who were her closest friends and smiled despite her sadness. Amara was perched on Sullivan's lap, as usual, while Larissa knelt on the floor between her husband Agin's legs, her head resting on his thigh in a sign of comfort. Belle became hyperaware of her loneliness as the feeling of longing grew inside her. That was what she wanted. To have the look of contentment that all of her friends had.

All her life, Belle had simply wanted to belong. Her parents had made sure she knew she never belonged at home. She'd fumbled through life, seeking validation in all the wrong places, until she'd met Larissa and Amara. They were the first true friends she'd ever had. They had taken her in, treated her like family from the beginning of their tentative friendship. Now they were her sisters. She couldn't imagine life without them. But that key piece was still missing—a partner to call her own.

But that was something she would never have. After all, what man would choose a thirty-year-old with a lifetime of trust issues and trauma? No sane man.

The couch dipped beside her as Ayden sat and slung one arm over the back of the lounge. Smiling at him despite the darkness weighing on her soul, Belle looked at his handsome face. It truly was a shame there was no sexual chemistry between the two of them anymore. He was the first man since Bryce that she'd began to trust. The one she'd had a real spark with.

"So, sweetness." He used her pet name on purpose. "Are you really going to give up and go home?"

She fought the urge to roll her eyes as she looked away from him. While Ayden had men and women begging—sometimes literally—to play with him, Belle didn't have that luxury. The men willing to play with her now were few and far between. She was pretty enough and experienced, but her height turned a lot of men off. At five feet ten inches, she was far taller than most women, even a lot of men. Most Doms preferred their women short, round and soft, not tall and toned like Belle. Thanks to genetics and her physical job, she would never be soft and round like she'd always wanted to be. She'd longed for a small, feminine figure.

"I'm going to finish my drink in peace then head home," she told him in no uncertain terms.

As Belle looked around at the scenes nearby, one in particular caught her attention. A big Dom, tall, muscular and intimidating—exactly her type—had a submissive strapped to a bondage table. With a plug in her butt and a vibrator in her pussy, the woman writhed against restraints as the big man ravaged her breasts with his hands and mouth.

He pulled away and stood over the women and Belle noticed it was Master Ambrose, the latest member to be voted in as Master by Haven's members. Though he was a close friend of Ayden's, she hadn't met him yet. She'd avoided him based on his size. Big men scared her now. Though she'd always been attracted to big, strong men, they now intimidated her and made her panic. All because of Bryce. The one reason she wasn't scared by her large male friends was because there was no sexual interest from them.

Master Ambrose had a reputation of being strict and firm yet fair. He was very popular amongst the female submissives. All the women she'd spoken to who had played with him said he was sweet yet stern, strong and caring. He also doled out punishments to misbehaving submissives. He was the kind of Dom Belle would have once drooled over and sought out.

But he wasn't the sort of man she looked for any longer. She preferred shorter men, ones who wouldn't be able to physically overpower her quite so easily as a big man would.

The man moved like a predator—large and graceful—down the woman's body until his mouth came down on her most intimate area. Belle felt herself becoming aroused for the first time in weeks as she watched, mesmerised by the scene. The woman cried out in pleasure and pulled against the restraints, her hips bucking against his face while he pinned her down with strong, knowledgeable hands. He looked up and said something to the submissive that had her eyes bulging, her head shaking.

What Belle wouldn't give to be that woman. The man looked like he knew how to work a woman into a frenzy.

Another man stepped into Belle's line of vision, speaking down to the submissive. He must have been the other woman's Dom. It wasn't uncommon for Doms to ask one of the Masters to step in a dish out a punishment or do a specific kink for their submissive if they weren't comfortable doing it. It required an extra layer of trust in the relationship. Just one more thing for Belle to envy.

After removing the vibrator, Master Ambrose replaced it with his fingers, fucking her until she threw her head back on a cry, her entire body shaking as she came forcefully. *Jesus fuck*. Belle's thighs clenched this time, but she couldn't tear her gaze from the scene. The woman lay on her back, completely sated, her chest heaving with strained breaths. But Master Ambrose wasn't done. He continued his movements and coaxed another orgasm from the woman. This one had her screaming loud enough that the sound travelled to Belle's ears and sent a shudder down her spine.

Belle's skin tingled, her clit throbbing as she watched the aftermath of the scene. The Dom and Master undid the restraints, both murmuring to the woman before Master Ambrose said something to the other Dom. He packed his things away, moving with unnerving confidence. Belle hadn't seen anything like it. He was beautiful and enticing — hot as fuck.

"I see Master Ambrose caught your attention," Ayden said, his smirk evident in his tone.

Belle startled, having forgotten he was beside her. Embarrassment washed over Belle as she realised that she'd been caught watching like a voyeur. Larissa smirked as well. Narrowing her eyes at her friend, she hoped that nobody had caught onto her arousal.

"He would love to scene with you if you want me to ask."

"No," Belle snapped. She would not do a scene with that man. He was too big, too dominant, too everything she was looking for. And far, far too intimidating.

"Did you just roll your eyes at me?" Ayden narrowed his gaze as he looked down at her.

"I am perfectly capable of setting up my own scenes. I don't need you playing matchmaker all the time."

The second Larissa and Amara's jaws dropped, she realised what she'd done. She'd just snapped at a Dom inside of Haven, without a good reason. A Master no less. That was a serious no-no.

Shit.

"You know what you need? You need to be reminded of your place here."

Belle tensed with fear. *Crap. Shit.* Looking at him, she shook her head. "No. I really don't. Please. I'm sorry, Sir. I'm just tired and… I forgot where we were."

She recognised the set of his jaw, that piercing look in his blue eyes, and sighed. She was doomed no matter how hard she grovelled. Tears of shame and disappointment burned her eyes.

"Fuck," she muttered.

"Fuck indeed, little sub." He stood and pulled her with him. "Come. You're getting a punishment."

Receiving sympathetic looks from her girlfriends and smirks from the Doms, she allowed Ayden—Master Ayden—to pull her away. Ayden was a sadist. He loved spanking unruly, misbehaved submissives. She'd been on the receiving end of it once and had hated every single second of it.

"I'm sorry I snapped at you, Sir," she said meekly while trying to blink away tears that blurred her vision.

"Don't cry. Only babies cry. Are you a baby?" She had learned from a very young age that crying got her nowhere. She saved her tears for moments when she was alone.

"You will be," was all he said.

Belle did her best to appear the good submissive. Once upon a time, she'd been a brat, but Bryce had trained that out of her, beating her down until she no longer found it fun to mouth off. The last time she had acted the brat, he'd restrained her, gagged her and set her on the couch, then left her for two hours while he watched a movie in the other room. It had left her feeling so alone, she'd cried until she felt sick.

Now Belle knew that was abuse. No good Dom would ever do that to a submissive. Especially one with abandonment issues. But at the time she'd been blindsided by what she thought was love. So now she obeyed without question. Because that was what Doms wanted.

Ayden led her through the main room towards the scene area where Master Ambrose had been. When he stopped, her heart dropped into her gut. He'd led her straight to Master Ambrose.

Fuck.

Masters and Mistresses of Haven were all expected to undertake basic tasks when it came to submissives and Dominants alike, but certain Masters had specific jobs. Agin was in charge of the beginner training programme for Doms, Sullivan was in charge of new male Dominants, Mistress Ashely the females, Ayden was in charge of helping new and unattached submissives and Master Harvey, the sadist, was the enforcer of all submissives. But now Master Ambrose had taken over some tasks as enforcer to the single females. And tonight, that included Belle.

Looking up to Master Ambrose, Belle had to crane her neck to meet his eyes. He was taller than she'd realised — about six feet five inches, she guessed. And built? The man was deliciously broad, had a chest she wanted to run her hands over, muscled shoulders she wanted to hang off, have her legs draped over. Her mouth watered as she looked him up and down, noting the fit of his black button-down, the way his dark jeans clung to powerful thighs. He was attractive, but more than that, he had a build that would make her feel feminine.

"Master Ambrose," Ayden said. "I have a disrespectful little submissive for you to punish, if you're up for it."

He reached back to grab her arm just hard enough to remind her she had no say in what happened to her, unless she used her safe word.

"This one mouthed off to me, forgetting her place in the hierarchy. She needs a reminder of where she stands."

Belle sucked in a breath and tried to ignore the sudden tightness in her chest. She deserved to be punished. She'd done the wrong thing in front of others. But all she wanted right now was to go home, curl up on her couch and cry herself to sleep.

Eyes shimmering in the dim lighting like two dark emeralds, Master Ambrose looked at her. Belle suddenly felt very, very small.

"It would be my pleasure, Master Ayden."

His voice was smooth, rich and deep, wrapping around Belle's exposed skin, enveloping her in a satisfying warmth. For a moment, she imagined what it would be like to have him whisper sweet nothings in her ear, to hear him murmur dirty words while he did unspeakable things to her. Ordered her to come.

Arousal trickled down her inner thighs when he shot her a half smile. How could she be so turned on by the simple sound of his voice?

He continued to watch her, assessing her with that deep green gaze. While he wasn't classically handsome, he was drop-dead sexy. His light brown hair fell over his forehead, cut just long enough for a woman to tangle her fingers in. His jaw was chiselled to perfection, his full pink lips appeared soft but it was his eyes that transfixed her. Two pools of pure forest-green held so much strength that they made her want to melt into a puddle at his feet.

Yes, he scared her. How on earth could she be attracted to yet fearful of a man at the same time? She really was broken.

"Give us a moment, sweetness." Ayden's voice broke through the silence before he and Master Ambrose stepped away.

Belle stood alone, hugging herself as tears of fear and disappointment in herself burned her eyes. It was just another reminder she was alone, in every sense of the word. God, when had she become so negative and needy? She was meant to be a strong, independent woman. She should be happy to be alone and not need a man. But she wasn't like that deep down.

Biting her lip to distract herself from the emotional turmoil, she forced the tears away. Belle would not cry. She didn't cry in front of others. She'd never cried during a scene. Not even during a spanking. She refused to cry in front of a stranger.

"Belle." Ayden tipped her chin up with a finger. "You understand why I'm doing this?"

Her bottom lip quivered as she nodded. "I'm sorry, Sir."

"I know you are," he said. "But we have rules for a reason."

He pressed a gentle kiss to her forehead. "This will be good for you."

Yeah, right.

"Come on, little sub," Master Ambrose said after Ayden left. "Let's have a chat."

"But..." She didn't want to talk. She wanted to get her punishment done so she could leave.

Judging by the hard stare he gave her, there would be no arguing with Master Ambrose. Closing her mouth, Belle obeyed and tried to ignore the sinking feeling in her stomach. She followed him to one of the quieter sitting areas near the recovery corner, specifically designed for people to negotiate in.

Seated beside Master Ambrose, Belle couldn't hide her surprise when he pressed his thigh against hers and slung one arm over the back of the lounge, behind her. He gripped at her chin with his free hand, firm but not rough, and forced her to look at him. Those gorgeous eyes held a hint of a smile despite his hard expression.

Arousal continued to flutter through her veins at his proximity. Her skin heated at the burning tears returning to her eyes. Belle fought the urge to crawl into his lap and cry. He was not the comforting sort of Dom, based on what she'd heard. Regardless, she suddenly couldn't wait to be spanked by this man. This Master.

Chapter Two

Ambrose ran his thumb along the gorgeous submissive's chin, watching while she fought the urge to speak. How had he never met her before? Ayden had mentioned her time and time again, yet hadn't introduced the two of them. Ambrose had to wonder if his friend was saving her for himself. While Ayden had assured him the two of them were strictly platonic, Ambrose had to wonder. After all, why else would he have not met Belle yet?

She was so soft and sweet in her submission. Mouth-watering in her genuine appeal. Yet beneath that inherent vulnerability that came with being submissive, there was a strong sense of self-confidence about her. Belle appeared to be a woman who knew herself and, no doubt, what she wanted. How could any man resist that? Self-assurance had always been a turn-on for Ambrose.

This cute woman had been having a rough time, according to Ayden. Lacklustre scenes, purposely choosing soft Doms, inexperienced ones that would not push her limits. Ones she would never submit to. To Ambrose, that said she was punishing herself for some reason. Ayden agreed and hadn't been able to figure out why. Self-sabotage was common in some people, although Ambrose had never understood it himself.

He had asked if she was a brat—if she was likely to act out during the punishment Ayden had allocated. But the other man assured him she wouldn't. That had Ambrose feeling relieved. Once upon a time, he'd loved bratty behaviour and back talk—he had found it endearing, charming and fun to deal with. Not anymore. Not since his ex-wife had ruined that fun for him. Back when things were good between them, she'd talk back and mouth off just to rile him up and receive a "funishment". Later, though, it became evident she was doing it to anger him. As a consequence, Ambrose now found that all bratty behaviour did was leave a bitter taste in his mouth.

But Belle wasn't a brat. The pretty woman had tears in her eyes that pulled at his protective instincts. Tears she was desperately trying to hide. He continued to evaluate her, trying to figure out if the tears were genuine or an act to get out of a punishment. But no, that wasn't the case. They were real tears. If he wasn't mistaken, they were tears of genuine fear.

Ambrose was aware of his size and reputation as a firm Dom. Had she been truly afraid of what he would do to her?

"Am I that scary?"

"What? No." She appeared almost appalled at the suggestion otherwise. "I just... Can we please get this over and done with? I'd like to go home."

He narrowed his gaze. One thing he would never tolerate was topping from the bottom. A submissive did not get to control the scene with him.

"I just finished a punishment. I'm thirsty. Please get me a bottle of water from the bar."

Her jaw dropped. "That was a punishment?"

He couldn't hide his smile at the expression on her face. She'd witnessed the scene, then. That explained the arousal he could see in her. The scene had been an intense one. That poor submissive. Her Dom said she'd held back an orgasm because she'd become embarrassed by the noise she made during a scene. Ambrose's mission was to make her come so hard, she was incapable of holding back her sounds. The Dom had just finished a scene with her and was fatigued — so he handed her off to Ambrose. In the end, she'd come so hard, she'd not only screamed, she'd been left as limp as a wet noodle. And she'd definitely not held back.

"I'm still thirsty," he stated.

Nodding after a little hesitation, Belle responded with a quiet, "Yes, Sir."

Standing gracefully, she made her way to the bar, each step more confident than the last. By the time she returned, her shoulders were squared, her chin set in a sign of confidence, tears nowhere to be seen.

Belle was a treat to look at. With long, wavy, raven hair that flowed down her back, she had ample breasts that would be the perfect size for his big hands. A small, slender waist flared out into hips that were made for cradling a man's body. Her body was definitely appealing. She would be the perfect size for a big man like himself.

But her pretty face was what held his attention. She had plump, pink lips, a slender, pointed nose, a stubborn little chin and the most beautiful eyes he'd ever seen. Big and the colour of melted milk chocolate, they were expressive and held a story—one he wanted to hear.

When she approached, the stain of fear returned to those hypnotic eyes. While as a Dom, he was used to seeing a little fear and anxiety in a submissive, this was different. This was genuine.

"Relax," he told her and took a sip of water. "I'm not going to beat you. You'll receive a light spanking at best."

Looking at him with those gorgeous eyes, Belle forced a smile. "You've never been spanked before, have you?"

He laughed to himself. In his early days as a Dom in training, Ambrose had tried being a submissive once. It was important for Dominants to put themselves in that position at least once, so they understood the amount of trust that came with handing over power to someone else. Ambrose had hated every second of his experience as a submissive. So much that the Domme topping him had never gotten to the spanking they'd planned. There had been absolutely no doubt in his young mind that he was a Dominant through and through.

"No, sweet girl, I've never been spanked."

"The build-up is often worse than the actual act," she explained.

"I do believe that is the case." He ran a hand over her hair, finding it just as soft and silky as he'd imagined. "But the mind fuck is all part of it."

"You're one of those Doms," she muttered and turned her face away from him. "Great."

"You don't enjoy a mind fuck?"

Her hair fell over her shoulder as she shook her head. "Not anymore."

With a gentle hand, Ambrose brushed her hair back over her shoulder. "What happened to you?"

"Nothing," she snapped, an obvious lie.

He left it, not willing to push her. He had a job to do—spank her, get her to feel the emotions she'd been keeping locked away then send her back to Ayden who could comfort her and give her aftercare.

After drinking half the bottle of water, he placed it on the small end-table beside the couch. "Ayden tells me you haven't had a good scene in weeks."

She gave him the cutest little frown he'd ever seen. "He shouldn't have told you that."

"As a Master protecting you, it's his job to share information with those who are doing a scene with you. And this was pertinent to your punishment."

She sighed. Such a sad sound of resignation.

"Care to share why you've had such lacklustre scenes recently?"

"I don't want to discuss it," she muttered. "Especially not with a stranger. Sir."

Fair enough. "We should become better acquainted then."

Unable to resist, Ambrose ran his knuckles down her cheek and pushed her hair behind her ear, exposing her long, slender neck that was begging for a caress from his lips. He trailed his knuckles down her throat, to her shoulder, along her upper arm. His gaze settled on her breasts, barely contained by the halter top she wore. He loved halter tops. It would be so easy to undo the straps and release her breasts for his own enjoyment. But that wasn't what the punishment tonight was about. He would save that for next time.

One long, slow blink from her. She was fighting for control.

"I'll share what Ayden thinks then, shall I?"

She didn't respond but sucked in a shallow breath when he moved his hand to the top of her breast, his knuckles grazing the soft skin before he removed his hand. It appeared she had sensitive breasts. That was good to know.

"He believes you are choosing soft Doms because you're afraid. Afraid to let go and hand over control to the wrong man. You're fighting for control, right now." He tilted his head and took her in. "Instead, you should be giving in to that feeling of arousal. Handing yourself over to me, at least a little. You know you can trust me. Ayden would never have handed your punishment to me if I were untrustworthy."

Ayden was supremely protective of Belle. It was evident in the way he spoke of her. But he'd also given Ambrose a little warning before leaving Belle in his custody.

Belle frowned again. He wanted to kiss that frown right off her pretty face. So, he did just that. Dipping his head, Ambrose pressed closed lips to hers, beaming inside when she gave in immediately. Lips softening beneath his, she parted them when he opened up and swept his tongue across the seam. He pulled back far too soon, smiling when she followed, seeking more.

Oh, he would definitely have fun with this responsive submissive.

"You strike me as the type of woman who requires control in her daily life but seeks submission in the bedroom."

The blush on her cheeks told him he was right on the money.

"I demand submission. Even with a brief scene. I get off on the power exchange."

Belle looked at him through her lashes, pupils dilating, all submissive and appealing. Her pink tongue darted out to wet her lips. *Fuck it*, he had to kiss her again. Placing his lips to hers, he ran a hand along her scalp, gently gripping at her soft, thick hair. She sought his lips out, this time. He teased, nibbling at her lips before he swept his tongue inside of her mouth. She yielded, giving herself over to the kiss in a beautiful way.

Continuing to kiss her, Ambrose brought his other hand up to caress her jaw, cupping it to hold her in place while he took his time. She placed her small hands on his chest, not pushing him away, instead keeping him where he was while she leaned further into him. The small moan that came from her throat had him hard as a rock in no time.

Fuck, I can't remember the last time I was so aroused from a simple kiss.

Belle was something else. Beautiful. Intriguing. Different.

A small whimper escaped her lips when he pulled back, breaking the kiss to see a trickle of disappointment in her eyes. He remained close enough to feel her warm breath on his lips and just watched her for a moment. Her cheeks were flushed a beautiful red over the light brown of her skin, eyes hooded, pupils dilated. Eyes that were so vulnerable, making it clear she wanted more, even if she wouldn't ask for it.

"That's a good girl," he said softly and ran a thumb along her now wet bottom lip.

Stick to the task at hand, man.

"Are you wearing underwear?"

Her jaw dropped, disbelief written on her face. "Excuse me?"

"Answer the question."

"I…I'm not wearing any."

His lips—and his cock—twitched in approval. He cupped her cheek, caressing her jaw.

"You're a delightful woman, Belle."

Her cheeks flushed further at the compliment and she avoided his gaze. She was clearly not comfortable taking compliments.

"I'm going to give you a choice," he said and removed his hands from her. "I can bend you over my lap here and deliver your spanking, or I can take you to that free spanking bench over there. It's up to you."

Usually, he wouldn't give the submissive a choice, but this one was sensitive at the moment. The last thing he wanted was to embarrass her or make her feel more uncomfortable than she already did.

Biting down on that plump bottom lip, Belle looked towards the more public area. Her eyes were dark and mesmerising as she looked into his, trembling ever so slightly. *Delicious.*

"Here, please, Sir."

Smiling, he tilted his head in a small nod. "Very well. Over my lap, please."

With a little hesitation, she assumed the position with the confidence of an experienced submissive. He shifted her hips into a more comfortable position over his thighs and flipped up her short skirt. Her ass was a perfect heart shape, two round globes just begging for his handprints. Rubbing one palm over the soft skin, he pressed the other to her lower back to brace himself.

"Tell me why this is being done."

"I was rude to Master Ayden."

"You'll receive ten swats. I want you to count for me."

She tensed, a minuscule movement he wouldn't have noticed if he weren't paying such close attention to her. "Yes, Sir."

He brought his hand down onto her right cheek lightly, gauging how much she could handle. The little squeak she gave was delightful, sending blood straight to his cock. She said "one" just loud enough for him to hear.

"Good girl."

Belle relaxed further at the term of endearment. He loved the way she responded to him.

Bringing his hand down on her left cheek, he rubbed the sting away and continued. By the time Ambrose reached six swats, she was wiggling beneath his hold. As he ran his hand over her heated skin after the eighth smack, he was happy to hear a sniffle. That was what the punishment was about — forcing her to let go and feel the emotions she'd been ignoring. To release them. One more and she sobbed, her body relaxing in his lap as she let go.

Ayden had been right — Belle had been holding on to some feelings.

"One more, sweet girl," he said before bringing down his hand.

A loud slap filled his ears and, straight after, the sound of an uninhibited sob. As her body went completely lax, Belle's shoulders shook as she sucked in a deep, shuddering breath. Ambrose pulled her up to sit on his lap, heart aching when he saw the look of pure devastation on her face. She covered her face on a silent cry, trying to compose herself with each sobering breath.

Belle really wasn't willing to let go and feel. *Stubborn little sub.*

"Let it out," he whispered as he pulled her against his body, wrapping his arms around her softness.

She leaned into him but shook her head. *Definitely stubborn.*

"That wasn't so bad, was it?"

Running his hands along her smooth thigh, Ambrose enjoyed the feeling of having a submissive in his lap. All too soon, Belle sat upright and swiped at her cheeks, her composure settling.

"Maybe you need a bit more to truly let go," he teased, smiling when he saw the appalled expression she shot him. "Don't worry, we're done for the night. I'll save that for next time."

"Next time?"

He just about broke at the expression that fell across her face. Did she think of herself as undesirable?

"Oh yeah." He kissed those soft lips once. "There will definitely be a next time, if you're willing, beautiful girl."

Cheeks flushing an adorable deep red, Belle avoided his gaze, clearly feeling shy.

"Did you enjoy your spanking?"

"I—yes, Sir."

"Honest little sub." He squeezed her no-doubt-tender bottom, thoroughly enjoying the squeak she gave. "How about you give me a proper kiss to say thank you?"

For a moment, she stared at him with those big, brown eyes. Fuck, she was beautiful. Her submission made her even more appealing.

Leaning forward, Belle kissed him, sighing into his mouth when he cupped her cheek. His cock hardened to a painful point as his tongue swept over hers. There was no doubting he was attracted to this woman, but more than that, he was intrigued by her.

* * * *

Head still spinning, feeling well and truly embarrassed, Belle sat on the lounge near her friends and pressed her thighs together. Wetness trickled between them as she'd walked away from Master

Ambrose. Her breath came in short pants before she'd managed to calm herself. She'd never been so aroused from a spanking. She had almost wanted to beg him to take her tonight. But she wouldn't. Emotions were crashing over her, too close to the surface. She needed to go home and let them out in private, like she always did.

She could only imagine what he would do with his hands and mouth on her. "*Next time*," he'd said. He'd asked her to meet him for a scene next Friday night, after his dungeon monitor shift.

"Make sure you tell Ayden you were a good girl," he'd told her, flashing that heartbreaker smile.

His smile had changed his face. He'd gone from darkly sexy to intensely beautiful in the flash of teeth. And it had made him far more approachable and less threatening than his cold, Dom stare.

"Looks like you had a good time," Ayden said as she adjusted herself to sit a little more comfortably on her burning behind.

"You're an asshole," she muttered, still fighting traitorous tears. "Master Ambrose said to tell you I was a good girl."

"Then I'll forgive you for your arsehole comment."

"I cried. Wasn't that the point of your little punishment?" she snapped, well aware she was being irrational.

Belle hated strong emotions. She preferred to ignore them until she was alone and there were no witnesses to her 'irrational' feelings. Right now, she wanted nothing more than to be held. Preferably by Master Ambrose, even though he intimidated the hell out of her.

Larissa must have spotted the tears she was blinking back because she asked Agin for permission to move then sat beside Belle, wrapping her slender arms around Belle's shoulders. She held her tight and pressed a quick kiss to her hair. Now, Belle really wanted to cry.

"I should get going," she said as she continued to fight the losing battle over her roiling emotions. "I need to get up early for work."

Larissa frowned but let go. "We're still on for tomorrow night though, right?"

Belle nodded. "I'll be finished at five, then I'll head straight over."

After bidding farewell to her friends, she hurried to the locker room, holding back the tears by a thread of sheer stubborn will. *Suck it up, girl.* She wasn't the girl who cried at the club. She wasn't weak.

"Belle." Ayden caught up with her when she exited the club. "Wait up."

Blinking rapidly to unblur her vision, Belle stopped but didn't turn to face him. "I'm going home."

"You're not driving while you're this upset," he told her and moved into her field of vision.

"Look, you did your Domly duty, just leave me alone," she snapped, moving around him to head towards her car.

"Tell me what's wrong."

The heat of anger boiled in her veins as she spun to face him. "You specifically sent me to get a spanking, knowing full well it would shake things loose in me. It always does. You know that. It's why I hate being spanked. You knew it would upset me, so mission accomplished. Now, I'm going home to cry in private where I feel safe."

"You don't feel safe here? With me?"

And now she'd said the wrong thing in the heat of the moment, like she always did. Guilt piled on top of everything else and made her bottom lip quiver.

"That's not what I meant. I just… Let me deal with things my way, would you?"

He didn't respond. He wrapped his arms around her shoulders and pulled her into his embrace.

"I hate seeing you upset, but you needed to feel tonight. That's why I did it. It's obvious you've been upset for weeks, but you've refused to discuss it with any one of us."

There was a good reason for that. Belle didn't discuss her emotions openly. If she did, it was with her girlfriends, because she knew they wouldn't judge her. Part of her knew Ayden was looking out for her. But the other part hated him a little for making her cry. Her friends all knew how much she hated crying. She avoided it at all costs. She'd learned from a very young age that crying got her nowhere. It made her appear weak. At least that was what her parents had always told her.

"I'm sorry I made you cry. But it's my job as a Dom to give a submissive what she needs, not what she wants. Tonight, you needed to cry."

Calming herself enough to stop the tears, Belle pulled back, understanding where he was coming from.

"Just because I understand it doesn't mean I like it."

He laughed. "I know, sweetness. But you'll feel better now."

She sighed in defeat. He was right. She did always feel better after a good, cathartic cry.

"How was Master Ambrose?"

"He asked me to scene with him next Friday."

At the slow, smug smile that spread across Ayden's face, she came to the realisation that he'd planned that all along.

"He'll be good for you."

"You did it on purpose, didn't you?"

"I've been wanting to introduce the two of you for months. You just weren't ready for him yet," he said with a wink.

"You know I don't need you to hook me up."

"But you do. You've been choosing the wrong men. You've been fighting submission."

The bastard was right. She'd been doing it because she was becoming afraid of men again. She didn't understand why—she'd had a good run in recent months, not panicking at all, not feeling intimidated by men. But suddenly the fear had returned, and she couldn't figure out why.

"Drive safe." He let her go with a kiss on the cheek.

* * * *

Greeted by the tell-tale beep of the security system, Belle entered her empty home. Locking the doors behind her, she set the alarm to night mode and made her way through the house. Once upon a time, she hadn't been anywhere near as paranoid about her safety. She'd lived in a nice, naïve little bubble. That had been completely shattered. All because she had put her trust in the wrong man.

Like a fucking idiot, she scolded herself.

After a long, hot shower, Belle changed into some soft loungewear and made her way to the kitchen to make a gateau for tomorrow's girls' night. Baking grounded her, allowed her to focus on nothing other than making sweets for those she loved. After that spanking, all she wanted to do was tune out. She didn't want to feel. Unfortunately, her mind had other ideas.

As she measured out the ingredients, Belle was reminded of her nanna. The woman who had taught her to love baking, how to be herself. The one who had taught her strength, kindness, intelligence and sensitivity. Mixing together the chopped hazelnuts, chocolate and sugar, Belle let the tears she'd been holding in fall down her cheeks.

Her thoughts drifted to Master Ambrose. He'd been so dominant, firm yet gentle. Sweet, even. Not at all what she had expected. When he'd kissed her, she had wanted to melt. She hadn't felt like that since… Hell, ever. He was exactly the sort of Dom she used to enjoy dating and playing with. Strong and sturdy, confident and so physically big that he made her feel small.

Curled up in his lap, she'd felt feminine. She'd always had a more masculine energy. It had been the bane of her mother's existence that she'd been a tomboy growing up. Skinned knees, dirty clothing and boyish pastimes had never given way to the dance classes, etiquette lessons and high teas she'd been forced into.

Belle was screwed up. She shouldn't have been thinking about her parents tonight. They should stay locked up in the past where they belonged. It was a good thing she had a psychology appointment booked for this Wednesday where she could let it all out. Belle had gone through years of therapy to get to a place where she didn't feel worthless, where their detrimental words didn't mean anything to her. Except they still did, deep down. She would always feel like the lost little girl who needed and never received the approval and love of her parents. Part of her would feel she had no value. That she was truly worthless, as they'd told her.

Slipping the cake tin into the oven, Belle then moved to the freezer and grabbed a tub of chocolate fudge brownie ice cream. Ice cream made everything better. She curled up on the couch, thankful the tears had now stopped. As she dug in, her mind wandered. As always at this time of year, she focussed on her grandparents. The only two people to ever say they loved her. This week had been the twentieth anniversary of Nanna's sudden death. The day that Belle's life had changed forever. She had been alone and unloved ever since.

Nanna and Grandad had practically raised her. They'd been the ones to show young Belle unconditional love and support, to treat her with absolute kindness and care, to nurture her. Much to the disdain of her arsehole parents. Her parents were apathetic people, uncaring and unloving. Had it not been for her maternal grandparents, Belle would have grown up to be a completely different person. But they'd instilled good values in her, showed her the worth of hard work, taught her to see the good in people.

Belle's father had always been void of emotion. He spent all of his time working, sometimes disappearing to the office for days on end. As she grew older, Belle realised he had spent most of his nights cheating on her mother. Not that she could blame him or be mad at him for it. Her high-functioning alcoholic mother cheated as well. It wasn't uncommon for her to disappear for days.

Belle hated that they were her role models. Watching Nanna and Grandad when she was little, she'd learned what a true partnership was. How a healthy relationship worked. Her ability for compassion and capacity for love came from them. Her honesty, too. While her parents had lied all the time, not ever thinking twice about it, her grandparents had always been honest, even when it caused friction between them and their own daughter.

To this day, her fondest memories were of gardening with Grandad and baking with Nanna. It was the reason she still enjoyed both activities. They helped her feel connected with her long-passed grandparents.

They'd been amazing to her, right up until the days they had died. Grandad went first of a sudden heart attack when Belle was ten, Nanna a few weeks later of a brain aneurysm. Belle still missed them so much it made her heart ache.

After their deaths, Belle had been raised by a slew of nannies and babysitters, none of whom stuck around long enough to make a connection with her. They were usually run off by Mother, who either accused them of sleeping with her husband or made passes at them until they didn't show up one day. When Belle had turned twelve, her parents had deemed her old enough to stay at home alone. They threw money at her to keep her quiet. She'd been relying on herself ever since.

On her eighteenth birthday, Belle had gained access to the immense inheritance her grandparents had left her, thanks to her grandad's very successful business. She had signed an offer on a house and moved out as soon as she could.

"You worthless, ungrateful brat." Mother had sneered at her when she told them the news.

Father had barely reacted, saying, "If you move out, you're on your own. No more financial assistance from us."

That pretty much summed them up. *Bastards*.

With a huff of exhaustion, Belle threw her head back on the couch. *Stop wallowing, girl*. She had always tried her hardest to be positive, to not get pulled into the abyss of negativity that always tempted her to focus on what she didn't have. But sometimes it was difficult to ignore. And tonight, she was drained. When she was drained, she focussed on negatives — it was just how her brain worked, no matter how hard she tried to change it. She reminded herself there were a lot of positives in her life. She was healthy, had a very successful growing business and a great circle of friends who supported her. But it wasn't enough.

Belle still craved what her girlfriends had. A man of her own. A partner in life. Someone to share with at the end of the day. Someone to complain to. Someone to love. A Dom who would claim her, need her, even.

That was her biggest problem. Nobody needed her.

Focus on tomorrow. Tomorrow is a new day. It will be a good day.

After all, tomorrow she was having a girls' night with the two women who were sisters in every sense of the word other than blood. That would get her back on the right track.

Chapter Three

The whole point of being the boss and owner of the clinic was that Ambrose got to choose his own hours. Unfortunately, as the owner, it was his responsibility to fill in at the last minute when one of his veterinarians called in sick. After one of the vets came down with a case of food poisoning overnight, she texted him at six a.m. to call in sick. He hadn't been able to find a replacement and was now working on a Saturday. He hated working weekends. There were always more emergencies on the weekend.

He was bloody tired after last night. After his punishment with Belle, he'd stayed at Haven until one a.m., tempted to work off his sexual frustration with a different submissive. For some reason, he hadn't been able to bring himself to do it. It surprised him. He'd never had trouble choosing a submissive, but each time he had looked at another woman last night, he had thought of Belle. Of the way she'd responded to his touch, her sweet kisses that had tasted of sugar and cherries. He'd stayed painfully erect until he'd gotten home and taken care of himself in the shower.

Had she been in a better headspace, Ambrose would have offered to play with her last night. But she had not been in the right mindset at all. He prided himself on being a good Dom. A good Dom didn't force a submissive into a scene she wasn't ready for. He'd seen the tears in her eyes as she had left the club, closely followed by Ayden. His fellow Master had refused to divulge any information on her last night, other than to reassure Ambrose she would be okay once she got home.

There was something about Belle that called to Ambrose, made his dominant instincts come to the forefront and want to envelop her in a cloak of safety. All day, he'd been thinking of her, wishing she had given him her number so he could check on her today. Instead, he was receiving updates from Ayden. It felt wrong. But the woman was private and seemed to be hiding something that kept the inherent sadness in her eyes. She was a puzzle he wanted to solve.

Making his way through the back room of the clinic, Ambrose unlocked the cage that held Ayden's golden retriever, Forrest. The big, goofy dog bounced out of the cage and jumped up to greet him with a big, sloppy dog kiss.

"Hey buddy, you ready to go home?"

Leading the dog to the treatment room where Ayden waited, he noted how poorly trained Forrest was. He darted down the hallways, sticking his nose into each empty room before he caught the scent of his owner waiting for him. Ambrose couldn't help but smile. Lucky for him, the dog was a total sweetheart, not an aggressive bone in his body.

Ayden received one of those 'I haven't seen you in years' greetings from the dog he loved as he squatted to greet him.

"Were you a good boy for Uncle Ambrose?"

"He was the best boy," Ambrose said as he handed the dog a liver treat. "He has all the nurses wrapped around his little finger."

Straightening, Ambrose looked to his friend. "As I suspected, it was a simple benign cyst. Nothing to worry about. He'll be more comfortable now that it's been removed, though."

"I assume it's just an age thing?"

Ambrose nodded. "He's getting to that age where he'll start getting skin tags, lipomas and random cysts here and there. There's no point in removing them unless they're bothering him."

"Thanks for doing that for me. I appreciate it." The other man smiled as he stood, leash in hand. "So, have you cooled down after last night? You were a little hot and bothered after dealing with Belle."

Ambrose narrowed his gaze as he regarded the other man. "I haven't been able to stop thinking about her. Have you spoken to her this afternoon?"

"She just texted me again. She's fine."

"That's it?"

"She tends to shut down when she feels strongly. I spoke to Larissa earlier and she said Belle spent most of the night crying. So, the spanking did the trick."

"Good," he said firmly. "If there was ever a woman who needed to let go, it's her. She was wound so tight I thought her head might pop off."

"And you were the perfect man for the job," Ayden teased.

"You're a manipulative bastard, you know that?"

There was no doubt in Ambrose's mind that Ayden had provoked Belle until she had snapped at him, just so he could introduce the two of them. For months, Ayden had been hinting that Ambrose needed a permanent submissive of his own. That he would help him find her. Apparently, he'd had Belle in mind the entire time.

"She told me you have a scene planned for Friday."

"We do, indeed."

"Don't take it personally if she backs out at the last minute. Like I said, she's been choosing soft and newer Doms. She may get cold feet."

An odd expression came over Ayden's face. One Ambrose hadn't seen in the months they'd been friends.

"I don't have anything to worry about, do I? There's nothing going on between the two of you?"

Ayden shook his head. "No. I'm just protective of her. She's got a traumatic history."

Ambrose crossed his arms and leaned against the treatment table. "So you've set me up with a headcase?"

"No, it's not like that," Ayden assured him. "She's got trust issues. It took me months to earn her trust and, even now, I'm not sure she's told me the full story."

Ambrose hesitated, wondering what he'd gotten himself into. His ex had been a headcase, unsure of what she wanted, constantly changing her mind. And she'd ended up cheating on him with a so-called friend of his. It had all but wrecked Ambrose's trust in women. It was why he no longer dated. He refused to be taken advantage of. Life was easier alone.

"Be warned, she may panic."

"Ashely mentioned that last night. Said the one time she topped Belle, she had a mild panic attack."

The Mistress had pulled Ambrose aside after Belle left, warning him to take things slowly with her. Ashely was known for dealing with submissives with issues such as anxiety and trauma. Though she could be as strict as the next Dominant, she was also good at reading others. She often did demonstrations on reading body language for newer Dominants and tops.

"Any more advice?"

"Just be yourself and I'm sure you'll get along." His smile dropped for a moment. "And be warned, if you push her too hard, you'll not only have to deal with me, but Agin and Sullivan as well."

Ambrose allowed himself to smile. It was obvious the men were protective of her, their submissives all being close friends. But he could handle whatever they dished out. After all, he'd dealt with some bad men in his life. Dealing with his mates in a bad mood would be a cake walk.

* * * *

Stretched out on Larissa's soft lounge that had always threatened to swallow her whole, Belle sipped at her Dr Pepper and listened to her friends discuss their weeks. Girls' night was exactly what she had needed. A night of gossip, good food, sugary drinks and her favourite dessert all shared with her best friends. People she didn't have to pretend with.

After working a full day of yard maintenance because one of her employees was ill, her body was exhausted. She felt odd. Everything hurt and ached. She'd recently made the decision to pull back on doing maintenance jobs herself because her body didn't recover as fast as it used to. She was only thirty, but she felt far older at times. Right now, her hamstrings were tight, her right knee ached and her lower back was so sore that she'd taken painkillers earlier in the day to relieve some of the pain. What she really wanted was a few days off to do nothing but rest.

"Do you at least have tomorrow off?" Amara asked with a frown once she'd finished lecturing Belle about the perils of working herself into the ground.

"Technically, but I have a mountain of paperwork to catch up on. Plus, tax is due."

"So no," Larissa said in a worried tone. "I didn't want to say it, but you look wrecked today."

"Gee thanks," she retorted with a scoff. "My body's just taking longer to recover. I know I can't keep going like this."

"I'm glad to hear you're finally making sense," Larissa commented from her perch on the other end of the couch. "Is there something else going on? You haven't been your usual perky self for a couple of weeks."

"The anniversary of Nanna's and Grandad's deaths came up. It's been twenty years now. But it's still affecting me. I haven't been sleeping well, either."

"Did your spanking with Master Ambrose last night help at least?" Amara asked with a wiggle of her eyebrows.

The other women knew all too well how a good spanking could relieve emotional turmoil.

Belle scowled. "I cried as I was leaving them again when I got home."

"He got to you."

"Yeah," she agreed, unable to lie to her friends. She also hadn't been able to stop thinking about him all day. "I haven't had a spanking like that since before the incident. It shook something loose in me. I'm still angry at Ayden for sticking him on me."

"But it was a good release."

Belle nodded at Amara. "I do miss the release pain used to give me."

"But you can't handle pain anymore." Larissa finished her thought.

She shook her head. "You saw how badly I panicked the last time I tried."

While she and Ayden had still been seeing each other, she'd tried a scene with more than light pain involved. The second Ayden had flogged her a little harder, she had lost her shit, descending into a full-blown panic attack in the middle of Haven. It was awful. Humiliating.

"But I got so fucking aroused, you guys. I couldn't tell you the last time I was that wet. I just wanted to hop onto his lap and take him for a ride."

The other women cackled with laughter.

"He wants to do a scene on Friday."

The chorus of oohs that came from her friends were amusing, albeit juvenile.

Rolling her eyes, she laughed. "Calm down, children. It's not that big a deal."

"Then explain why that big smile has appeared on your face," Larissa teased. "I haven't seen that for a very long time."

"If ever," Amara agreed.

"I can only imagine what he'll do if he intentionally arouses me." Dropping her head back, Belle tried to ignore the tingling in her lower body at the memory of the calloused hand caressing her naked ass. "Fuck me, I was throbbing at the end of it. He knew how to touch me. How to kiss — holy fuck, the man can kiss."

Finishing her drink, she placed the empty glass on the coffee table. "The problem is that I don't want to drop."

Now that she had depression and anxiety, she was more prone to subdrop, especially after an intense scene. Not that she'd tested that theory in a while.

"Sweetie, if he's as good a Dom as everyone says, he'll take care of that. He'll take care of you."

Belle sighed. "I know. And I want that, I do. I just struggle with the thought of someone else taking care of me."

Because she'd spent her entire life taking care of herself. She'd never relied on a man.

"You've never really had a man take care of you, though," Larissa said. "When you truly give yourself over to a man and let him give you what you need, it's so rewarding."

"You've done it alone for long enough. It's time for you to open yourself up to the possibility of dating again," Amara said.

Belle thought it over, biting down on her bottom lip. "I think you're right. I've let my trust issues rule my life for long enough."

Her friends remained silent, letting her work through her thoughts without interruption.

"I want to belong to someone so badly. I want what you guys have. A man who loves me. A true partner in life. Someone who will always have my back. Someone who will protect me."

Belle had never had a normal relationship. She'd jumped straight from casual fuck-arounds in her early twenties to being manipulated and controlled by Bryce. She'd never had a healthy relationship. And the more she thought about it, the sadder it seemed.

It was all because of her parents and the trust issues they had caused for her. After spending a lifetime feeling unwanted, she'd thrown herself into a serious relationship with a man who wanted her—or so she had thought. Instead, she'd ended up more damaged than when she'd entered it. All because she'd been so desperate to belong.

Still, she had always hoped one day that she could move past it and become a regular, functioning woman in a relationship. One that could hold on to a real man. Have a tangible, successful relationship. Now that she'd met him, part of her hoped that Master Ambrose would be that man. There was something about him. He had a way about him that had her wanting to fall to his feet and worship him. He seemed like the kind of man who would take care of her. As well as incredible dominance, there was a certain softness to him, a kindness. The way he'd held her while she wept last night had made her feel treasured. Like he cared. But that was crazy. They didn't know each other — he didn't care about her. Belle had been reading too many damn romance novels.

"There's that dreamy smile again," Amara teased.

Belle retaliated by throwing a pillow at her friend's head, grinning when the other woman lost her balance and fell back against the couch.

"You know we just want you to be happy. However that looks."

"I know and I appreciate it."

Belle's phone rang. An unknown caller on a Saturday evening. She almost didn't answer it, but some niggling in the back of her mind told her to.

"Belle Winters?"

"Yes..." Dread filled her when she recognised the voice, one she hadn't heard in almost two years.

"It's Officer Skinner. I'm sorry to be calling you so late, I just heard the news and wanted to check on you."

"News? What happened?" Panic fuelled her racing thoughts that got away from her.

"Nobody has contacted you?" A quiet curse. "Bryce was released yesterday."

Her heart dropped. "What?" The question came out a squeak.

"It appears he pulled some strings and got out early."

"But… He had six months left on his sentence. I was supposed to have another six months…"

She'd had time to decide if she was going to sell her house and move. She'd had another six months of safety left. Now, that was gone.

"I'm sorry, Belle…" The rest of the officer's words were lost in a haze as Belle's mind drifted.

Chilled to her core, she felt the phone slip from her hand then lost all feeling in her body, as though she'd been dropped into a pool of ice water. Her chest constricted as she struggled to breathe. Her heart froze, shattering as she began to panic. Her friends spoke, their words not getting by the sound of roaring blood in her ears.

Bryce was out of gaol. He would come for her. He would finish what he had started. He'd told her as much when she'd seen him in court.

"I'll get you, you bitch," he had sneered from his spot in the dock. *"I'll do more than send you to the hospital next time."*

"He's out," she managed to rasp before her throat constricted and she lost track of everything.

* * * *

Tears had dried on her cheeks when Belle came to, aware that she'd had a panic attack. Huddled in the corner of the couch, her friends touched her, murmuring sweet words of encouragement. As her heart rate slowed, her breathing returned to normal and she gained the feeling back in her body. But she remained emotionally numb. Her mind had shut down. She didn't know what to think, how to feel.

"Sorry," she mumbled. "I'm sorry I reacted that way."

"Don't you dare apologise," Amara snapped, her fierce tone forcing Belle to look at her. "You suffered a serious trauma at the hands of a monster. That monster is now out. If you hadn't panicked, I would have been worried."

Larissa ran a soothing hand over Belle's hair and smiled as she held her. "Do you want to stay here tonight?"

"She's staying here tonight." Belle looked up to find Agin kneeling beside her. His dark eyes were fierce as he looked at her, his hands resting on her ankles.

Had he witnessed the panic attack? Oh God, how embarrassing.

"You'll stay here as long as you need," he said, giving her ankles a light squeeze.

Belle started to shake her head, to insist she would be safe at home, but Agin gave her a short, stern shake of his head. A Dom look.

"No argument, Belle."

As much as she hated to admit it, she didn't want to be alone. Not tonight. Staying with friends would be the best thing for her.

* * * *

How the fuck could I have been so blind? Belle replayed the night of the incident in her mind as she lay in the guest bed, curled up on her side, her hands fisted beneath her chin. There had been warning signs in

Bryce's behaviour. Her friends had brought them up. In the beginning, he had been everything she'd ever dreamed of. He was smart, kind, sweet and seemed to genuinely care for her. But after a couple of weeks, his behaviour had changed. He became more controlling, insisting she spend all her spare time with him. Belle, naïve and desperate for validation, had thought that meant he loved her, that he hated being apart from her. Now she knew the truth. That he had wanted to control her.

After a couple of months, he'd tried to control how much time she spent with her friends. That was when she'd put her foot down. He'd gotten so angry that he hadn't spoken to her for days until she had caved and apologised. Fuck, she'd had no spine. She'd been a true idiot to fall for his act. She'd stuck around for six months, hoping to win his love, but she never had, no matter how hard she'd tried.

Then she'd walked in on him cheating and everything had changed. Later, she discovered he'd been cheating with several different women throughout their entire relationship. Cheating was a crash-and-burn offence for Belle. She would never forgive someone for that.

After witnessing him fucking his secretary, she'd felt so betrayed that she had just left without saying a word, unsure if he'd even noticed her presence in the office. She texted him once she'd returned home and told him never to contact her again. Ignoring his calls and texts that had followed, she had stayed at home and broken down, feeling like a complete fool for falling for his act. Instead of leaving her alone, he'd broken into her home. The one place she had felt safe.

He'd confronted her in a rage, calling her every degrading name under the sun. Then he'd grabbed her, threatened her, hit her. When she had refused to take him back, he had completely lost it. His face had contorted with rage unlike anything she'd ever seen. And he had proceeded to beat the absolute shit out of her.

Blow after blow had come until she had passed out from the pain. He'd waited for her to regain consciousness then had beaten her some more, continuing the cycle all night long. The next thing she knew, she had been waking in the hospital in absolute agony. In the weeks that followed, she'd regained her memory of the night, though part of her wished she hadn't. Even now, two years later, she had nightmares about the incident.

After calling her an ambulance, Bryce had fled the scene and taken off for two days before turning himself in to the police. He had claimed he didn't remember a thing about the incident. Said he'd blacked out. His family had hired a well-respected psychiatrist and psychologist to diagnose it as a stress-induced psychotic break. And it had worked. He'd gotten a reduced sentence because of it.

Now the bastard was free. And Belle was left terrified. What the hell was she supposed to do now? *Move.* She had to move.

Her friends had all offered to have her stay sat their houses, even talking about a roster. But she wouldn't do that to them. She wouldn't become a burden that others had to take care of. She was a grown-ass adult. She would look after herself. She always did.

Come tomorrow, she would suck it up, go home and deal with her issues like a big girl.

* * * *

Waking early the next morning, Belle found Agin already up and sitting at the dining table with a mug in hand. He immediately stood when he spotted her and began to make her a cup of coffee. It made her smile. Agin was a service Dom and enjoyed taking care of others. It also made his career choice as a social worker obvious.

"Morning," she greeted him, her voice croaky, throat sore from all the crying she'd done last night. It had been a rough couple of days for her emotions.

He greeted her with a warm smile. "How are you feeling?"

"Better."

Agin gave her a sceptical look and waited. She really needed to get some less perceptive friends.

"Fine, I'm still upset and anxious. But I'm dealing. I'm processing it."

Handing her the mug, he gestured for her to join him at the table. The stone was startingly cold against her bare forearms as she leaned forward to take a sip of her drink. The hot liquid slid down her throat as she sipped, hoping it would melt the ice that had surrounded her heart.

"Have you given any more thought to what we discussed last night?" Worry was evident in his tone. "You're more than welcome to stay here as long as you need."

She didn't need to. What she needed was her own home, to be surrounded by her own things where she felt comfortable. Bryce wasn't going to take that away from her.

"I appreciate the offer, but I think it's best I return home and deal with this myself."

"Belle..."

"I'm a big girl, Agin. I know everyone sees me as this damaged, broken person, but I'm not fragile."

Lips flattening into a thin line, he regarded her for a quiet moment. "Do you really think we see you as damaged and broken?"

She scoffed. "Of course you do."

And why wouldn't they? She *was* damaged and broken.

"None of us see you that way," he said fiercely. "You forget that I was there for the incident. I witnessed your strength first-hand. You're an amazing woman, Belle. You're a survivor. I have never once seen you as weak or fragile. You are strong and brave and intelligent. If anyone is capable of dealing with this alone, it's you. But you don't have to. You have all of us to lean on. Let us help."

Warmth wrapped around her like he'd given her a big, comforting hug. His words meant the world to her. She'd had no idea he saw her in that way.

"I understand your choice to deal with it alone, but never forget you are *not* alone. We are all here for you. Always, sweetheart." His expression became stern. "If you feel worried or scared, I expect a phone call. So do Sullivan, Ayden and Grayson."

She frowned. They'd talked about her last night. She hated when people talked about her behind her back.

"Yes, we discussed it. Because we're your family and we love you. We are going to protect you, even when it makes you mad. And you know you would do the exact same thing for any one of us."

He had her there. Letting out a sigh, she rested her chin on her palm and looked at him.

"I'm serious, Belle. If we find out something happened and you didn't contact one of us, we will be having a very different conversation. We're not screwing around with your safety."

"Yes, Sir," she mumbled as she brought the mug up to her lips.

She felt like she'd just been scolded. But also cared for. Loved.

Larissa soon joined them and tried to talk Belle out of staying at home alone. Her independence was the one thing Belle would not give up. Once Agin seemed satisfied Belle was going to do the right thing and contact them if she got scared, he left the two women alone.

"I'll call you tonight, okay?" Larissa said as Belle went to leave. "If I feel you're not okay, I'm coming over to stay the night."

Belle shook her head but smiled. "I'll be fine. I'll even sleep with a knife under the pillow to protect myself."

She'd meant it as a joke, but it fell flat. After all, for weeks after the incident, Belle had slept with a cannister of pepper spray beneath her pillow. That was something none of her friends knew.

"Really, I'll be okay," Belle assured her. "I'll speak to you tonight."

And with that, she headed home to sort her life out. Alone.

Chapter Four

The next few days and nights were filled with anxiety. Belle didn't sleep properly—her slumber contained constant nightmares of Bryce breaking into her home again. Absolutely exhausted, she'd organised to take the afternoon off work to relax and partake in some self-care.

After packing up her trailer, she took a moment to look down at her dirt-streaked clothing. No matter how careful she was, Belle always ended up covered in dirt. *I can't do anything right, can I?*

She locked the trailer, making her way to the driver's door, when a voice she hadn't heard in years brought her to a standstill. *Fuck.* Father was walking towards her through the car park of the large office building she'd been working on. He strode forward, looking as pompous and self-important as ever. Dressed in an immaculate business suit, as always, his hair was neatly styled, not a single hair out of place. His handsome features were skewed into the stern expression he wore permanently. Belle could count on both hands the number of times she'd seen her father smile.

As they grew older, she realised why her father never had trouble finding women to cheat with. He was a rich, successful businessman with youthful, handsome features. But he wasn't a happy man. Happiness had never been on his radar. He was too power-hungry. An emotionless robot. A bastard.

Of all the days to see Father, why did it have to be a day when she looked like the filthy runt he'd once called her? She'd been five at the time, but the words and images of him saying it had stuck in her mind. It was the first time she remembered him being outwardly cruel to her.

"Belle." His voice was as cold and detached as ever.

"Father." She tried to return the ice in her voice but failed.

Steeling herself, Belle tried to close off her emotions, to protect herself. She pushed back the feelings of failure and inadequacy she always had when faced with one of her parents. How did he always manage to make her feel like a worthless child when she was in his presence? Years of therapy and she still had no idea why she allowed him to have so much power over her.

He looked her up and down, expression not changing, eyes not even flickering with the slightest amount of warmth towards his only child.

"You're looking...well."

The pause hit its mark, right in her heart. The fucking prick made her feel worthless beneath his judgemental gaze. Belle tried harder to close herself off, to pretend his words and judgement meant nothing to her. But they did. They probably always would.

"As do you," she responded cordially. "How is Mother?"

"Well." His lips twitched in the faintest hint of a smile. "She remains busy with her little projects."

Those little projects were charity events she headed and organised with her circle of socialite friends, all just as vapid as she was. Always pretending to be a woman with a heart, Mother had most of society fooled. She'd built a name for herself in the city as one of the most charitable women around. But Belle knew it was all a lie. She never cared about the causes she was raising funds for. Couldn't have cared less about the organisations she claimed to help. But all her socialite friends worshipped the ground she walked on and that was what mattered to her. Being queen bee.

Father's business associates also admired her for her charitable ventures. They were both always seen doing the right thing in public, while in private they were monsters.

"And you?"

"I'm well. Business is good. I was just here on an acquisition."

"I'm glad you're both doing well," she lied. The vindictive part of her, the part that ate at her soul, wanted to wish them ill will. She didn't want them to succeed. She wanted them to fail.

Fidgeting with her keys, feeling exponentially uncomfortable, Belle waited for him to speak again.

"I thought you were focussed on design now, that you'd gotten out of maintenance work."

There it was. The jab at her career that came every single time they spoke. Neither parent had approved of her career choice, no matter how successful her business was. She earned into six figures now because she had worked her arse off to make sure her business was a success. But that made no difference to her parents.

"Getting dirty is not an appealing career choice. No child of ours should be sinking so low as to do menial labour," Mother had once said to her.

"You have been given every advantage in life and you choose to be a gardener? I thought we taught you to aim higher," Father had concurred.

Her failure to live up to their expectations was the only thing her parents ever agreed upon.

"I fear allowing you to spend so much time with your grandfather had an undesirable effect," Father had said.

Despite the fact that Grandad had franchised his business and become a multi-millionaire before Belle was born, her parents still looked down on him because he continued to do 'menial labour' despite the fact that he didn't need to work. He enjoyed his work, just like Belle did. Nothing would change that.

"I do both," she told Father firmly. "I enjoy both sides of my job."

Belle had picked up the landscaping contract for a new business development in the central business district. It was a huge deal, a great step forward for her design business. Not that she would ever tell her parents. They didn't deserve to hear of her triumphs.

Her father pursed his lips as he looked down his aristocratic nose at her. Belle braced for more negativity. Luckily, his phone rang. *Saved by the bell,* she thought with intense relief.

"I have to take this," he said as he glanced at the screen. "Take care of yourself."

Empty words.

"You too." She forced a smile and released a long, slow breath as he walked away from her.

Striding away with that arrogant swagger like the professional arsehole he was, he didn't once look back at his daughter who he hadn't seen in two years. Belle got into her car, locked the doors behind her and looked down to her shaking hands. Filled with rage, she was also upset. But she wouldn't cry. She wouldn't give Father that power.

Why does seeing one of my parents still make me feel this way? Angry. Sad. Defeated. Worthless.

Anyone else who treated her so poorly had been cut out of her life years ago. She no longer cared for their opinion of her. But it was different with her parents. She would always seek their approval. That broken child that still lived inside of her would always hope for their love and affection. The adult in her knew she would never receive it and tried to move on. Still…this was her father. The one man who was supposed to love and protect her. Yet he'd never done either of those things.

Feeling like the needy little girl she'd once been, Belle blinked away the tears that burned her eyes and ignored her phone when it made a sound. Then it rang. It was the security company who monitored her system at home, notifying her the alarm had been triggered.

"Yes, please call the police," she told the operator as her heart jumped into her throat. "I'm twenty minutes away."

Lungs burning as she tried not to panic, her throat constricted, that familiar feeling of fear crawling up her spine while she tried to focus on the road. Continuing to drive home, well aware she was on the verge of panicking, Belle tried to control her mind which instantly flashed to memories of Bryce breaking into her home.

It couldn't be Bryce, though. She'd gotten the violence restraining order she'd had against him renewed first thing on Monday morning. Surely he wouldn't be so stupid as to break it.

The police were still at her home when Belle arrived, pulling into her long, circular driveway behind them. She greeted the female officer who approached with a friendly expression, glancing at the large male officer who stood beside the car on his phone, giving her a smile and firm nod when he spotted her.

"I'm Officer Jenowski," the female officer said. "We've done a perimeter check and didn't find any signs of forced entry. The front door had been opened. The alarm must have scared off the would-be burglar."

An immediate sense of relief washed over Belle, but it wasn't enough to put her mind at ease.

"The security firm said you may have footage from the front-door camera before it was vandalised."

Belle looked over the officer's shoulder and noticed it had indeed been smashed. Pulling out her phone, she played the last file of footage to show the officers. It showed a large, tall, broad man, built like a brick shithouse, as her grandad would have said. With confident strides, he approached the front door, his face covered by a baseball cap and hoodie, his hand quickly covering the camera before the footage cut out.

She froze in place, heart slamming against her ribs as she watched the footage again. It was Bryce. It had to be. He had the exact same build, the same swagger. The man also wore gloves, proving it had been a planned break-in, not some random who got angry and decided to take it out on her house. The officers both commented and made notes of the footage.

"It's not much to go on, but there was a similar break-in down the road on Monday. It could be the same offender."

Belle opened her mouth to tell them about Bryce, about all the worries she had about him attempting to hurt her again, but fear took over and stole her voice. She remained frozen when nothing came out. *Fuck.* Another car pulled in the driveway. Ayden.

Appearing furious, he stalked towards her and wrapped an arm around her shoulders as he introduced himself to the female police officer and greeted the male one, whom he appeared to already know. Since he owned her security company, she wasn't all that surprised to see him. Leaning into his body, she sought the comfort of someone she cared for.

"Have you told them yet?" He shot her a Dom look, as if he knew she'd chickened out.

When she shook her head, still unable to speak, he proceeded to tell the officers about the incident. Lucky for her, they took it seriously when she told them the man in the video looked like Bryce. After finalising details, they left.

Fear licked at her spine as she unlocked the electronic lock on the wooden door and let herself in, very aware of Ayden stepping in right behind her. She headed for the kitchen, making coffees for both of them before she even tried to speak again. Tongue tied, she clammed up even as she sat on the lounge beside her friend.

"Do you want me to stay with you tonight?"

Shaking her head, she rejected his offer. She was an adult. She could stay in her own home alone. Except she was terrified.

"Belle," he prodded her. "I can tell you're on the verge of a panic attack. Let me pick up Forrest and we'll stay here tonight. You'll sleep better knowing we're here with you."

One stray traitorous tear rolled down her cheek. She swiped at it, looking away from him to hide her expression as her heart began to thaw, fear taking over completely. He moved, wrapping his arms around her shoulders. She crumbled into her friend. She allowed Ayden to hold her, trusting him to take care of her as she allowed panic to take control, replacing the sadness and frustration she'd felt earlier.

"One of my guys will be here with a new camera soon. I'll install it and then pick up Forrest. You can come with me if you want to."

She shook her head, sniffed and wiped away another stray tear. "I'll be fine. I'm not that broken."

His face changed to speak a level of anger and ferocity that she'd never seen in him before. "If I ever hear you refer to yourself as broken again, I'll put you over my knee and spank you myself."

Struck by his tone, Belle's eyes widened and she inched away from him, wrapping her arms around herself. She hadn't meant to make him angry. But she had. Maybe she was the asshole all along.

Ayden released a breath and pressed a kiss to her forehead. "Why don't you take a shower while I wait for the camera?"

Pulling her to her feet as he stood, Ayden patted her on the butt. Without a word, she did as she was told and hoped it would help her centre herself again.

It didn't.

* * * *

Absolutely exhausted, Belle curled up on the couch with Forrest's big head resting in her lap. She might have been exhausted, but she was calm at last. Ayden's beautiful dog had always had the ability to relax her. And she got her fill of puppy cuddles whenever she saw him too.

"You're spoiling him, you know," Ayden said, amusement thick in his tone as he stretched out on the other end of the couch.

"I'm his favourite aunty. It's my job to spoil him." She kissed the top of the sweet boy's head and smiled. "Isn't it, Forrest?"

She was rewarded with a lick on the cheek that made her smile.

"Oh yes, you're the best boy ever, aren't you?" Looking into those big, brown eyes, she rubbed his face in the way he loved. "I love you so much."

A few moments of silence passed before Ayden spoke again. "So, are we going to talk about it?"

Damn Doms and their need for communication.

"No."

"Belle…"

"I don't want to talk, Ayden," she snapped. "My day went from bad to worse and now I'm trying to stave off another panic attack by focussing on the present. Just leave it. Please."

In her periphery, she saw him frown. Curling up further, she wrapped an arm around Forrest's big body before he could leave her.

"What else happened?"

Ugh. Idiot. She hadn't meant to let that slip. With a sigh, she looked down to Forrest who now had his eyes closed while he enjoyed the soft strokes of her hand on his head.

"I saw my father today," she said quietly.

"Oh, sweetness."

"Don't." Her voice cracked. "Don't pity me."

"It's not pity, Belle," he snapped. "It's empathy."

Shaking her head, she looked at the television, not willing to see that expression on his face. The one that would make her heart shatter.

"You're going to shut down on me, aren't you?"

"Of course," she responded in a monotone. "It's what I do."

Each time she felt strong, painful emotions, she shut down. Because every time she'd shown emotion at home, she had been either ignored or yelled at. Called pathetic, weak, pitiful, a nuisance.

"Babies cry," her parents used to say. *"You are not a baby, so stop acting like one."*

There had always been so much venom in their voices when they said that to her.

"Forrest, move, buddy."

The dog slid off her lap and Ayden slipped in beside her. He wrapped his arms around her and pulled her into his warmth. She didn't bother to fight it. One thing about Ayden was he was a comforter. He loved holding others. Touch was his love language. And, right now, she needed to feel loved. Needed to feel like someone cared for her. If only for a moment.

* * * *

That night, with Ayden in her home and Forrest in her bed, curled up behind her, Belle slept like a baby. The previous night, she'd barely slept a wink. Every single noise had her waking in a panic on high alert, waiting for the alarm system to go off. At three, she'd given up on trying to sleep and begun working on a new landscaping design for Amara and Sullivan's property for their wedding.

Despite getting a deep sleep, she dealt with anxiety all day. The constant constriction in her chest, her heart rate spiking throughout the day, being on the verge of bloody tears. It was exhausting. As she packed up after her final job for the day, she received a phone call from Officer Jenowski, the officer who had attended her home yesterday.

"We arrested the perp we believe to be responsible for the break-in at your home," she told her firmly. "He fits the profile and has admitted to two further break-ins in the area this week alone."

"Are you sure it's him?" Belle had remained certain it was Bryce in the footage.

"He was caught trying to break in a few doors down from you wearing the same hoodie as the man in the footage you sent us."

Unable to feel even the slightest sense of relief, Belle got into her car, locking the doors immediately.

"Thank you for letting me know," she told the officer.

"If anything else happens with you, call us."

Belle hung up, her gut churning, a wave of nausea rolling over her as she started to drive home. Bryce had an alibi for the break-in, according to the officer. She had no choice but to believe the man responsible had been caught. She had to trust the justice system would do its job. Except she knew it didn't work. If it did, Bryce would still be locked up. Instead, he was free. And she was terrified of being alone in her own home.

Chapter Five

The scents of leather, sweat and sex hit Belle harder than she'd expected when she entered Haven that night. All afternoon, she'd been trying to focus, to get into the right frame of mind to scene with Master Ambrose tonight. But the phone call from the police had thrown her for a loop and she'd been struggling since.

The sense of anticipation and excited anxiety was now joined by utter nervousness. Perhaps she should have cancelled tonight. But no, she had made plans and she would follow through with them. Besides, being at Haven surrounded by people was far safer than being at home alone.

Heading for the submissive section, Belle paused. Master Ambrose hadn't told her where to meet him. He'd said he would find her after his dungeon monitor shift finished at ten. Fidgeting with the bottom of her bustier, she scanned the room and didn't find anyone she knew. No doubt every one of her friends was already off having fun of their own.

She continued to head towards the submissive section, and bit her bottom lip, trying to focus on getting her head right. She calmed a little further until a large wall of a man stepped in front of her, forcing her to stop dead in her tracks.

"Excuse me," she said, suddenly feeling very small and intimidated.

"Well now." The deep, rich timbre of a voice rolled over her in a pleasant wave. "I'd hoped you'd be a little more excited to see me."

Her heart leapt when she recognised Master Ambrose's voice. Craning her neck, Belle looked into those intense, beautiful eyes of dark emerald that belonged to the object of her affections. Her breath caught in her throat. He was even more handsome than she'd remembered.

"Master Ambrose. I'm sorry, I didn't realise it was you."

She offered him a confident smile despite the butterflies now thudding around her stomach.

He cupped her face with one big, gentle hand, sending heat spiralling through her veins. "You can make it up to me."

He lowered his head and took her lips in a soft kiss. *Oh, what a kiss.* Nibbling on her lower lip, he ran his tongue across it before pulling back, leaving her wanting so, so much more. The fear and intimidation diminished, replaced with pure arousal. He gathered her hand in his and tugged gently.

"Come on, I got us a room upstairs."

"Upstairs already?"

She took a peek inside herself and tried to figure out how she felt about that. Excited. Nervous. A little scared. Sure, there were dungeon monitors around all the time. She wouldn't be alone with this large, intimidating almost stranger. But still...

He offered her a smile. "I thought you'd be more comfortable negotiating in private, but if you're not, I can find a quiet area on the main floor."

A little hesitation and she swallowed against her dry throat. She could do it. She could be alone with this man. This Master. The mere fact that he'd offered to find somewhere more public put her mind at ease.

"Upstairs is fine," she managed to get out, although her voice remained a little too quiet and timid for her liking.

Master Ambrose led her to the fairy room. It had been named that by members because of the hundreds of multicoloured fairy lights that were set up along the walls and ceiling, wrapped around the furniture, forming tendrils of rainbow that oscillated in the darkness. It was named the Romance Room.

The lighting gave the entire room a feeling of sweet romance. The canopied four-poster bed helped with the ambiance. Slow, instrumental music played in the background from speakers in the corners of the ceiling. Each private room had a different theme and different feel to it, but this was one of her favourites.

After closing the door behind him, Master Ambrose moved to stand behind her and her nerves kicked into high gear. Staying in place, Belle clasped her hands at the small of her back and straightened her back, waiting for him to speak.

"I took a look at your limits list."

She flinched. A limits list for each submissive at the club was available for the Dominants to look over, making initial negotiations a little smoother. Belle was ashamed of how extensive her list was now. All thanks to that piece of shit, Bryce. Mentally shaking her head, she forced all negative thoughts from her mind and focussed on the present. Tonight was about having fun. Getting to know a new Dom — a Master.

"Belle." His voice was stern. "We all have limits and triggers. As your Dom, it's my job to avoid them and make sure tonight is enjoyable for us both, as well as keeping you safe."

"I know, I just." She gave a small sigh. "My limits list didn't used to be so long."

A gentle hand ran over her hair, sending a shiver of need down her spine. He smiled, not a hint of anger or frustration in sight. She'd been given a hard time by some Doms for her hard limits. Others had flat-out refused to play with her because she could no longer handle anything other than mild pain.

She saw a flicker of anger flash in his eyes and prepared herself for the verbal slap. It never came. Instead, he ran a finger down her cheek, along her neck before his hand curled over her bare shoulder.

"If you are ever with a Dom who makes you feel bad about having limits, find another Dom."

Good answer. She smiled at his encouraging words. After dealing with the wrong men, she'd almost forgotten what it was to deal with a good Dom. Too many of them had called her names. *Frigid. Ice queen. Tease. Worthless.* That last one always hit home. Because, deep down, she did feel worthless. Rationally, she knew that was just the trauma speaking, but still, it was hard not to believe it when somebody else said it.

"What was that thought?" he asked gently.

"I've had altercations with a few Doms because I've called off a scene due to their attitude. It just makes them meaner. But I refuse to play with someone like that."

She was rewarded with a blinding smile. "Good girl."

Her entire body was bathed in a warm glow at the term of endearment. Oh, how she loved being called a good girl. It made her feel as though she'd done something right, for once.

"Other than what is on your list, is there anything else you wish to avoid tonight?"

Belle shook her head. "I'm good with anything that's not listed. I'll try almost anything once."

"Fair enough." Removing his hand from her, he shifted his weight. "Now, for my rules. When we're together, I expect you to keep your eyes on me at all times, unless I instruct otherwise."

She caught his eye immediately and was rewarded with another gorgeous smile. This one was filled with heat. God, he was beautiful to look at. It made her inside flutter.

"While we are in the main room, I may institute high protocol. But I will always be clear about what I want. You will never have to guess with me."

That gave Belle a sense of relief. Some Dominants weren't clear in their instruction, and it made her nervous when she had to guess what they were after. It left her on edge the entire time they were together, and she wasn't able to let go and enjoy herself.

"Yes, Sir."

"You are not to wear underwear of any kind while we're together."

He took a step forward and slipped a hand beneath her skirt. Sucking in a deep breath when his fingers touched her mound, his touch feather-light, she found herself impossibly aroused in an instant.

"Nice and smooth," he murmured his approval. "I like that."

"I aim to please," she teased, letting out a nervous little laugh before he withdrew his touch.

"Then I'm sure you'll please me over and over tonight." He took a step back. "Now, strip for me, please."

Belle's pupils dilated at his gentle order and she moved to disrobe. Her bustier came off first, releasing ample yet perky breasts. Peaked with pink-brown nipples that he couldn't wait to taste, her breasts were absolute perfection. Shimmying out of her skirt, she bent to fold it neatly on top of the bustier and stood with her hands clasped behind her back once more.

All week, Ambrose had been fantasising about what her sweet little body would look like, and he had not been disappointed. Blood rushed to his cock as he looked her up and down, taking it all in, one tantalising piece at a time. Her body was taut, muscular and toned, while remaining soft and curvy in all the right places. She had an hourglass shape with skin that appeared soft and smooth and biteable. Her waist curved in before flaring out to wide hips that were made for his body to settle between. As she shifted her weight, she parted her athletic thighs slightly, clearly self-conscious beneath his assessing gaze. It gave him a peek of her pussy. The outer lips hid everything. He couldn't wait to discover her. But he had all night. He would definitely be taking his time.

Ambrose reached forward, pulling her long hair over her shoulders to let it fall over her breasts. He couldn't hide his grin when he looked down at her. As he'd thought, her hair just covered her nipples. She looked like a sexy mermaid.

"Very nice, sweet girl."

Her cheeks flushed at the compliment, and she responded with a quiet, "Thank you, Sir."

He loved the sound of 'Sir' coming from her lips.

"Come with me."

He led her to the other side of the four-poster bed, watching as her eyes widened at the array of toys he'd laid out on the bed for her to go through. She looked at them, a hint of hesitation and anxiety showing on her face. Wouldn't she be surprised to see his dungeon at home where his collection was all out on display? The collection he carried with him in the club was nothing.

"Anything you absolutely do not want to use, put it to the left. Any toys you're curious about or that are a possibility for future play, move to the centre. Anything you're okay with for tonight, move to the right. Got it?"

With a quick nod, she bit down on her plump bottom lip and regarded the toys. He stood to the side, leaning against a post, and watched Belle as she made her way through the items. He became more aroused, his cock pressing against the cold zipper of his jeans uncomfortably as he watched her fluid movements. Everything this woman did came with grace and confidence. He'd always loved that in a woman — it was a huge turn-on for him.

As he'd expected, the heavier floggers and crops went to the left, with one crop remaining in the centre as a maybe for the future. Clover clamps to the left, a definite no, tweezer and alligator clamps to the right. An array of dildos and plugs followed suit. The medium-sized ones went to the middle, the far larger ones to the left.

All bondage-related items went straight to the right, without a hint of hesitation. So, she liked bondage. That pleased him immensely. He'd always loved bondage, having a submissive helpless against his torments, writhing in blissful agony.

All the toys were laid out mostly as he'd expected, save for a few surprises, like the fact that one of the harsher crops had made it to the middle pile as a possibility for future play. Judging from her limits list, Ambrose assumed she either didn't like or was triggered by pain. Now it appeared she just preferred not to experience it. While he was not a sadist, he certainly enjoyed dealing out erotic pain when he got the chance. It drove a submissive higher, often getting her lost in subspace. And that filled a part of his dominant side that not much else did.

Stepping beside her, Ambrose ran a hand down her bare back, leaving it to rest on the spot where her spine dipped. She turned her head to look up at him.

"I hope that's okay. I don't like pain much anymore."

There was that word again. *Anymore.* Something had definitely happened to her. They would be discussing that later.

"You did well. I just wanted to be sure where your limits lay." He dipped his head and stole a quick kiss, pulling away before he was tempted to go deeper. "Sit on the bench and wait while I pack these away."

He packed the toys in his bag, making sure to keep them in the order she'd put them in. Belle sat propped on the edge of the small bench that sat against the far wall and watched his every movement. Arousal was evident in her gaze. Most of the hesitation she had previously shown had melted away, replaced with the delicious anxiety that most submissives felt when waiting for a scene to begin. When he came to stand before her, she bit on her lower lip and peered up at him through her lashes. That look alone just about drove him wild.

"Do you have any questions or concerns about tonight? Anything else I should know about?"

She appeared so small and vulnerable as she looked at him. Submissive. She was absolutely beautiful.

"I'm good, Sir."

"Very well. What is your safe word?"

"Red."

"Red," he repeated. It was the club's safe word as well, easy for him to remember.

"If you become overwhelmed and need a break, you may use yellow." Gripping her chin between his thumb and finger, he kept a hold of her gaze. "Though we're both experienced, we are new to each other. You *will* use your safe words." He bent to meet her gaze dead on. "If, at any time, I feel you are uncomfortable and not using them, I will call the scene to a halt and we will be done." He paused for effect. "Is that understood?"

"Yes, Sir."

"Good girl." He offered her a smile and straightened. "I'm sure you've heard a few things about me. Most of them are true. I'm a strict Dom."

Her pupils dilated at the comment, her cheeks blushing a gorgeous pink. His heart filled with hope. He'd heard she preferred a strict Dom, one with a firm hand, one who gave her rules to obey. That was definitely him.

"I will not tolerate back talk or bratty behaviour. Can you abide by that for me?"

Her smile faltered for a moment. "I'm not a brat anymore."

Implying that she once had been. He couldn't help but wonder what exactly she'd been through to halt her bratty tendencies and her enjoyment of pain. But now was not the time to dwell on it. He had some pleasure to dish out.

"I require verbal responses. The correct answers are 'yes, Sir' and 'no, Sir'. Nothing else. If you wish to ask a question, you may ask for permission to speak." He gave her a smile of amusement. "I may or may not give you permission."

"Yes, Sir."

"For now, you do not have permission to speak unless it is to use a safe word," he told her, gripping her chin a little harder to emphasise his control. "I expect to hear moans and sounds of pleasure. But I will not tolerate begging."

Her jaw clenched at the word. *Interesting*.

"This body is mine for the next few hours. You will get what I give you, nothing more. Is that understood?"

He could see when she slipped further into that submissive zone. Her eyes became softer, her body relaxing before him. "Yes, Sir."

Bending to meet her face, he paused. *Fuck*. He could smell her arousal. His nostrils flared as he sucked in the heady scent, his cock hardening further as desire tore through his veins, taking him higher and higher with each heartbeat. She did enjoy a hard Dom, didn't she?

"If you disobey me, you will be punished."

That delicious fear returned to her eyes. Her lips parted as she took a deep breath.

"I will not go over your limits, Belle, I can promise you that." A look of relief flashed across her face. "But I will push them. The second you are uncomfortable, I expect to hear 'yellow' from those pretty lips. I have no interest in toying with your safety and well-being."

Her expression told him she understood the severity of his tone. He meant every word. He didn't say things he didn't mean—he chose his words carefully, especially when dealing with a submissive.

"Let's begin, shall we?" Straightening, he removed his hand from her face. "On your feet."

Belle stood with her back and shoulders straight, a faint smile on her lips. With a smile of his own, he realised the top of her head reached his shoulders. If he wrapped his arms around her right now, he would be able to rest his chin on the top of her head. He wouldn't have to bend so far to kiss her. To play with her. She was the perfect height for him.

To test his theory, he dipped his head and kissed her. Tilting her face ever so slightly, Belle met him half-way. Her lips were pillow soft and silky smooth beneath his, opening as she sighed into the kiss. She brought her arms up around his shoulders, holding on as she let him control the kiss. He brought his own hands up to rest on her hips. He slipped his tongue inside of her mouth and pressed his body against hers, revelling in the feeling of her soft little body as she yielded.

Fuck, the woman can kiss. He might very well become addicted to her by the end of the night.

His heart swelled at her small whine when he broke the kiss. Resting his forehead on hers, he breathed her in for a few moments. As much as he wanted to tie her down and fuck the life out of her, he had to take his time. To learn what she did and didn't like. And he would take his time. He intended to torture them both a little tonight.

Chapter Six

With her arms restrained above her head, legs kept apart by a spreader bar, Belle waited, pressed against the bed post with her anxious heart in her throat. *What the hell is he going to do to me?* After kissing her into a frenzy, he'd stopped, leaving her so aroused that every inch of her skin felt tight. Her clit throbbed, begging for his attention. And now he stared at her, watching her squirm, his gaze intent. Like a predator with its prey. And right now, she felt like prey. Tied up, helpless, more aroused than she had been in months.

It was on the tip of her tongue to ask what he intended to do tonight but that was part of the beautiful torture of being a submissive…the lack of knowledge, the mind fuck. Handing her body over to a man for him to use as he pleased. It was what she craved. What she'd been missing.

So far, this man had proved to be a talented and careful Dom. He was calm, controlled and so stern and strict. His dominant nature sang to her submissive one.

When he gave an order, she obeyed immediately. With one mere look, she'd ended up pressed against the bed post, knowing what he was after. After one simple kiss, she'd been wet. There was just something about him that she liked.

She continued to wait, adjusting her feet so she was more comfortable. His gaze scanned her body, taking her all in. Arousal dripped down her inner thighs, her poor neglected clit throbbing with a desperate need to be touched.

Master Ambrose closed the distance between them, his big, warm hands coming up to cup her breasts. With her nipples bunching, she bit back a moan when he ran his thumbs over each one. Belle sucked in a breath and fought the urge to close her eyes and enjoy the sensation.

Eyes on him at all times, she reminded herself. That was going to be harder to obey than she'd initially thought.

He pinched one nipple before dipping his head to wrap his lips around her right nipple. She parted her lips on a quiet gasp, dropping her head back as arousal tore through her veins. Oh God, it was so good, her knees went weak. Hot and wet, his tongue teased, licking around the peak before he moved to the left and repeated the intoxicating movements. He teased, sucked, sucked a little harder then teased again. By the time he'd finished his ministrations, she was panting and writhing in ecstasy. He let her nipple go with an audible pop and straightened to capture her gaze.

"You're an absolute delight, princess."

Her insides melted at the term of endearment. She'd never been called princess before and had always found it patronising. But coming from Master

Ambrose, it had her wanting to drop to her knees at his feet.

Anxiety rose in Belle's chest when he pulled something from his pocket. A pair of alligator clamps with little weights on each end. *Oh, fuck, yes.* She loved nipple clamps. They made her wish she could handle more pain without panicking. Clamps combined with a little extra pain always used to send her deep into subspace, giving her a physical and mental release unlike anything else.

Bending, he bit down gently on her left nipple, the action eliciting a gasp from her. Pulling at the restraints, Belle wanted nothing more than to thread her fingers through his hair and hold him in place. He sucked on the nipple so hard it hit the roof of his mouth. Her pussy clenched in response as she let out a small whimper. She'd never had overly sensitive breasts but, right now, they were on fire with need, taut and tingling.

He attached the first clamp, smirking at her small sigh when she felt the bite of pain. After sucking on the other nipple, he attached the clamp and received a small cry this time. With a devilish grin, he straightened before looking her dead in the eye. He flicked one of the weights, eyes glinting with amusement when she squeaked in response.

"For someone who doesn't enjoy pain, you sure seemed to enjoy that."

Her cheeks flushed. She wanted to try so much more with him.

"Let's see just how much you enjoyed yourself, shall we?"

He dipped one hand between her thighs and touched her, barely dipping inside to graze her clit. It sent a shockwave of pleasure shuddering through her entire body. She pulled at the restraints in frustration, trying to seek more contact but, of course, was unable to.

"Well..." His voice was a rumble in her ears. "I'd say you're having a wonderful time."

She moaned as one finger slipped inside of her easily. "Yes, Sir."

Whining when he removed the finger almost immediately, she opened her eyes to find herself staring into his heated forest-green gaze. *I could get lost in those soulful eyes. So unbearably masculine in their beauty.*

"Let's see how much more I can get out of you."

He dropped to his knees, parting her pussy to run his hot, wet tongue over her clit. Crying out in blissful agony, she almost came right then. *Oh God. Oh fuck.* Her skin felt too tight as he drove her higher with a few well-placed licks. He was going to kill her. This was how she'd die. She hadn't even come yet and she was floating among the clouds.

Head dropping against the bedpost, Belle closed her eyes and whimpered as he sucked her clit into his mouth. One finger invaded her entrance at an excruciatingly slow rate before it curled inside of her. He found her G-spot in seconds, massaging it, pulling a low, slow moan from her. That was a sound she hadn't heard in far, far too long.

Pressure built in her core, her breath coming in pants as she teetered on the edge, needing just a little more... His finger and mouth disappeared, his body heat moving away. She opened her eyes—he was returning to her with a slim vibrator in his hand, a G-spot vibe similar to one she owned.

He pushed one hand into her hair and closed it into a fist, holding her where he wanted her. Taking her mouth in a delicious rough kiss, Master Ambrose groaned when she gave into him completely. She tasted herself on him, moaning at the eroticism of the act. When he pulled away, she followed, wanting more. He smirked and kept his gaze on her as he slipped the vibrator inside of her ever so slowly, filling her with a desperate need.

"Hold it in for me, sweet girl."

She blushed at the term of endearment then froze. There was no way she could hold a vibrator inside of her. She was so wet, it would be sliding out of her at any moment. *Fuck*. The vibe came to life and all thoughts were wiped from her mind. *Hold it in*. Clenching her inner muscles, she held on as tight as she could. The mere thought of disappointing him filled her with dread.

Master Ambrose tilted the vibrator until it hit her G-spot. Her entire body flushed as she struggled to hold herself up, overcome with such an intense pleasure that she thought she might burst.

"There, huh?"

The man sounded far too pleased with himself. Releasing her hair, he moved his hand down to tap lightly on her clit. Heat surged through her, carrying the tingle of arousal through her veins. Arousal peaking, her chest heaved as she cried out with each heavy exhale.

"You have permission to come, princess. Whenever you're ready."

His words were a trigger — her orgasm hit her like a tidal wave, washing over her senses before she lost complete control. Crying out, she clamped her eyes shut on the white lights that filled her vision. Master Ambrose didn't stop. His finger danced around her clit, rubbing up and down one side, over the top before moving directly over the top of the oversensitive bundle of nerves.

Arousal peaked at the border of pleasure-pain as he continued to torment her, not letting her come down. Her cries turned into whimpers as her muscles went lax. The vibrator continued to pound on that sweet spot inside of her, forcing her arousal to build again. Sweat beaded on her forehead, a small drop trickling down her back as she sucked in a harsh breath. A second finger joined the first, rubbing over the top of her clit, pushing her higher towards bliss. Her knees threatened to give way, but she managed to stay standing, fighting the wave that threatened to crash over her. *Almost... Just a little more...*

It hit like a fury, crashing over her, bathing her in a warm glow. Belle's eyes burned from the overwhelmed tears that threatened to breach her closed lids. The intensity of the orgasm was too much for her to handle. She gave a keening cry as her knees buckled, her muscles turning to jelly, and she lost herself.

She came floating back down to her body to find Master Ambrose removing the restraints, gathering her in his arms. Holding her close, he kissed her long and slow. Marking her. Taking everything she had to give him.

Fuck me.

She was in real trouble with this man. This Master.

* * * *

Watching the little sub's responses, Ambrose removed the spreader bar and adjusted her stance for her. She'd come so beautifully, with her whole being, not holding anything back. It was stunning to witness. The fact that she had given herself over so willingly filled a part of him that hadn't been touched in years.

He couldn't stifle his grin when she hissed in a breath as she moved her arms and grabbed at her breasts when the clamps moved. Chuckling at her response, he smiled deeper when she gave him the cutest little frown he'd ever seen before correcting herself.

"Nice save, princess," he said with amusement. "Now get on your knees. It's my turn."

"Yes, Sir," she responded eagerly and dropped at his feet.

With a lick of her lips, she looked up to him for permission to touch, grinning when he nodded at her. She undid the button of his jeans and lowered the zipper. His throbbing cock sprang from its denim cage, bobbing up and down in front of her mouth. He always preferred to go commando at the club because it was a real time-saver. There was no use in having a submissive fumble with his underwear when she gave him a blow job.

Not waiting for instruction, Belle dove right in. She grasped the base of his cock with one small hand, her hot, wet tongue running along the underside in a long, slow lick. The base of his spine tingled when she wrapped those lush lips around the head of his cock and sucked.

Fuck!

Her mouth was warm and wet as she took him in a little further with each bob of her head. Bringing down one hand to fist in her hair, he looked down at the exact moment she looked up at him, eyes vulnerable.

"You're very good at this, little sub."

Smiling around his cock, she broke his gaze and got back to work with a determination he didn't see in enough women. He kept his hand fisted in her hair, not to control her movements, but to remind her he was in control. To keep her on edge.

He closed his eyes and enjoyed the sensations as she swapped between licking and sucking, driving him mad. The woman had one talented mouth. At one point, she sucked him so hard, it felt like his dick was caught in a vice. He hissed in a breath and forced himself to stay in control.

Get a hold of yourself, man. You're a Dom. A Master. Don't come like a horny teen.

Sucking on his cock, Belle drew him in until the head hit the back of her throat. Then she fucking swallowed. *Christ.* That was it. He let go and moved her head back and forth as she sucked harder until his orgasm was about to take over.

"I'm going to come," he warned her.

With her free hand, she grasped at his hip in response as she buckled down and sucked until his cock twitched and throbbed. His entire body tingled, his balls drawing up against his body as a rush of pleasure and heat washed over him. He came in her mouth, trying not to thrust too hard. Without pause, she swallowed, even moaning as she peered up and watched his reactions closely.

Fuck. She was so sexy, and she had no idea. With one last, long, hard suck, she let him go and licked her lips before settling back on her heels, shooting him a sultry look.

"Thank you, Sir."

Breathless, he pulled back and smiled down at her, cupping her chin in his hand. "Thank you, sweet girl. Now, get in the centre of the bed, on your back, hands above your head."

He kicked off his shoes as he undid the buttons of his shirt and slipped it off. Grabbing a condom, he sheathed himself before joining her on the bed. On his knees, he sat beside her and took a minute to enjoy the view. She was laid out like a virgin sacrifice for him, her hair splayed out around her head, knee bent, thighs pressed together, that naughty little grin on her face. She appeared very pleased with herself.

Holding himself up on his arms, he hovered and bent to kiss her. Belle gave herself to him, her soft lips moving against his. Her sweet little tongue darted out, testing the waters before he deepened the kiss with a groan. She tasted like sugar and cherries. Absolutely delectable. Reaching up, he clasped her cuffs together while blindly reaching for the restraint he knew was there. He broke the kiss and attached it, pulling to test the strap. As he moved up to loosen the strap so she would be more comfortable, the sneaky little submissive took the opportunity to kiss his chest. She pressed her silky lips against his skin, her tongue flicking out for a taste. It sent a shiver across his body.

Moving back to his initial position, he captured her mouth again, devouring her with an insatiable hunger. He enjoyed the way her thighs parted and wrapped around his hips in invitation, holding him close. He slipped his cock through her folds, grinding his hips so his cock ran along her clit. She gasped into the kiss and tightened her legs around him, arching her back in a helpless move.

It was so damn tempting to thrust into her, but he still had things he wanted to do before he fucked her. He intended to give her so many orgasms tonight that she forgot her own name.

Chapter Seven

Belle looked down when Master Ambrose pulled back from her. His erection, long and hard and thick, bounced in front of him. How the hell was he still hard? He'd just come, for crying out loud. She couldn't help but take it as the highest compliment that he was aroused again already.

"So," he said as he leaned forward on his hands. "You enjoy sucking a man's cock, do you?"

"Yes, Sir," she responded, her voice still husky from her earlier orgasm.

She'd always loved giving a blow job. There was something incredibly erotic about sucking a man's cock while he thrust in and out of her mouth. Making him come by using only her mouth had her feel a sense of pride and intense arousal.

"Lucky for you, I enjoy eating pussy."

Oh God. A man going down on her could be hit or miss. Lowering his head, he brought his mouth so close to her pussy that she could feel his warm breath on her sensitive skin. Yet he didn't touch her.

"Unlucky for you, you're not allowed to come until I give you permission."

Belle froze. Fear licked at her spine as she looked down into his intense gaze. He was serious. She'd never been good at controlling her orgasms. In fact, she was plain bad at it. Contemplating her punishment, she felt her eyes burn, panic rising in her soul. She couldn't imagine any punishment this Master dealt out would be enjoyable. And the last thing she wanted was to disappoint him.

He closed his over her clit and she almost lost her mind.

He drove her higher and higher towards bliss with his tongue and lips, his teeth soon joining the party. Belle's moans turned into cries as she fought the urge to come. Her entire body burned with desire, skin painfully tight, the need to come causing her to tremble and shake all over. Two fingers invaded her cunt and he bit down on her clit.

Shit. Fuck!

Unable to hold back, she felt the wave of orgasm threatening to crash over her all too soon. Pulling at the restraints, she tried to close her thighs on him but he pushed them back with a ruthless force and continued his torture. Biting down on her lip hard enough to hurt, she tried to stave off the orgasm. It worked for all of two seconds. The man was too good. She was going to fail.

Hold it in, girl. You can do it.

He curled his fingers inside of her and everything stopped. Removing his hands and mouth from her, he prowled up her body, propping his hands on either side of her head. Chest heaving, face tingling, she looked up at him in utter confusion while he smiled down at her.

"I almost forgot these."

These, what?

She opened her mouth to ask just as he undid one of the nipple clamps. Blood rushed back to the abused peak, pain radiating through her.

"Jesus, fuck," she cried out as she fought against the restraints, desperate to soothe the pain.

The bastard actually grinned as she whimpered when he kneaded her breast. His mouth came down on the nipple and tears burned her eyes as he sucked gently, licking away the pain, soothing the hurt. Sighing in relief when the pain subsided into a dull, pulsing ache, she felt herself sinking into the bed.

"Get ready," he warned before removing the other clamp.

Pain tore through her breast, almost too much as he repeated his movements on the now-throbbing nipple. Crying out as he licked away the hurt, she continued to pull against the wrist restraints. She'd forgotten how bad removing clamps could be.

Belle sucked in deep breaths, eventually noticing that her threatening orgasm had subsided throughout the ordeal. That was, at least, until he resumed his former position and licked over her aching clit. Everything tensed inside of her, cunt clenching around his fingers, her entire body tingling and trembling, lungs burning as she tried to suck in air, desperate for anything to help stave off the orgasm. She couldn't disappoint him. She *wouldn't*.

Then she did. It was all too much. He sucked her clit between his teeth and bit gently, tongue flicking over the top of the throbbing nub. Crying out as the orgasm took over, crashing violently on top of her, Belle lost control. Sinking further into the mattress, the force of the orgasm knocked all the air out of her lungs. Her entire body shook and spasmed, sending her spiralling.

Once the glorious agony had worn off, the realisation that she'd disobeyed a direct order hit her. Hard. She'd come without a Master's permission. She'd let him down. Let herself down. She'd been a bad submissive.

Her breath came in harsh sobs as she fought the urge to cry.

"I'm sorry, Sir." Her voice was ragged. Then she remembered his other order not to speak. "Sorry," she muttered as she avoided his gaze.

Bad submissive, she scolded herself. *This is why nobody wants to play with you.*

Blinking away tears the wave of shame brought, she scolded herself once more, called herself all sorts of names. *Pathetic. Worthless.* Could she have fucked up anymore?

Master Ambrose continued to hover over her, watching her with an inscrutable expression, his face a mere inch from hers.

"I'll admit I didn't give you much of a chance, but a deal's a deal." With a slow, sexy as sin smirk, he said, "I owe you a punishment."

He tilted his head ever so slightly, no doubt catching the pure disappointment written all over her face.

"But the punishment can wait. Don't beat yourself up, sweet girl." He kissed her gently. Too quickly. "I wanted to test your limits. Turns out you're not good at orgasm control. Now I know."

Shaking her head, she turned her face away from his to avoid his eyes. It was one of the ways she'd always failed. She'd never been able to control her orgasms, to hold them off. Closing her eyes to hide from him, from the world, she bit her lip before it could quiver and betray her.

Worthless. Completely, utterly, absolutely pathetic. This is why no man wants you. You can't obey one simple order.

One large hand cupped her cheek, forcing her to turn and look at him. "It's okay, princess. Don't fret."

His lips grazed hers as he spoke. "Now I'm going to take you. As I please." He lowered his voice to a husky whisper. "And there is nothing you can do about it."

Her empty pussy clenched, wanting nothing more than to be filled. A sad whine escaped her lips. *God, could she get any needier?*

"Now, there's a nice sound." He grinned. It changed his face completely.

The man was beautiful.

He positioned his cock at her entrance and slipped inside, pausing for a second. She gave another panting whine and tried to move her hips, to take more of him in, but his hands held her hips in place by force.

"Uh-uh, sweet girl." He chuckled. "You know that's not how this works."

She did. She was utterly helpless. Only able to take what he gave her. To please him. And that was what was important right now, pleasing him. Especially since she'd just disappointed him. Belle ached with the need to please him.

Giving up the fight, Belle slipped into that submissive state she'd avoided for so long. He kissed his way down her neck in teasing nibbles and gentle bites, pushing his cock inside of her at a frustratingly slow rate. And she took it, like the good girl she wanted so badly to be.

"Fuck, you're tight," he whispered in her ear, pushing himself to the hilt. "And you're all mine."

As her inner muscles clenched around his cock, the words rang in her ears. *You're all mine.* Oh, how she wanted to be his. Giving a groan of appreciation, he pulled out slowly then pushed back in, his cock pushing past her sensitive passion-swollen tissues.

"Now you have permission to come whenever you like."

* * * *

Holding on for the ride of her life, Belle came three more times until she fell back, boneless, on the mattress. Master Ambrose had ordered her to wrap her thighs around him and had proceeded to fuck her senseless. She had come so fucking hard at one point she had screamed and lost herself completely. Vaguely aware of him following her, growling out his orgasm, she tightened her thighs around him and moaned as he continued to thrust inside of her, allowing her cunt to milk him dry.

The bed swallowed her whole as she drifted away, unable to move but for the heaving of her chest as she sucked in air. It was all she could do to keep breathing. He'd fucked the life out of her.

Feeling his warmth as he wrapped around her, lying down by her side, she turned her head and let out a light hum of satisfaction as she nuzzled into his shoulder, more content than she ever had before. Emotionally spent and physically exhausted, almost numb, she had nothing left. All she could do was feel. And she felt amazing.

Don't fall asleep, she reminded herself.

The last thing she wanted was to fall asleep with a virtual stranger, no matter how comforting the man was. And he was comforting. And the absolute most incredible Dom she'd ever met. Right now, she felt truly cherished.

Lying flat on the bed holding the sleeping little subbie in his arms, Ambrose had an overwhelming sense of contentment. Belle was so damn responsive, so generous in her submission. There was just one negative he'd noticed. She constantly checked the door, looking for a dungeon monitor, only looking away once she'd seen them walk by. She didn't feel safe with him — that much was obvious. And it was fair enough considering they were virtual strangers to each other. But that would change. He would play with her again and again until she was completely at ease in his presence.

Right now, he was lost in Domspace. He didn't want to think of the traumas she might have dealt with in her past, so much she was flighty and clearly untrusting of others. But he would bring it up the next time they saw each other.

Belle's breathing sped up as she woke and stirred a little in his arms. Coaxing her out of her sleep, he ran a hand up and down her back and continued to hold her, to kiss her hair. Suddenly, her entire body tensed. Her breathing stopped.

What the hell?

A look of sheer terror fell across her face as she pushed off him, sitting up to scramble away. Definitely the reaction of a traumatised — abused — woman.

"Belle," he said, using his Dom tone. "Stop."

Freezing, she looked at him like he was a monster. It was a shard of ice slicing through his gut. He'd had a woman look at him that way before, decades ago...

Her eyes darted around the room as she huddled into herself at the end of the bed, her back pressed against a bed post.

"You're safe. You're at Haven."

Too slowly, recognition came to her eyes as she looked at him, finally seeing him. Her eyes shifted to the small window in the closed door. A face appeared and hovered for a moment. After she nodded, they disappeared, and she uncurled her limbs.

"You're okay, princess." He didn't dare move right now, though everything inside of him was screaming to hold her. "You're safe."

The term of endearment had its desired effect. Her eyes softened and she stretched her legs in front of her while watching him carefully. She remained scared. Of him. It was a punch in the gut to realise. He knew he was a big man but scaring women triggered a trauma from his own adolescent years, bringing back awful memories. Memories that threatened to swallow him whole.

"I'm sorry," she whispered as she hugged herself. "I just..." A deep, shuddering breath as those heartbroken eyes looked away from him. "I'm sorry."

He waited for her to continue, but she didn't. She let out a heavy sigh and continued to hug herself, curling her legs up to wrap her arms around them.

"Can I touch you?"

Her face crumbled as she whispered, "Please."

That was all the permission he needed. Moving closer, remaining aware not to move too fast, Ambrose sat with his legs crossed and pulled her onto his lap. She went willingly, her skin cold to the touch. He pulled out the blanket that had been wrapped around her earlier and placed it over her shoulders just as she began to shake.

Trying to comfort her, Ambrose pressed a soft kiss to the top of her head and just held her, murmuring sweet words of reassurance over and over, trying to get her to believe she was safe. Something bad had happened to this woman, something that had involved a man—that was evident. And it broke him to think about some piece of shit daring to harm this amazing woman. It filled him with a fury that he hadn't felt in years.

* * * *

Sometime later, Belle stirred in his arms and pulled back to rub her tired eyes.

"Feeling better?"

"Mm-hm." She nodded.

"Stay here." He lifted her off his lap and moved to grab a red sports drink from his bag, smiling when she accepted it eagerly and guzzled half of it without taking a breath. "Better?"

"Yes. Thank you."

Settling beside her, Ambrose ran one hand over her soft hair to soothe himself more than her. It worked.

"How are you feeling?"

"Sore," she answered before biting her bottom lip. "And embarrassed."

Belle rested her elbows on her knees and leaned forward. "I'm sorry I panicked. I didn't mean to fall asleep on you. I should have known..."

"Did I do something to trigger you?"

She looked at him, appalled. "No!"

One small, slightly calloused palm touched his face in a sweet gesture that threatened to melt his heart.

"It wasn't you. I just..." She gave a small huff. "I don't want to talk about it tonight."

He watched her for a moment, wondering how hard he could push before she ran from him, before deciding against it. Right now, it wouldn't do anything other than alienate her. She was still skittish. They didn't know each other well enough for her to open up to him. Not yet.

Then it hit him. The realisation that he wanted to see her outside of the club's walls. He wanted to know her — really know her. *Shit*, he wanted to date her. He had a connection with Belle that he hadn't felt in years. One he hadn't expected.

Getting back to the task at hand, Ambrose leaned forward and cupped her cheek, loving the way she leaned into his touch. Belle wasn't truly afraid of him — she'd just panicked. That filled him with a deep sense of relief.

"Did you enjoy yourself tonight?"

Her cheeks blushed a gorgeous pink over the light brown of her skin as she smiled sheepishly. "I really did, Sir."

She gave him a tentative kiss. He kissed her back lazily, moving his hand to cradle her nape to hold her against him. He explored her mouth, teasing her, tasting her, enjoying the heady scent of her arousal.

"I've never come so hard in my life," she told him when he pulled away. "I think you may have broken me for other men."

"Good," he replied. "That's something I like to hear."

He gave her another quick kiss. "I thoroughly enjoyed myself too. I've never had a submissive like you."

She peered at him through her dark, thick lashes, disbelief in her soulful eyes. Did she really believe herself undesirable? She was amazing. Such a sweet submissive. Intense, giving and so fucking hot his cock had been rubbed raw from how many times he'd taken her. Ambrose continued to watch her without speaking, just touching her. He cupped her cheeks in his hands, thumbs tracing her jaw and lips. Lips that quivered beneath his touch. Looking into her eyes, he saw tears gathering there.

Oh hell. She was dropping.

He wrapped the blanket around her tightly and moved to sit with his legs crossed again, pulling her into his lap to her previous position. When she didn't fight him, he smiled to himself.

"Lean against me, princess. I've got you."

Slowly but surely, she relaxed and leaned her full weight against him. He rocked her and rested his chin on the top of her head, tightening his arms around her, hoping she would feel safe and secure in his hold. Because she *was* safe with him. He felt a deep-seated need to protect all submissives he played with, but it went deeper with Belle. Something about her intrinsically called to his protective nature.

"I'm sorry. I disappointed you," she mumbled and let out a shaky breath. "I didn't mean to."

Disappointed him? What on earth was she talking about? She'd exceeded his expectations for tonight. Had taken him on the ride of his life.

Then it hit him. She'd come without permission earlier. That had been hours ago, and she was still holding on to it.

"Oh, sweet girl, no." He leaned back and placed a finger beneath her chin, forcing her to look at him. "I told you, I was testing you. I wanted to see if you could control your orgasms. I was only teasing."

She looked at him unconvinced, tears still blurring her beautiful, melted chocolate eyes.

"You didn't disappoint me at all. I promise you." He pressed a soft kiss to her forehead, one that left his lips tingling with the need to kiss her elsewhere.

"Really?" She sniffed. "I'm sorry." A rapid swipe at her eyes. "I probably should have warned you I'm prone to subdrop."

"Even if you weren't, I'm sure you'd be dropping. We got a little intense tonight."

"A little intense?" She let out a cute giggle. "I'm pretty sure I lost consciousness at the end."

Grinning, a sense of pride caused his chest to swell, his ego enjoying the subtle stroke of her quiet words. Pulling away, she rested her hands on his chest and watched him, her gaze focussed on his smile.

"You're beautiful, you know that?"

The blush and sheepish expression he received was gorgeous. Unable to resist, he kissed her again. A quiet knock at the door told him it was time to leave. The club would be closing soon. With a hint of regret, he broke the kiss and caressed her cheek.

"It's time to go." He patted her on the butt. "Stay here for a bit while I clean up, then we'll get you dressed."

Chapter Eight

Belle sat on a lounge in the submissive section of Haven the next night, nervous to see Master Ambrose again. After standing with her in the car park last night until her drop had lessened, he had texted her earlier in the day to check in and see how she was going. Luckily, she hadn't dropped any further and was feeling good tonight. That subdrop last night had been horrid to go through. Almost crying in front of him had made her feel awful. Embarrassed even.

Her fellow submissive and friend Ellie approached the area, heading straight for Belle. The twenty-six-year-old's bottom lip was stuck out in an adorable pout that made her look much younger than usual and she rubbed at her butt. Though she had done a lot of research into the lifestyle and discussed it with Belle and her friends, Ellie was still considered a newbie. After being introduced to Amara through Sullivan—who she worked with—Ellie had become a fixture of their group. And Belle adored the younger woman.

Belle enjoyed the innocence Ellie had when it came to BDSM. She hadn't been jaded by bad experiences yet. But there was also a darkness in her, an age that didn't belong in such a young woman. She'd been through some traumatic experiences in her short life, but Belle hadn't discovered all of her past yet. She'd taken the woman under her wing while at Haven, keeping her safe when she could, being her company in the submissive section most nights.

"What happened to you?" Belle asked with a little smirk.

"Master Ambrose just spanked the shit out of me because I mouthed off." Sitting gingerly beside Belle, Ellie squirmed as she tried to find a comfortable position to sit in.

Belle felt a pang of envy in her chest. She missed the days when she could deal with a good, hard spanking for punishment...the reminder of it each time she felt the ache as she sat. She'd always been so fulfilled after a little beating.

"What did you say to him?"

The other woman's pale cheeks flushed. "He touched my lower back because I was in his way, and I didn't think before speaking. I called him a pervert and told him to ask before he copped a feel."

Laughing as her friend blushed further, Belle leaned back in her seat. Ellie was a brat. She was used to holding her own amongst men given her job as a gym trainer, and the fact that she was friends with all the Doms in their group. She was also too smart for her own good. Not many Doms could get her to submit, but it was always fun for Belle to watch them try.

"Master Ambrose hates brats, I know that. But it just came out before I realised what I was saying.

Apparently he's in a mood." The younger woman continued to sulk.

"Thanks for that. I've got a scene with him tonight."

Ellie's dark eyes widened as her mouth dropped open. "Whoops. Maybe he got it out of his system with me."

Belle could only hope. She wasn't in the mood to be pushed too far, not after last night. She'd spent all day working again. Her body ached, and her mind was mush. She just needed to submit and let go.

Master Ambrose appeared in her line of sight not a second later, striding towards her with those long, powerful legs, a stern expression on his handsome face.

"It's a good thing I don't judge you based on the company you keep, princess," he teased before bending to kiss her.

Biting her lips, Ellie narrowed her eyes at him, but held back her no doubt snarky retort. *Smart girl.*

"I know better than to talk back to a Master," Belle said with a smile as Ellie stared daggers at her.

Master Ambrose gave her a smile of approval. "Are you ready?"

"As I'll ever be."

She took the hand he offered and said goodbye to Ellie.

As she followed him through the main room, he led her straight upstairs again. That surprised her. She'd asked the single submissives she knew about him earlier in the evening and found out that he had a tendency to do public scenes rather than private ones. She'd prepared herself to be taken in public tonight. Apparently, they were going to play in private again instead and that suited Belle just fine. She was more than happy to keep him all to herself.

* * * *

Entire body tingling with arousal, Ambrose took a step back and watched the writhing submissive in front of him. Restrained on a cross, she wriggled her hips, head swaying back and forth as she went up on her toes while he flogged her lightly. He remained very aware to only strike her with light blows and, even so, she was well on her way to subspace.

He moved to stand in front of her, checking her cuffs again, running a hand along her heated back, grinning when she whimpered in response to his touch. Her back arched to seek more. She was amazing. After already coming a couple of times earlier in the night, she was ready to go again. But Ambrose had been purposely holding back on that side of the play. He detached the butterfly strapped to her pelvis and tugged it off. She gave a low whine in response.

"Now, now, princess. You'll get there again, eventually," he murmured in her ear while brushing his fingers over her hair. "You just have to earn it."

Most women would be begging and pleading for release by now. But not Belle. Belle didn't beg. She was far too stubborn for that. He tossed the flogger onto his toy bag, moving to stand by her side, one hand on her front, one on her back, to keep her grounded. Moving them up and down her supple skin, Ambrose enjoyed the low moan she gave at his touch. When she got like that, he knew she was simply feeling and responding in kind. She had very little control over the sounds she made.

He moved his hand to cup her ass, giving the sensitive skin a squeeze as he leaned forward to press his lips against her throat. Her head dropped to the side, giving him better access. He sipped at her flesh, licked, tasted, biting down gently where her neck met her shoulder.

"Master," she moaned.

"Shh, sweet girl," he whispered in her ear before biting down on the shell of it, just hard enough to sting.

Lost in a sea of sensation, Belle turned her head to look at him, eyes glazed over. She didn't speak but her eyes said it all. She needed to come, was teetering on the edge, unable to get there herself.

"You've been such a good girl tonight," he murmured, grazing her smooth pussy.

She jumped and writhed in response, trying to seek the friction she so desperately wanted. Fuck, she was beautiful.

"I'll give you what you need, princess."

Thrusting two fingers inside of her soaking wet cunt, he moaned himself when her inner muscles clenched around his digits. *Christ.* He barely held on to his control as he thrust in and out of her, using the heel of his palm to press hard against her clit. Belle cried out, her head falling back as she tipped over the edge.

"That's it," he said, lost in the moment. "Come for me."

Her entire body trembled as her cunt clenched around his fingers. He kept them buried inside of her, curling them to drag out her orgasm until he'd wrung her dry. She was gone, lost in subspace. And it was stunning.

Keeping one hand on her at all times, Ambrose went about undoing Belle's restraints. He wrapped a soft blanket around her and scooped her into his arms, surprised by how light she was. She went with him, wrapping her arms around his shoulders, burying her face in the crook of his neck in a heartbreakingly sweet sign of trust.

He opened the door to the private room and asked the service submissive on duty to grab his bag and meet him downstairs. Carrying her down the steps, he made it to the recovery corner and found a quiet seat. He pulled her arms from around him and settled her in his lap, tightening the blanket around her trembling little body.

Clint, the service submissive, found him and dropped the bag beside Ambrose.

"Get me a scotch, a red sports drink and a bottle of water, please."

"Yes, Sir." The young man nodded and hurried away with his head held high.

Ambrose looked around the room and spotted Ayden, tilting his head to gesture for the other man to join them. Hopefully, if Belle saw a friend nearby when she came to, she wouldn't panic as she had last night.

"Looks like you gave her a good time." Ayden kept his voice low as he sat opposite Ambrose.

"A good time was had by all," he said, his voice still thick with arousal, cock throbbing with the need to release.

He was hard as a rock beneath Belle's supple body, but he wouldn't be doing anything about it tonight. Not with her. She was definitely done for the evening.

Returning with his drinks, Clint asked Ayden if he wanted anything, showing a hint of disappointment when the other Master said no. It was no secret that the submissive had grown a little too attached to Ayden. It was something all the Masters and Mistresses had to deal with, treading that fine line between mentoring the subs and treating them well while maintaining a certain distance so they didn't get any ideas of forming romantic relationships. Especially with submissives like Clint, who were prone to sub frenzy.

"When is your shift over?" Ayden asked the younger man.

"Eleven, Sir."

"Since you've been well behaved tonight, come find me when you're done. If I feel so inclined, I'll reward you for your good behaviour."

"Yes, Sir. Thank you, Sir." The other man beamed as he trotted away with a skip in his step.

Part of their jobs as Masters was to reward the single submissives who worked at the club for a discount in membership fees. As a result, most of them took the subs under their wing and often rewarded them for good behaviour and punished them for the bad. Since Clint was new to the lifestyle, he hadn't had much experience with the more senior Dominants, yet drooled over each Master and Mistress. Tonight, Ayden was throwing him a bone — perhaps literally.

"How'd she do?" Ayden asked, protectiveness evident in his quiet tone. "Did she panic at all?"

Ambrose had told him about the incident the previous night. "She hasn't panicked tonight, but that's why I brought her down here to wake up. I couldn't handle it if she panicked with me tonight."

"That bad?"

"It was awful," he told the other man. "I've seen it before, and it brought back some very unpleasant memories for me."

"You think she might not panic if I'm here when she wakes."

"Exactly." Taking a sip of his scotch, Ambrose rested back in his seat, running his hand up and down Belle's back in a soothing motion.

The two men chatted for a while before Belle began to stir in Ambrose's arms. He couldn't help but worry as he felt her body tense and prepared himself to catch her if she panicked. But she didn't. Instead, she lifted her head to look at him, a dreamy smile on her pretty face.

"Princess," he murmured.

"Mmm," was all that came from her.

She closed her eyes and snuggled into him like a milk-fed puppy. All soft and warm and cuddly.

Ayden smirked. "Looks like she's okay."

He nodded in agreement and pressed a kiss to the top of her head. Her eyes were still open, but she wasn't quite back with him yet. Passing her the sports drink, he popped the top open.

"Have a drink, it'll help."

"I don't want help," she whined. "I just want to stay like this."

Ayden's chuckle sounded and she turned to look at him with a cute frown.

"Shut up," she mumbled before taking a sip of the drink. "Master, he's making fun of me."

She whined again and continued to snuggle into him. Ambrose found it rather amusing himself.

"Is she usually like this when she's in subspace?" he asked his friend.

The other man shrugged. "I wouldn't know. I've never seen her in subspace."

"Never?" He couldn't hide his shock. She'd slipped so easily tonight, he assumed it was a regular occurrence.

"She never trusted me enough to let go." He stood and slapped Ambrose on the shoulder. "Be careful with that, my friend."

Continuing to run his hand over her blanket-covered back, Ambrose smiled down at the woman in his lap. If she trusted him enough already to go into subspace, he needed to tread lightly. The woman clearly had trust issues. The last thing he wanted to do was earn then break that trust. He had to be careful.

* * * *

Unable to wipe the smile off her face the next day, Belle was walking on air. Each time she thought of Master Ambrose, her soul soared. Last night, she'd hit subspace for the first time in over two years and it had been an amazing experience. Even before the incident, she had rarely trusted a man enough to take her to subspace. And, even when she did get there, it was short lived and had never felt like last night had. She was light and free and happy. So fucking happy.

Ambrose had continued to hold her until she woke enough to stand on her own two feet. He had then walked her to her car and had given her a sweet kiss she'd never forget. She'd even slept well, dreaming of him — of his hands on her body, his smile when she pleased him, his voice in her ears, his arms wrapped around her as he held her securely. She felt so safe with him.

Struggling with the cake plate and bag that held containers of cookies, Belle noted the strange car in Ayden's driveway and frowned. She didn't recognise it. If Ayden had company, why would he have told her to visit now? Because that was Ayden — he always had time for his friends. And he probably just wanted the sweet treats she'd baked for him.

This time, she'd baked him a special cake and a bunch of cookies to thank him for taking care of her during the week and for installing the new camera. He didn't have to do it, but he had, because he was a good man and a great friend.

She let herself in the unlocked front door, grinning when Forrest came bolting down the hallway to greet her with one loud bark, as usual.

"Hey puppy," she greeted him. "Let me put this down and I'll give you a proper cuddle."

Ayden walked in as she entered the open-plan kitchen and dining area, in a casual outfit of jeans and a jumper. To her surprise, Ambrose followed him, gorgeous in jeans and a fitted black sweater. He smiled when he saw her. She responded in kind, unable to keep her cool around him.

"Why hello, sirs," she teased, looking at Ambrose. "If I'd known you were the company, I'd have brought extra cookies."

She placed her things on the kitchen bench and bent to greet Forrest properly. "How's my favourite puppy?"

Scratching his neck as he threw his head back in expectation, she laughed as he enjoyed the attention.

"What did you bring me today?" Ayden asked as he rubbed his hands together.

"Your favourite chocolate chip cookies, some sugar cookies and my famous triple-choc layer cake."

"The big, fat cookies, not biscuits?"

She nodded, smiling as he practically drooled and opened the cookie container.

"All right," he said as he pulled a cookie out of the container. "Ambrose, mate, you have to try one of these. Belle is the best baker around."

Instead, Ambrose closed the small distance between him and Belle and wrapped an arm around her waist, his other hand cupping her cheek in a possessive move.

"How's my princess today?"

Her cheeks heated at his words. "Tired after slaving away in the kitchen all day." She shot Ayden a look. "You'd better appreciate the things I do for you."

He offered her a grin and shoved a piece of cookie into his mouth.

Turning her head to look back at Ambrose, she was taken aback when he dipped his head and stole a kiss. It was over far too soon. He hummed his pleasure as he pulled away and licked his lips.

"You taste like cookies."

"I may have eaten four of them while I was working on the cake." She giggled.

Actually giggled.

Taking a cookie from the container, Ambrose bit into it, eyes widening as he looked at Belle. "Damn, Belle. This is the best cookie I've ever tasted."

"I told you," Ayden commented.

Blushing at the compliment, she pushed her hair behind her ears and leaned into Ambrose.

"So, what did I interrupt?" Belle asked.

"Ambrose just took out Forrest's stitches. Now I owe him dinner as a thank you."

She looked up at him. "You're a vet?"

"Mmm-hmm. I own the clinic that's apparently down the road from you."

Belle knew the clinic. She drove past it every day. Now that she thought about it, Ambrose being a vet made sense. Outside of the club environment, he was far more approachable. And, she'd noticed, always smiling. He had a friendly, kind, caring aura about him. And Forrest loved him. The big lug was leaning against the man's leg with his tongue lolling out the side of his mouth as he enjoyed the scratches the big, scary Master was handing out. Although right now he wasn't scary or intimidating at all.

"I can see you being a good vet," she commented and accepted the piece of cookie he held to her mouth.

"Thank you, princess."

"Okay, you two." Ayden feigned disgust. "Enough with the lovefest."

"Aww, are you feeling left out?" Belle teased as Ambrose moved his arm from around her waist. "Poor baby."

Ambrose laughed, an open, melodious sound that had her heart skipping a beat. His entire demeanour changed when he laughed. She got a peek into the man he must be. He wasn't at all what she had expected him to be outside of Haven.

"So, you do have some brat in you," he commented. "Who knew?"

"Apparently she used to be quite the brat," Ayden said before biting his tongue when she widened her eyes at him.

"What changed?"

Everything, Belle thought glumly. She shrugged. What had changed was Bryce had beaten the brat out of her. He'd put her down until she no longer wanted to act out and tease him or have fun with him. He'd made sure she became the most compliant, obedient submissive around. He'd beaten down her spirit outside of the bedroom, too. But she'd worked hard and endured a lot of therapy to gain her sense of self back. Apparently, that meant her brat was also coming back. But Ambrose wouldn't like that. Master Ambrose hated brats. Everybody knew that.

Ayden went to speak again, but Belle shot him a pleading look. *Please don't say anything.* He frowned but kept his mouth shut.

"I should go." Wanting to flee, she grabbed her empty shopping bag and gave Forrest a little pat goodbye. "I'll see you both later."

Without waiting for replies, she left, making her way to her car before she realised Ambrose had followed her. She sucked in a breath, her nerves setting her anxiety alight as she waited for the questions that would inevitably come.

"Relax, Belle." His tone was gentle yet firm.

He wasn't mad, but he was something. Belle could see it in his eyes. He reached one hand up to touch her and she froze. She couldn't help it. She knew he wouldn't harm her, but she still reacted to his size. With a frown of disappointment, he dropped his hand.

"Do you really think I would hurt you?"

No, she didn't. But she also hadn't thought Bryce would hurt her. And he had. So badly.

His eyes flashed but he didn't move. He waited for her to speak.

"I'm sorry. I know you're not like that..." she hesitated, not knowing how to finish the sentence without revealing what had happened to her. And she was not ready to admit that to him.

"Go to dinner with me?"

Her eyes widened in surprise, a blush heating her cheeks. "What?"

"You know, like a date. When two people are attracted to each other, they share a meal, get to know each other."

She laughed, unable to stop herself from smiling up at him. Oh, she wanted to date this man. She really did. And what did she have to be afraid of? *Loss of independence, loss of safety, my sense of self. No. That won't happen again.* She wouldn't let it. She'd learned her lesson.

"Just dinner, nothing more," he said in a calm tone. "I'll even let you meet me at the restaurant."

How bad was it that he'd already picked up on the fact that she didn't want to be alone with him? *Pathetic*.

"Okay," she answered, before smiling despite the unhealthy amount of trepidation she felt. "I'd like that."

"Then it's a date." He bent his head and kissed her on the cheek in a gentle caress. "Drive safe, princess."

Slipping into her car, she gave him a small wave before driving away. She had a date. Becoming excited for it, she couldn't wait to text Larissa and Amara to tell them. This was a big step for her. She hadn't been on a real date since before the incident. He'd asked and she'd accepted. And hadn't recoiled at the offer, hadn't even thought about it.

That was progress.

Chapter Nine

Sitting in the back corner of his favourite Italian restaurant, Ambrose watched the front door, waiting for Belle to arrive. Since it was obvious that she wasn't ready to be alone with him yet, he'd arranged to meet her. Hopefully tonight would change her mind and she would realise she had nothing to fear when it came to him. He would protect her against the world if he had to. And he wanted to date her. He hadn't been able to get her off his mind since they'd first met. It was a compulsion, his desire to see Belle.

She was different than other women. More complex than most he'd played with at Haven. He'd found that most submissives were interested in him for a couple of nights then were happy to move on, away from his intensity. Yet he felt something different with Belle. She wasn't intimidated by him outside of the club. Instead, she appeared more interested. That alone intrigued him. But, more than that, he wanted to help her. To work through her trust issues. Because they were obvious.

Over the past few days, Ambrose had put two and two together and figured out she'd been in an abusive relationship in the past. He didn't know to what extent, but the markers were there. Yet her friends wouldn't discuss it with him, not even Ayden. He had to respect that. She deserved to keep some things quiet until she was ready to share with him. He just had to be patient. He could be patient.

Belle appeared in the doorway and his heart actually skipped a beat at the sight of her. Though her nerves were evident as she clutched her purse and spoke to the waiter who greeted her, she still brimmed with confidence. She scanned the room, a smile spreading across her face when she spotted him. He smiled back, unable to stop the light feeling that twisted around his heart and made him think of the future. A future with her.

Jesus, man, get a grip.

Sauntering through the room, she appeared confident and sexy in a fitted black dress that dipped low enough to show off her cleavage and stopped mid-thigh to display those shapely, toned legs.

Ambrose stood and greeted her with a gentle kiss, brushing his knuckles over her jaw. "You look beautiful."

"Thank you." Her cheeks reddened in an adorable blush. "You don't look so bad yourself."

Smiling at her teasing tone, he was happy to see she was at least comfortable enough to play with him. Pushing her seat in behind her, he returned to his own and grinned across the table.

Tonight, he had to remember not to push her, although he would pry a little. He would get to know the single most intriguing woman he'd ever met on a far deeper level. Then he would convince her to go out with him again.

* * * *

"So, tell me about your family," Ambrose said after their food arrived.

Belle froze. Though the question was a normal one for a first date, she appeared as though he'd just asked for her deepest, darkest secret.

"There's not much to tell," she said then took a sip of her drink. "I'm an only child and I'm not close with my parents." There was a flash of something in her eyes that he couldn't quite catch. "My friends are my family."

Tilting his head, he regarded her for a moment. Had her parents abused her as well? Was that where her trust issues came from? Her issues had been caused by a man, but they could have also been exacerbated by childhood trauma.

"I have noticed you're very close with your friends. They have nothing but wonderful things to say about you. Especially Ayden."

Belle grinned, her eyes lighting up, dancing with humour. "There's nothing going on between us, if that's what you're getting at."

"He assured me the same thing, but I had to wonder. What happened between the two of you?"

She shrugged, a fluid movement of her toned shoulders that had her hair spilling over her shoulders to hang down her back. He wanted to wrap it around his fist and feel the silky tendrils against his skin.

"Nothing interesting. He wanted more than I was willing to give initially. We played a bunch of times but, after a couple of months, it just fizzled. The spark was gone. We remained friendly enough, but after Amara and Sullivan got together, it became evident we were going to be seeing more of each other and we grew closer. Now, he's like the annoying big brother I never wanted."

Ambrose chuckled. "I'll have to tell him you said that."

"You've seen us together," she said with raised brows. "Do you really think I don't tell him how annoying he is all the time?"

Letting out a proper laugh this time, he ran a hand over his hair. He delighted in her snarky honesty.

"Anyway, tell me about your family."

Time to open up. To show her he was trustworthy. "I'm also an only child. No extended family. My dad died shortly before I was born so it was just my mum and I for a long time. We're very close."

Ambrose adored his mum. Didn't know where he would be without her. Almost losing her at seventeen had been a wake-up call. He'd taken her for granted for far too long, as all teens did. After that, he had taken it upon himself to protect her.

"She was my everything growing up, but I still acted as teens do. Acted out, fought her on everything. Then I came close to losing her and I realised just how lost I would be without her."

"Did she get sick or something?"

"Or something." He shook his head, fighting the flashbacks that crashed into his mind. His mum on the floor in a pool of her own blood, unconscious while the piece of shit she called a boyfriend continued to yell at and beat her.

"She didn't date while I was growing up, and only found a boyfriend when I was seventeen and getting close to leaving home. She did not make a good choice. He was mentally and emotionally abusive, but she couldn't see it. Then one day I came home from karate class to discover her on the floor. He'd beaten her to a pulp." He closed his fists against the rage that threatened to take over. Even twenty years later, it still got to him.

"Anyway, the man she's now married to is the polar opposite of that piece of shit. Once I realised he wasn't going to ever hurt my mum, he took me under his wing. He taught me how to treat a woman, how to respect a woman. He led by example. He treats my mum like a queen."

"Sounds like a good man." Her voice was quiet and almost timid as she spoke.

He looked up and noticed she'd paled considerably. Reaching over the table, he gathered her cold hand in his and ran a thumb over her knuckles.

"What happened to you, Belle?" he asked. "Tell me."

Melted chocolate eyes glistening with tears, she shook her head rapidly. "I can't."

Pressing his lips into a firm line, Ambrose fought the urge to push. He had to trust that she would tell him in time. When she felt comfortable enough with him. At least tonight had been a step forward.

"I'll wait until you're ready," he told her. "But my patience will only stretch so far, Belle. I want to help you, but I can't do it if you don't open up to me about your past."

She let out a low huff and her shoulders went slack. "I'm estranged from my parents. They're the reason for my trust issues. It takes me a lot to let people in, to trust them enough to open up. Just so you know," she added in an icy, closed-off tone.

Well, he certainly hadn't expected that. Or her defensive attitude.

"I spent my entire life being told I was worthless. A mistake. A burden. An interruption to their lifestyle. I always knew I wasn't wanted. If you want to go further with me, you need to remain aware of that. If you push too hard, I will push back."

Heart breaking for the beautiful child she must have been, Ambrose squeezed her hand a bit harder. Belle was so warm and caring and gentle. She gave herself over completely during sex, while holding back in every other aspect. It made sense now.

"Please tell me you had someone love you growing up."

Her face softened, a small smile spreading across her lips until it reached her eyes. "My grandparents were amazing. They cared for me most of the time because I was so unhappy at home. But they both died when I was ten and I've been alone since."

The sadness returned to her eyes, and he wanted to kiss it away. To scoop her into his arms and hold her, letting her know she was cared for. That she deserved love.

"Let's talk about something else. I didn't mean to get all depressing."

"To be fair, I did start it."

She gave him a very forced smile.

"Tell me about your work."

Soon enough, the awkwardness of their conversation was forgotten as they settled in, discussing their careers and social lives. Belle relaxed as she spoke more of herself and her friends, even laughing often. Now that Ambrose'd had a peek into her past, he was determined to get to the bottom of her trust issues. To make her realise that he was a man of his word, that she could trust him. He would make it his goddamned mission in life.

* * * *

Perching on the edge of her couch, Belle nervously bit at her already too short fingernails while waiting for Ambrose to pick her up. She'd swallowed her fears and agreed to let him drive her to Haven tonight. After dinner on Wednesday, he'd gone full Dom on her and insisted he would treat her as she deserved to be treated.

"Belle," he'd said sternly. "I will treat you like a slut in the bedroom, if that's what you want. But everywhere else, you will be treated as a woman should be. With honesty, respect and chivalry. That includes me picking you up for our dates."

He'd been so forceful yet sweet. How could she say no?

Fiddling with the pepper spray inside of her small handbag out of habit, she waited while the nerves built and tried to overrun her good mood. Ambrose was a good man. He was different from anyone she'd dated in the past. He held out chairs for her, opened doors for her and actually listened when she spoke. He asked questions to get to know her on a deeper level. And that scared her. The thought of truly knowing someone.

What if he decided he didn't like what he found? He would abandon her just like everybody else.

Shaking her head, Belle let go of the pepper spray and ran her hands over her face. It was fine. She could do this. If she didn't give him a chance, she might miss out on something that had the potential to be great. And he'd already proven he liked her. He'd asked her out on a second date before the first had even finished.

The more she discovered about Ambrose, the more she liked him. Belle had done her due diligence and asked around about him, receiving nothing but good reports. Last night, she'd asked Ayden extensive questions about his friend, and he had insisted Ambrose could be trusted, that he was nothing like Bryce. His mother's own experience with abuse had opened his eyes to the ways of the world. He would be the last man to treat Belle poorly.

She'd also noticed that Ambrose hadn't tried to control her, not like a lot of Doms she'd known. Almost every man she'd been with, even before Bryce, had tried to control her movements, her clothing, how she acted in public. One man she'd dated briefly had even tried to control how she acted in front of her friends at Haven. Not by instituting high protocol, but by flat-out telling her what to say and what to think. Needless to say, she'd broken up with him on the spot, in a public manner, so there would be no taking advantage of her again.

Belle had chosen some duds in the past. At least those days were behind her. She was far smarter now. Far less naïve, even if a little jaded. She'd found a good one in Ambrose—she knew that deep down. He was firm and stern when in Dome mode, yet so kind, sweet and gentle with her. He was playful, generous, caring and a great listener.

On Wednesday night, they'd stood in the restaurant car park and talked for almost an hour before she got too cold and he ushered her into her car. He didn't interrupt once she got started on the unfairness of the landscaping industry, telling him she'd been turned away from far too many jobs simply for being female. Instead, he'd sympathised with her and had shown compassion.

Headlights lit up her driveway and she jumped off the couch, heading out to meet him. After locking everything, she turned and found him approaching the alcove by the front door.

"You didn't have to get out. I was coming."

"Belle," he said in that stern tone that told her she'd done something wrong.

The frown on his face proved it. No *princess* for her tonight. The date hadn't even started and she'd fucked it up.

"Remember our conversation the other night?" She nodded. "Me treating you like a lady includes me knocking on your front door and escorting you to the car." He set his jaw and reached for her hand. "Remember that for next time."

"Yes, Sir," she replied quietly.

"I'm not mad at you, princess." He touched her cheek. "I'm mad at the inadequate men you've dated in the past. What sort of man doesn't greet his date at the front door?"

"Uh, most men." She scoffed, barely biting back a "duh."

"Then you have been with the wrong men, sweet girl."

A shiver ran down her spine when he pressed his lips against hers. Oh, she really had been with the wrong men. No other man could kiss like Ambrose.

"Come on. I've got quite the night planned for you."

She swallowed at his low tone, then he flashed her a wicked grin.

"Yes, you should be scared. You're getting punished tonight."

"Oh shit," she muttered as she followed him to his car.

"Oh shit, indeed."

Chapter Ten

Belle swallowed past the nervous lump in her throat as she lay on her back in the centre of the bed in a plain private room. With her pelvis tilted up, a wedge beneath her hips, her ass was on fire. This was not how she had been expecting the evening to go. On the drive in, she had sassed Ambrose, feeling bold because they'd only just entered the Dom/sub dynamic. He'd given her five swats as they entered the club and it had forced her straight into submission.

She was so fucking aroused. All he would have to do was touch her pussy and she would come. But he wasn't touching her. He stood and watched her, his intent gaze roaming her body, taking in her naked flesh. She must have looked quite the sight, with her arms restrained by her side, her legs parted, knees up, all aroused and becoming more frustrated by the second.

"How are you feeling? Any discomfort?" he asked as he ran his big hands up and down her legs.

She shook her head and felt the bed slip out from beneath her as she sank further into the submissive headspace. "No, Sir."

"Good." He bent over her, the fabric of his shirt grazing her oversensitive skin as he gave her a soft kiss that ended far too soon. "It's time for your punishment."

Her stomach dropped as though she were riding a rollercoaster. And she was...each damn scene with Master Ambrose.

"You thought I would forget?" He creased his forehead as he looked at her with raised brows. Fuck, he was sexy.

"I was hoping you'd forget," she teased.

"Bad girl." He dipped his head and ran his hot tongue along her slit, sending a shudder of need throughout her entire body as she gasped in surprise.

Wiggling her hips, seeking more, she moaned in disappointment when he straightened with a wicked grin on his face. Instead, she received a small, stinging slap to her inner thigh.

"Now that you're nicely aroused, I can get to work."

She looked at him in a silent plea. His eyes darkened to a forest-green as he rested his hands on her knees.

"You're going to get a lesson in edging."

Heart dropping to her gut, dread replaced arousal. The one time she'd tried edging, she had hated it so much, it ended up feeling like torture. Being forced to the edge of orgasm over and over only to be denied was not fun. She'd ended up crying before the scene was over.

But this was a punishment. He intended to torture her. *Well done, Sir.*

"You're going to love and hate every second of it."
He actually grinned at her, the bastard. "Since you're
unable to control your orgasms, I thought it would be a
suitable punishment, no?"

Opening her mouth to speak, she realised nothing
nice would come out and closed it. Instead, she
frowned at him.

"Oh, princess," he teased. "Don't be like that."

He tickled the insides of her thighs, running all the
way down to her pussy before dragging back up to her
knees. He taunted her. Teased her. She already hated it.

"You do not have permission to speak now." His
smile disappeared, intensity taking over him as he bent
to brush his lips against hers. "Just lie there and let me
have my fun."

Belle clenched her fists at her side as dread mixed
with arousal. A whine was already building in her
throat as his fingers left a burning trail along her skin.
He grabbed something from the bed where he'd
already laid out a few toys. Craning her head, she tried
to see what he was doing but received a cold stare. *Crap.*

She swallowed hard, closing her eyes for a moment
as she tried to calm herself. If he was going to torture
her and not let her come, she needed to be far less
aroused. Without waiting, he sucked her already
throbbing clit into his mouth. Hard. *Fuck.* He continued
to run his hands up and down her inner thighs, along
the outside to grasp at her tender ass cheeks where he
squeezed. That pulled an involuntary squeak from her
and she scowled.

Hearing a sound, she lifted her head. It was the all
too familiar sound of lube being squirted from a tube.
Coldness trickled over her anus then something hard
and cold pressed against it. Oh God, he was going to

put a plug in her. While she'd never enjoyed anal sex, she found that play, especially with plugs, was incredibly exciting. The feeling of fullness being fucked while wearing a plug made it so much hotter. Pushing back against the plug, she saw him smile while he watched what he was doing.

"That's my girl, take it in."

The plug went in with a silent plop and she sank deeper into that submissive space. Anal always made her submit. There wasn't much sexually that made her feel more vulnerable than having someone touch her back there. It was so intimate, so naughty. The damn thing began to vibrate, forcing her to suck in a deep breath at the wave of sensation that she rode. It had been months since she'd engaged in anal play. And it felt so different. Her hips started to rise after a few moments, seeking more — or less — she couldn't tell. A firm hand pressed against her pelvis, holding her down.

"No moving, princess."

After giving a frustrated groan, she complied and tried to keep still. It was bloody hard, but she fought the urge to squirm as he touched her. Master Ambrose slipped a finger inside of her and she just about lost her mind. Skin taut and hot, she felt so aroused she thought she might burst.

Soon enough, her breaths were coming in gasps, her chest heaving as she struggled to keep it together. As her inner muscles clenched around his fingers as they thrust in and out far too slowly, every inch of her skin tingled and burned. His tongue joined the party, light flicks against her clit that sent her higher and higher. Just a little bit more...

It all stopped. His tongue and fingers left her body and the vibration stopped, leaving her feeling empty. With a pathetic whine, she looked down and noted the absolute focus on his face. Then she saw arousal—he was aroused. Good. If she was suffering, he should be too.

He slipped a small vibrator into her pussy, its low, constant vibration clashing with the vibrations of the anal plug when he switched it back on. Biting down on her tongue to stop from crying out, she writhed her hips, unable to stop herself. He moved to play with her breasts, kissing, licking, sucking and biting his way around the swollen mounds.

The man really was planning on torturing her tonight. Rather than trying to fight it, Belle gave in and prepared herself for a long ride.

After hours—that felt like days—of torture, Belle had finally had enough. She'd been brought to the edge of orgasm so many fucking times, only to be let down. She'd moved past painful arousal and towards anger. Frustration swirled through her as she came down again, Master Ambrose's lips and hands leaving her. The vibrator came out next, the third he'd used on her tonight. The bloody man was more attuned to her body than any lover she'd ever had. But tonight, that wasn't a good thing. She'd hoped to be allowed to come, just once, to get a little satisfaction. But each time she got close, he'd sensed it and stopped playing.

Drown him.

She wanted to hit him, to sob, to scream, to cry. Instead, she focussed on the anger she felt towards him.

Letting out a groan of frustration, she closed her eyes to avoid him. She couldn't look at him. Every inch of her hurt. Her clit throbbed and ached, her pussy hurt, her ass burned and her breasts were on fire with desire. Her entire body was one, big, throbbing bundle of nerves just begging for release. One simple intimate touch and she would come. And the bastard knew it.

Hurt him.

Master Ambrose stood at her feet, not touching, just looking. She wanted to beg for him to touch her, to please her. But she wouldn't. She would never beg again.

"I think you've had enough for now," Master Ambrose said in a low tone.

She tuned him out. The bed shifted beneath his weight, but she didn't bother to open her eyes to see what he was doing. It didn't fucking matter anyway. He was going to do whatever the fuck he wanted. Nothing she wanted mattered. Fuck him. He was a dick.

"Open your eyes, princess."

No, she wanted to snap.

"Belle." A firm, authoritative tone. "Open your eyes."

Unable to disobey the gentle yet direct order, she opened her eyes and found his face an inch above hers. He lowered his body onto her, the fabric of his shirt and jeans scraping against her painfully tight, heated skin.

Belle let out a low whine and writhed beneath him, trying to get any form of friction. Anything that would get her to come.

"You're allowed to touch me now." A twitch of those lips she both loved and loathed right now. "If you want to, that is."

Lifting her arms, she found he'd removed the restraints. She wanted to touch him, to hold him close, but she also wanted to hit him, call him names and tell him to go fuck himself. But that would lead to more punishment and even she wasn't that stupid.

Without warning, his cock thrust inside of her, on a single slide, and slammed against her cervix. The mild pain and the extreme pleasure were an excruciating mix that had her coming in an instant. A finger tapped against her clit and she completely lost control of her body.

A high-pitched, keening wail filled her ears. *Fuck, is that me?* She'd never made that sound before. Her entire body trembled and spasmed uncontrollably beneath his as she rode out the absolute most intense orgasm of her life.

With a couple of long, hard thrusts, Ambrose pulled the last few dregs of her orgasm before joining her in pure bliss. A wave of pleasure rolled over his entire body, his cock pulsing inside of her as he felt the orgasm from the top of his head right to the tips of his toes. He collapsed on top of Belle, unable to catch his breath, well and truly spent.

Chest heaving, he pushed himself up on his hand and brushed the hair from her sweat-slicked forehead. She'd come so hard that her entire body had thrashed against the bed, against him. Glazed eyes looked up at him, a dreamy smile softened her face as her hands slipped over his shoulders before dropping to the bed. She was definitely gone now.

"You're amazing, Belle."

Sobbing in reply, she closed her eyes and hid from him.

Reluctantly withdrawing from her still trembling body, Ambrose moved fast to remove the condom and pack away his toys and her clothing. Heart still pounding, he drew his little sub into his arms, settling on the loveseat with her in his lap. He smiled as she immediately settled into the position.

His heart swelled with pride. She had done so well tonight. Reaching for the soft blanket he'd set out earlier, he wrapped it around her body as she trembled with aftershocks.

"You did so well, Belle," he murmured as he ran a hand over her soft, silky hair. "I'm so proud of you."

"Thank you, Master."

He paused. It was the first time she'd knowingly called him Master. And it sounded so right coming from her lips.

"I want you to be my submissive, princess. Exclusively."

Making a happy sound, she ran her hand beneath his shirt to touch his bare chest. He loved how tactile she was. Always touching him, especially his skin and hair. He'd forgotten how nice it was to just sit and cuddle after a scene.

"Would you like that?"

She hummed lightly. "I'd love that," she murmured, lifting her head to look at him. "I really like you, Sir. You're special to me."

It might have been the endorphins talking, but he loved hearing those words from her.

"So, you'll be mine then?"

She giggled that amazing, innocent sound. "Silly Master." She rested her forehead against his temple. "I was already yours."

"That's my girl." He kissed her. Now for the question he'd been avoiding all week. "Why didn't you tell me about the break-in?"

She sat up straight.

"Yes, I heard. And not from you." He ran his knuckles gently over her cheek. "I want you to tell me these things."

Tears glistening in her already glazed eyes as she looked down at his chest, her bottom lip dropped into a pout. "I'm sorry. I didn't mean to… I just…"

"You're used to dealing with things alone."

He'd have to be an absolute moron not to see that. It was glaringly obvious Belle dealt with things herself, especially since she'd grown up with zero parental support. It had to be a lonely life.

"You know me too well already," she murmured.

"Is that such a bad thing?"

She nodded, still pouting.

"Why? I want you to rely on me, Belle," he said and kissed her forehead.

"I can't."

"Why?"

"Because of *him*…" She shook her head and pushed at his chest.

"Hey, it's okay, I'll stop." He wrapped his arms tighter around her, glad when she didn't protest any further. "Just get some rest."

"I'm sorry, Master." She sniffed.

Fuck. He'd made her cry.

You're a grade-A arsehole.

"It's okay. I'm sorry." He began to rock her. "Just get some rest, princess."

After kissing the top of her head, he rested his chin on it and continued to rock her into a sense of security. Because she was always safe with him. He just had to get her to see and believe it.

Belle tilted her head just enough to press a series of soft kisses onto his very sensitive throat. "My Master," she mumbled and settled against him.

He ignored the thoughts that rose to the forefront of his mind, the question of what had happened in her past, of who 'he' was. Now was not the time to question her. Now was the time to make her feel safe and secure. So he did, murmuring sweet words to her, kissing and caressing the sweetest little submissive he'd ever known until she fell asleep in his arms.

Chapter Eleven

Head still spinning from the insanely intense orgasm he'd just had, Ambrose sat with Belle curled up in his lap. She was thoroughly sated and still off with the fairies. It had been a more intense scene than he'd intended. He hadn't expected it to hit him quite so hard. He could feel himself dropping as he continued to stroke Belle's hair.

She stirred in his lap. He smiled when those glassy eyes looked directly into his. Fuck, she was beautiful. And his. All his.

"Master?" The way she said the word pulled at his heart.

She said it almost tentatively, as though it was special to her, yet difficult to say.

"You back with me?"

"Mmm," she responded as she straightened and rubbed her eyes. "I think so."

"Here." He handed her a bottle of sports drink. "You panted and screamed so much you must be dehydrated."

After drinking the entire bottle, she gasped a few deep breaths.

"Wow, bit thirsty, were you?" he teased.

She scoffed. "Well, some asshole tortured me for hours without a break." Her face dropped when she registered the words she'd spoken. "I'm sorry, Sir."

"Relax, my sweet girl," he said with a gentle smile, continuing to run his hand over her hair. "We're done with the scene. From now on, when we're not in a scene, you can tease and sass me all you like. I'll even let you call me names."

Giving a sigh of relief, she melted back into his hold. "I wanted to call you a lot of names towards the end there."

"I'm sure you did. You even muttered 'bastard' just before I gave you your release."

Wide, chocolate eyes stared at his. "I did? I didn't realise."

"You'd be amazed at the things you say when you're in subspace."

"I usually remember most of it."

"Do you remember what I asked you earlier, just after we sat?"

She frowned, her lips pursed before she shook her head. He suddenly felt very nervous. What if she took it back? Had only agreed to be his sub in the hat of the moment while the endorphins were running high? He didn't get nervous around women and he didn't exactly like it.

"I asked you to be my submissive. Exclusively."

"Oh."

His gut dropped at the single syllable. Because this wasn't just any woman he was asking. This was Belle, the one woman he felt a deep connection with. The woman he wanted to be his own. If she said no, it would gut him.

"I thought I dreamed that," she said and wrapped her arms around his shoulders, letting the blanket fall. "Of course it's a yes."

Her smile lit up his world.

"Really?"

"I mean, I don't understand why you want me. You could have any woman here. But yes. I would love for you to be my Dom. As long as it's exclusive. I don't share."

Her stern final words filled him with pure joy. He didn't share either. He had shared submissives during scenes in the past but never when dating them. And he would never be sharing Belle.

"I only want you. It's as simple as that." He dropped a kiss to her swollen lips. "I want this beautiful, intense, strong, fun, teasing, unbelievably responsive woman that I love having curled in my lap."

The blush that overtook her cheeks drifted down to her chest pleased him more than he could say. Before she could speak again, he kissed her, so deeply it made his head spin.

* * * *

Belle opened her eyes to find herself still curled up in Master Ambrose's lap. Her Master. Smiling to herself as she uncurled from his tight hold, she inhaled his masculine scent. He smelled of soap, man and sunshine. It was comforting.

She had a Dom of her own. A Master to call hers. And she felt no trepidation whatsoever. That alone proved how far she'd come in recent months.

Sitting up straight, she stretched her legs out, feeling like a limp, wet noodle. She'd come so hard she'd lost herself and she still hadn't fully come out of it. A fog clouded her mind.

Looking to Master Ambrose's handsome face, she ran her fingers over the contours of his face, tracing the laughter lines around his eyes, the straightness of his nose, the slight bump on the bridge, the lines where creases appeared each time he grinned at her. God, she loved his smile so much. His grin was something else. Tracing his lips, she smiled when he opened his mouth and sucked on her finger. The act set her alight, jolts of arousal shooting straight to her clit.

How on earth could she still be turned on? Surely, she'd run out of orgasms.

"How are you feeling?" he asked when she removed her finger.

"Amazing," she answered, feeling a little silly and giggly.

His cheeks creased as he smiled just for her. "How about we get you dressed and home then?"

She nodded in agreement and stood on shaky legs, looking around for her dress. Finding it on the floor, she bent to pick it up, wobbling when the entire room spun around her. Ambrose caught her by the hips and steadied her.

"How about you sit on the bed and wait for me to pack up?"

Once he was done, he helped her dress and waited while she stood. She tried to walk, finding her legs too heavy, her feet dragging on the floor.

"Well, fuck," she muttered.

Ambrose grinned down at her, slung his bag over his shoulder and bent to pick her up. "Up we go."

He scooped her into his arms as though she weighed nothing. Throwing her arms around his neck, she giggled and peppered his face with kisses.

"You know if you give me another minute, I'll be able to walk again."

"I'm not so sure about that." He laughed. "Besides, I enjoy carrying you."

"I know I'm heavier than a lot of women. I'm not easy to carry."

It was a simple fact. She was tall and carried quite a bit of muscle. One of those alone made her harder to carry than a small, round woman.

He rolled his eyes. "I'm stronger than a lot of men. I lift weights far heavier than you every day, Belle."

His tone shut her up. He was probably right. She knew he enjoyed weight lifting for exercise and no doubt pushed himself to the limit. Tightening her arms around his neck, she settled in and enjoyed the feeling of a man—her man—carrying her.

* * * *

The drive to Belle's house was spent mostly in silence as she tried to gather her thoughts and sober up. Fuck, she was adorable lying there in his passenger seat, all relaxed and sleepy. Although he'd known tonight would take a lot out of her, he hadn't quite expected her to take so long to recover. It looked like he would be spending the night with her. And wasn't that just a shame? He couldn't wait to feel her soft little body pressed against his first thing in the morning. To wake up with her in his arms as she stirred and woke.

Helping her out of the car, he took most of her weight while her bare feet dragged on the pavement. With her purse and shoes in his hand, he reached for her keys and unlocked the security screen door. He couldn't hide his frown when he saw the electronic keypad attached to the wooden door.

Someone had done a number on her. Her security was next level. While he averted his eyes when she entered the code, the second beeping of an alarm system greeted them when she opened the door. Tomorrow they were definitely going to be having a conversation about her past.

Belle took a step forward, stumbling a little. He lunged forward to steady her before picking her up to carry her throughout the house.

"Bedroom?"

She pointed to the left. "Off the front lounge," she said then pouted. "I can walk, you know."

"Actually, you can't." He laughed when she scowled at him.

"And whose fault is that?"

"That's why I'm taking care of you. I feel guilty," he teased.

Belle slapped his chest playfully as he made his way into the master bedroom. He set her on the bed and looked around the room. Off-white walls with a deep blue trim, dark floorboards and plain light fixtures were offset with splashes of colour on the furniture. The bedding was a pastel rainbow doona cover with bright red pillowcases, the bedside tables were dark wood decorated with multicoloured candles and photo frames. Even the drapes were a deep blue with rainbow trim. The room was so much like Belle. Practical yet playful, warm and inviting.

Leaning over, he unzipped her dress, pulling it down until she stood for long enough to let it slip down her naked body.

"Do you need the bathroom before you go to bed?"

"Nuh-uh." She shook her head and pulled back the doona before pausing to look at him. "Will you stay with me?"

His heart leapt at the question. "Of course I will."

The smile she gave him was heartbreaking in its beauty. Strong yet vulnerable. He reached into his bag and pulled out a pair of boxers, hastily changing before slipping into the bed beside her.

"You came prepared," she murmured as she cuddled into his body.

"I'm always prepared."

She made that cute hum sound that he loved. "My little Boy Scout."

"Little?" He raised his brows.

Grinning in response, she snuggled into him, pressing a kiss to his bare chest.

"Thank you for tonight, Master," she said. "I had fun."

"I'm glad. Now get some sleep." He kissed the top of her head. "I'll be right here if you need anything."

"Mmm. I really like you. You're special."

Oh yeah, he was falling for her already. "I think you're special too, princess."

He settled in with a sweet armful of woman, her scent in his nose, her taste on his lips. He went to sleep with a dream. He woke to a nightmare.

Chapter Twelve

Belle woke with a violent shake. A rush of adrenaline had a sheen of sweat erupting across her exposed skin. Why the hell was she naked? She didn't sleep naked. What had happened? The nightmare that woke her had been so violent, she felt like she was still stuck in it.

Something moved behind her—a body. She froze. There was someone in her fucking bed. It hadn't been a dream. *Fuck.* Panic tore through her entire body, setting her veins alight. Belle scrambled out of the bed with a shriek, her butt crashing to the floor as she scurried backwards until her back slammed against the wall.

Think, Belle, think! She couldn't. Her mind a complete mess, her brain shutting down as she tried to make sense of what was going on. The man in her bed sat up, casting a big, dark shadow across her as she wilted beneath his gaze. It wasn't Bryce. That had just been a dream. This man was built differently, leaner, with broader shoulders and shorter hair. But there was a very real, very large man in her bed.

A heavy wave of fresh panic crashed over her and she curled into herself, trying to protect herself from whatever the big stranger might do. Her entire body tingled as it called out for oxygen. She tried and failed to suck in a deep breath, only managing to rasp in panicked gasps.

"Belle." A deep voice, firm yet gentle. "You're okay."

Ambrose. *Master.*

The silhouette of his large body slid off his bed, keeping his distance as he kept his movements slow and non-threatening. Knowing it was Ambrose didn't make her feel much better. She still panicked.

"You're at home. You asked me to stay the night. Do you remember that?"

Somewhere in the recesses of her shutdown mind, she did remember asking him to stay the night. She should have known better. Should have known she would wake and have a panic attack.

Her vision threatened to turn into a pinpoint as she continued to stare at him, trying to focus on his face in the darkness, on the fact that he looked at her like she was a wounded animal.

"You're all right, sweet girl," he said. "Just breathe." *Breathe.*

"Breathe with me," he ordered in a firmer tone. "Deep breaths."

He sucked in a long, deliberate breath. Through the darkness, she saw his chest rise and fall and took in a gasping breath of her own. Trying to focus, she aimed to follow his movements, failing miserably.

As she panicked further, her vision began to blur. Through the rushing of blood in her ears, she vaguely heard him swear under his breath and move. He lifted her frozen body and set her between his knees, pressing his warm chest against her freezing cold back.

His lips touched her ear as he spoke in a hushed whisper. "Now follow me. Breathe. In...and out... In...slowly...and out..."

Eventually catching on, she began to follow the movements of his chest, sucking in a breath through her nose, letting it out through pursed lips.

"Good girl," he murmured, his chest rumbling against her. "In through the nose... Out through the mouth." Ever so gently, he ran his hands up and down her bare arms, keeping time with his breathing. "In...and out..."

Belle found herself calming down. She regained the feeling in her extremities and face. Her chest stopped screaming for air, though it continued to ache.

"That's my girl. Just focus on your breath. Nothing else matters. You're at home. You're safe. I've got you."

Holy shit. She hadn't had a panic attack like that in months. It had come on so hard and fast, she thought she would never come out of it. And by herself she wouldn't have. And she'd just done all that in front of Ambrose. Tears of embarrassment and shame burned her eyes while negative thoughts crept into her mind. *Pathetic. Weak. Pitiful.*

"Belle. Stop," he snapped.

That shut her mind down again. He wrapped one arm around her shoulders from behind and pulled her back against him.

"Just stop," he said in a softer tone.

Safe. She felt safe.

They sat like that for a while before he shuffled. "Come on, let's get back to bed."

Without a word, she followed. As she lay down in bed, a sob escaped her throat. He pulled her body into his and hushed her, telling her she was okay over and over. But she was far from okay. She was broken. So irrevocably broken that she couldn't even spend the night with the man she was falling for in her own bed.

* * * *

Ambrose woke to a cold, empty bed. No sweet little submissive curled against him as she had been most of the night. He sat, finding the ensuite door open and Belle nowhere to be seen. Sounds coming from the kitchen caught his attention. Quickly dressing in a pair of sweatpants and a T-shirt that he kept as spares in his toy bag, he relieved himself then made his way to the kitchen. He found Belle pottering around, making breakfast, a vacant stare on her face.

She smiled when she spotted him and scraped scrambled eggs onto two plates. Despite her smile, she appeared to be hurting. Vulnerable. Fragile. The dark rings beneath her eyes told him she hadn't gotten much sleep after the panic attack. That worried him.

"I was just about to wake you," she said with faux confidence. "I got hungry. I hope you like bacon, eggs and toast."

"The bed was cold without you," he replied. "I'll eat anything you make."

Unable to help himself, needing to feel her in his arms, Ambrose moved to stand behind her. Not noting a single hint of fear, he wrapped his arms around her waist and buried his face in her neck, inhaling her sweet cherry and vanilla scent. She paused her movements and leaned back against him for a few moments. *Good*. She wasn't afraid of him, just afraid in general. He could work with that.

"As nice as this is," she mumbled. "I need to get the bacon."

He let her go to dish up the remainder of the food. Once done, she turned to lean against the island bench and held out her arms.

"You can come back now, please."

With a smile, he stepped into her hold, letting his hands drift down to her tight, perky ass. He gave it a quick squeeze which earned him a giggle. Moving his hands to rest on her hips, he held her gently, allowing her to dictate the length of the hug.

"How are you feeling?"

"Fine." That was an obvious lie. "I made you coffee too. There's milk in the fridge if you want. Or I have a thing that froths the milk that I can use with my machine."

"Black's fine," he said.

Letting go of Belle, he grabbed both plates and carried them to the dining table nearby, while she followed with mugs in hand. He sat back and watched as she dug into her food with the gusto of a woman who had been thoroughly loved the night before, though she refused to look at him the entire time she ate.

"What have you got planned for the day?"

"No plans." She shrugged. "I might do some gardening. How about you?"

"I thought I might spend the day with my sub." *Get to the bottom of her panic attack.*

"Is that right?" Raising one elegant brow, she regarded him with a smirk.

"Only if she wants to, of course."

"She does."

A few moments of silence followed as they finished their meals. The food hit his stomach, which still churned with worry. *Time to rip off the Band-Aid.*

"Are we going to discuss what happened last night?"

Avoiding his gaze, Belle shook her head. "We don't have to."

"I prefer that we do."

She gave a small sigh and dropped her cutlery to look him directly in the eye.

"How often do they happen?" He took a sip of coffee and waited.

"Not often." Resting her elbows on the table, Belle clasped her hands together and sat back. "I have depression and anxiety, as well as PTSD. I'm prone to panic attacks because of that."

"Mmm-hmm." He figured as much. "And having me in your bed last night triggered you."

A faint nod. Pushing his chair back, Ambrose patted his thigh. He didn't want to have this uncomfortable conversation with her so far away, where she was able to stay disconnected from him.

"Come here, please."

Sticking her chin out stubbornly, she narrowed her gaze. "I don't need comforting."

"But I do." He'd never been afraid to admit when he needed comforting or was feeling weak. Right now, he felt both. Because what he was about to ask was already bringing back some awful memories for him.

Belle hesitated for a moment and bit on her bottom lip before standing. She moved to sit on his lap, a little awkwardly at first, until he wrapped his arms around her and pulled her against him so she had to lean on him.

"Tell me what happened to you." No response. "I know you were abused, Belle. It's evident. I need to know what happened so that I don't trigger you again."

Her hair fell over her face as she looked into her lap and laced her fingers together.

"I can't," she whispered.

Was she ashamed? He remembered his mum being ashamed after her abuse too, even though it made no sense to him. Nobody should ever be ashamed of surviving abuse or assault.

Brushing her hair over her shoulder, Ambrose touched her cheek, trying not to take it personally when she shied away from his touch. But it was difficult.

Damn the piece of shit who'd done this to her.

She was fragile right now, not willing to open up. He didn't want to push her too hard, but he also needed to know the truth. He needed to help where he could.

"I told you my mum was in an abusive relationship." His throat threatened to close over the deep, raw emotion that was suddenly at the surface. "It started out slowly, progressed into verbal and emotional abuse. By the end of their relationship, he was trying to control everything she did. But Mum pushed back. One night, while I was at karate practice, she told the bastard to leave." He sucked in a deep breath, his chest constricting against the action. "His response was to beat her."

The image of his mum lying in a pool of her own blood filled his mind. The sound of her dull moans rang in his head. Her face battered and bruised and swollen, smeared in blood… Ambrose tightened his arms around Belle, seeking the comfort he needed. He forced a smile when she wrapped her arms around his shoulders and leaned against him.

"I came home and found her... She was unconscious. He stood over her, yelling at her, tried to kick her..."

Belle gasped.

"I lost it. I gave in to my rage and we fought. It wasn't pretty." It had ended with Ambrose choking the man until he passed out. "Mum had swelling and bleeding on the brain and was put into an induced coma for a week."

"Oh, Ambrose." Wetness appeared in her voice as she held him, running her fingers through his hair. He closed his eyes and enjoyed the comfort. "I'm so sorry that happened."

"For years afterwards, Mum had panic attacks. She would wake in the dead of night screaming. I did what I could to help but she was afraid of me, her own son. All because I was a man." His voice broke as he felt his heart breaking all over again at the awful memory of his own mother crawling away from him. "All because some piece of shit dared to touch her."

The familiar rage threatened to build in him again. But he bit it back. Because the last thing Belle needed to see right now was an angry man.

"My point is, you're exhibiting similar behaviours. Don't think I haven't noticed how you are when we're alone. Constantly checking for a dungeon monitor, looking for exits, clutching at what I assume is pepper spray in your purse—just in case I lose my shit on you."

She bit her lip and avoided his gaze. "I didn't realise you noticed that," she whispered.

"Belle, if I'd known you were at risk of having a panic attack, I would never have stayed last night. I would have organised for one of your friends to stay with you."

"But I asked you to stay. I wanted you to stay." She tightened her arms around his shoulders, and she pressed her forehead against his temple. "I want you to stay with me."

"Then tell me what happened so I can help. I don't want to trigger you again, princess."

She smiled at the term of endearment and pulled back to look at him properly.

"It was my last boyfriend. He started out as a regular Dom, then soon became controlling and manipulative. He didn't like the fact that I was so independent." She let out a small huff. "To cut a long story short, I caught him cheating on me, left him and he broke into my house and beat the shit out of me."

Ambrose tightened his hold on Belle and tried to push back his strong emotions. The mere thought of someone laying a hand on his sweet girl was enough to send him into a mad rage.

"That was two years ago. But I still have flashbacks sometimes. Moments of weakness."

"It is *not* weakness," he growled. "You were involved in a severe trauma. Betrayed by someone you trusted."

"I know." She sighed. "I know that rationally. But I still have moments where I feel weak for giving in. Like I'm letting him win knowing he still affects my life. The thing is, I've been doing well up until a couple of weeks ago. He got out of gaol early and it's made me paranoid."

"That makes sense."

"What happened with your mum? With the man? How did she cope with it?"

"He was deported back to New Zealand. He luckily hasn't attempted to contact her since."

He flattened his hands on her back and looked into her worry-filled eyes. Not a hint of tears in sight. This amazing, strong woman had held it together so well. He was so proud of her.

"I have a restraining order against Bryce that's still standing. I just have to hope he's not stupid enough to dishonour it."

"Is he the reason you're selling your house?"

"I can't stay here now that he's out. It's not fair. I've lived here since I was eighteen. This is my sanctuary. My safe haven."

"It's not fair." He offered her a gentle smile. "I suppose Ayden has already suggested increasing your security, getting more cameras?"

She gave him a nod. "I'm considering it, I just..."

"You don't want him to win."

It made no rational sense, but emotionally, it did. Mum had been much the same. She'd refused to be scared out of her own home and still lived there to this day. Had the bastard stayed in Perth, it probably would have been a different story.

"Yeah," she whispered. "I know it doesn't make sense."

He brought one hand up to cup Belle's face. "It makes perfect sense. I want you to know I admire your strength and resilience. A lot of people would have given up after something like that. But you fought. You continue to fight."

She smiled a sincere smile before she kissed him sweetly.

"How are you feeling, right now?"

"Other than a little embarrassed and ashamed, I'm fine."

Ambrose frowned. She had nothing to be embarrassed or ashamed about. She should be proud of herself.

"Even though you're alone in your home with me."

Her eyes widened at the realisation and her arms loosened on his shoulders. "I am. Why do I feel so comfortable with you?"

"Because I'm special," he teased, using her words from last night against her.

She smirked and hit him playfully on the shoulder. "I knew I shouldn't have told you that."

"Well, you can't take it back now. It's out there," he teased again. "I meant what I said too, Belle. You're very special to me. I care for you. I adore you."

The blush that pinkened her cheeks pleased the man in him, made the Dom in him feel even more protective. He made a mental note to tell her how he felt more often.

"From now on, if anything happens to you, if you get scared or worried or have another panic attack, you tell me right away. If you're alone, you call me. I'll be here in minutes."

Belle remained silent, clearly fighting with her independence and trust issues.

"I'm serious, princess." He caught her gaze and gave her a serious look. "You call me. You let me care for you."

"Yes, Sir."

Chapter Thirteen

Stretching out her long legs, Belle watched the sun set over the garden that was her pride and joy. Rays of sunlight shone down on the native plants while honeyeaters flittered around, chattering as they headed to their roosts for the evening. Her heart ached at the thought of leaving this place. Her special garden that she'd put so much time and effort into making something to be proud of. She loved her quiet property. She would miss it endlessly. But she wasn't safe here anymore. Each night, because she didn't feel safe being home alone, she'd invited Ambrose over. But when he'd left her, she'd been on edge. She hadn't slept well in days.

Even now, with Larissa beside her, she still wasn't at ease. In her own fucking home. It wasn't fair. But she'd found a few properties in the area that suited her needs. She just had to make that final decision to make an offer on one. But she also didn't want to rush into anything.

This morning, though, as she'd been leaving for work, she found her rubbish bin had been tipped over, trash strewn all over her driveway. She'd made the instant decision for Ayden's people to install cameras on the front of her house so that she could see anything like that happening.

"Do you think I'm doing the right thing with Ambrose?" Belle asked her friend and sipped at her hot chocolate, trying to warm up her chilled core.

"Absolutely," Larissa said from her seat beside her. "Inviting him into your home and letting him work on your trust issues with you is the smartest move you could make."

"I wasn't so sure at first. But I really do feel safe in his presence. Even when he's here and we're alone. I feel safer than I do with you." She glanced at her friend. "No offence."

"Because you know he has the ability to protect you if Bryce ever does show up."

That was true. Ambrose had two black belts and decades of martial arts experience behind him. He was well and truly strong and fit enough to defend her. Belle couldn't help but feel guilty, because while she did like him—a ridiculous amount—she didn't want him to feel like she was using him. She did adore the man. The more she got to know him, the deeper those feelings went.

"Have you spoken to the police again?"

Belle nodded. "They called me yesterday. Bryce had an alibi for the time of the break-in. They believe the guy they caught is responsible for the break-in here."

"But you still think it was Bryce."

Belle looked at Larissa. "I've lived here for twelve years and there's never once been an attempted break-in or incidence of vandalism. Suddenly Bryce is out and I've experienced both? It can't be a coincidence."

"Is that why you don't want to be home alone at all?"

A small nod. "I haven't had any alone time this week. But I'm strangely not missing it."

Larissa grinned and shook her head. "I don't think you realise just how social you are."

Raising her brows, Belle regarded her friend with a look of derision.

"I'm serious." She laughed. "You say you need your alone time, but you also need social time. You're always happy to spend time with us. There's a reason why you're at Haven every week. You need human interaction."

Shifting in her seat, she placed her glass of wine on the table. "Now Amara is a more private person, more withdrawn than us. She needs time to herself, or she goes off the rails. She can't handle being around others constantly. But you're built different. I think you spent so much time isolating yourself growing up that you just got into the habit of being alone. But you don't truly enjoy it. You're not wired that way, and neither am I."

Her words gave Belle pause. Because Larissa was right. Belle had spent more of her formative years alone out of necessity. She didn't spend time with her parents, didn't have any close friends as a teen. Hell, she hadn't had any close friends until she'd met Larissa and Amara five years ago. She knew that now.

"You think I'm making up for lost time."

"I know you are. I also know you've missed having a partner of your own. Someone to spend your evenings with. And now that you have Ambrose, you're enjoying it."

Her friend's honest words made sense. "I don't want to become reliant on him. I don't want to cling to him just because he's a good guy and he's showing interest in me." She let out a small sigh. "I did so many things wrong with Bryce, I don't want to repeat it."

"But you've learned from that experience. How many times have men shown interest in recent years and you've shut them down, not because you were afraid of commitment but because you weren't interested?" Larissa pointed a finger to get her point across. "Besides, we pointed out the wrong things you were doing. You just didn't listen. If you were doing it again, I would be pointing it out, wouldn't I?"

Belle smirked because it was true. Her friends had always been very vocal about the red flags Bryce's actions threw up. She'd just chosen to see his potential rather than who he actually was.

"I am not the sort of friend who will sit idly by and allow you to make mistakes, am I?"

It was true. Larissa had consistently warned her against Bryce but had never once said "I told you so" when things with him had gone to hell.

"Okay. What's your honest opinion of Ambrose then?"

"I like him. A lot. I liked him before you started seeing him. He's a different man outside of the club, though. On the few occasions I've seen him, he's always been very sweet, courteous and kind. He seems like a genuinely good man. Now, inside of Haven is a different story. The man scares me sometimes."

Belle laughed. "I know what you mean."

"The first time I met him, he scared the absolute shit out of me. I nearly peed my pants." Larissa's eyes danced with laughter. "I'd just mouthed off to Agin because I was feeling particularly bratty."

"Of course." Belle laughed.

"He took one look at me and told me if I were his sub, I'd be getting a beating right then and there in the main club room. And he said it with a smile on his face, which just made it scarier."

"He threatened me the other night while smiling." Belle shuddered at the memory. "It gave me chills."

"What did you say to him?"

"I told him he was too old to be working late nights at the clinic by himself." Belle grinned at Larissa's open and loud laugh. "He threatened to tie me down and spank me so hard I wouldn't be able to sit for days."

She shuddered at the memory of the image it had put in her mind. The calm expression on his face as he'd delivered the threat with a friendly tone. "It ended up turning me on so much I mounted him on the couch instead."

Larissa let out a hearty laugh and slapped her thighs. "That's proof you're recovering. Can you imagine if any other man had said that to you?"

She didn't even want to consider it. The mere thought sent chills of discomfort down her spine.

"He's going to introduce me to more pain as well. I want to see if I can get back to where I once was."

"That's not going to trigger you?"

Belle shook her head. "It hasn't so far. He used a cane on me last night. I froze when I saw it, began to panic, but Ambrose was great about it. He put it down even before I said yellow. He could see me panicking before I felt it. He watches me so closely."

"That's a good Dom right there," Larissa pointed out.

"I guess that's why he's a Master."

"Indeed." Picking up her wine glass once more, Larissa gave her a cheeky smile. A bratty one. "Now, give me all the gory details of what you've been doing each night."

Belle did, telling her friend all about the scenes they'd done so far. How Ambrose would slip into Dom mode without warning and instead of worrying Belle, it made her melt. By the end of the night, she realised Ambrose had slipped his way into her heart. She cared for him, missed him when they were apart. And she had no issue with being alone with him.

* * * *

The next night, Ambrose arrived to pick up Belle at seven on the dot. As instructed, she waited for him to knock on the front door and opened it with a sneaky smile on her face. His eyes widened the moment he saw her, just as she'd hoped.

"Holy shit, Belle."

She'd dressed up tonight. Or down, technically. Wearing a deep red lacy bralette and matching thong, she'd paired the outfit with a pair of sky-high black heels, black stockings and a matching garter belt. The outfit made her feel incredibly sexy and daring. She hadn't worn anything too revealing in a long time. But Ambrose had given her the confidence to do so tonight.

"Do you like it?" She peered at him through her lashes, knowing full well what the look did to him.

"Fuck me," he said on an exhale. "Let's just stay here tonight."

He placed his hands on her hips, fingers digging into her firm flesh, sending a shiver of arousal through her.

Oh, he made her feel so absolutely claimed whenever he touched her with such intensity. Dipping his head, Ambrose gave her a kiss of pure possession. His erection pressed against her mound as he moulded his body to hers. Tangling his fingers in his hair, Belle returned the kiss with the same ferocity, tongue exploring his mouth, licking against his. A low growl sounded from his throat when she moved a hand between them to grasp his erection through his dress pants.

Pulling away far too soon, he removed her hand from his crotch, laughing when she whined in response. She pouted too, wanting to stomp her foot in a little tantrum.

"I have an extra surprise too," she teased and grabbed his hand.

Guiding it between her thighs, she moved her feet apart just enough to expose herself. His eyes widened as he touched her pussy and discovered the thong she wore was crotchless.

"Fuck," he growled and brought his mouth down on hers again.

Belle squealed in delight when he picked her up and forced her against the wall while ravaging her mouth. She made a move to undo his belt and pants, but he took over and was inside of her in seconds. Pulling away from his mouth, she cried out in bliss as he lifted her, wrapping her legs around his waist, and thrust his unsheathed cock inside of her.

They'd decided last night to get rid of the condoms since they were exclusive and she had an IUD to protect her against pregnancy, but fuck, she hadn't expected it to feel so raw and primal. She'd never had unprotected sex before. The slide of his velvety skin against her wet channel felt like nothing she'd ever experienced.

"Christ, princess." He groaned into her ear as he thrust into her over and over. "You feel fucking amazing."

"So do you," she said breathlessly and held on to him. "I can't. I'm not going to last."

"Neither am I."

Ambrose moved one hand down to rub her throbbing clit and she came not a second later, barely able to breathe while she clung to his shoulders. He followed her soon after, growling out his orgasm, thrusting hard and deep inside of her cunt while she squeezed his cock. Fuck, she'd had quickies before but nothing like that. That had been primal—pure need and attraction had driven it. And she wanted to do it all over again.

Letting her down to her feet, Ambrose did up his pants and belt.

"Stay here," he ordered and disappeared. He came back with a damp washcloth and cleaned her up. "Now that we've taken the edge off, I can do what I planned to at Haven."

He was planning while she was still trying to catch her breath. "How can you even think about that right now? I'm wiped out."

Grinning at her, he kissed her, all hungry and aroused. "When it comes to you, Belle, I'm insatiable."

He planted another kiss on her lips before wrapping her up in a coat. Pulling her out of the house and into his car, he gave her a little smack on the butt. He taunted her on the drive to the club, fingering her, playing with her ultra-sensitive clit. She soon realised wearing open panties around this man was a very bad idea.

* * * *

Every inch of Ambrose's body throbbed in time with his heartbeat as he watched the scene before him. Belle was fucking incredible. Strapped to a cross, her hips writhing and arching, she followed the cane, seeking more pain. He decided to give her a little break and pressed his body against her sensitive arse, enjoying the gasp she gave. Her head came to rest on his shoulder, her face pressing against his as she sought a kiss.

Teasing her for a moment, he licked her lips, bringing his hands around to cup her breasts. Erect nipples pressed into his palms as he kneaded her flesh and pressed a series of kisses to her bare throat. He smiled against her skin when she tilted her head, baring herself to him. He loved how much she trusted him already. She put her body entirely in his hands when they played. And slowly but surely, her emotions too.

He pressed his throbbing cock against her ass, teasing himself a little before stepping away. Picking up a heavier flogger, he got to work, flogging her gently, waiting until her upper back was a beautiful pink, the same colour of her cheeks when she blushed.

Ambrose moved to stand behind her, pushing her hair over her shoulder to expose her ear. "Are you ready for more, princess?"

"Yes, Master. Please."

Her voice was husky and filled with arousal. *Gorgeous.*

"Just say the word and I'll take a break."

He took a step back, prepared himself, making sure he was focussed on her face as well as her body. He needed to be extra careful with her tonight. She'd asked him for more pain, so she could get used to enjoying it again, but it was going to take time. He refused to rush. He had to remember not to lose himself and to take it slow.

Whack. The flogger came down on her back and she cried out quietly. After a couple more hits, he moved to assess her, noting the quick nod she gave to keep him going.

Fair enough.

He continued, flogging her again and again, adding a little more strength to each round. As well as dealing with more pain, Belle had learned to trust him more, trust that he wouldn't ever treat her like that asshole had. Whenever she'd safe-worded with him, apparently, Bryce had ignored her and kept pushing. He was everything that was wrong with men.

Adding a little more muscle, he flogged her again, noticing the hitch in her breath immediately. He dropped the flogger and moved to her side, one hand on her lower back, the other on her chin.

"Yellow," she whispered before her glazed eyes found his.

"That's my girl." His heart swelled with pride. "Do you want to stop?"

Her lashes came down slowly as she shook her head. She didn't want to stop but she needed to. He wasn't willing to push her any further tonight. She was done feeling pain for the evening.

Ambrose pressed a soft kiss to her cheek. "You're done for the night, sweet girl."

Bending to undo her ankle restraints, he heard a small whimper and sniff. She hid her face from him and stifled her tears. His brave little sub didn't cry. She'd admitted that she saw it as a sign of weakness. But he didn't. All he saw when he looked at her was a pillar of strength.

"I'm incredibly proud of you, Belle," he whispered and petted her, running his fingers through her hair. "You did well tonight."

Vulnerable eyes looked at him, glistening with unshed tears.

"I'm going to reward you upstairs."

"Really?"

Was there anything sweeter than a hopeful submissive?

"Really." He detached her wrist cuffs and gathered her into his arms. "Kneel for me while I pack up my stuff."

She obeyed without question, looking towards the crowd they'd attracted with a small smile. Ambrose slung his toy bag over his shoulder and gestured for her to stand, wrapping an arm around her shoulder as he ushered her upstairs to an empty private room. The fairy room again.

"Sit on the bed."

Pulling out a tube of healing ointment from his bag, he stripped off his clothing, loving the way she opened her mouth to speak before clamping it shut. He loved how hard she fought to obey him. But he also loved her bratty little outbursts. Though they never happened at the club, they did at home.

After rubbing the ointment onto her sensitive and no doubt stinging skin, he got onto his back in front of her.

"Ride me, princess."

Fuck, she was absolutely beautiful when on top. Like a goddess, she rode him, used him for her own pleasure before dragging him down with her.

Running his hands up and down her stocking-clad thighs, he watched her as she sat back, his softening cock still inside her hot, wet cunt. Her fingers dug into his chest as she struggled to catch her breath.

"Holy shit."

"You can say that again." His head was still spinning, his legs and toes tingling.

Collapsing on top of him, Belle rested her head on his chest and let out a breath of contentment. While he thoroughly enjoyed playing with and having sex with Belle, he treasured the aftermath, where she was all limp and sated, cuddling into him, seeking comfort and reassurance from him. There was nothing more vulnerable about her than the moments that followed sex.

He brushed her hair off her face and ran one soothing hand along her back. Lifting his head, he pressed a kiss to her hair. As he expected, she lifted her head and sought a proper kiss, that cute little smile on her face as she asked silently. Unable to resist, he cupped her cheeks in his hands and kissed her softly.

He had fallen for this woman. Hard and fast and completely.

Chapter Fourteen

Enjoying the early winter sun beating down on her, Belle knelt on the ground and went about pulling stubborn weeds from her favourite park. Pride Park was a large public park in an inner-city suburb and had been her first major landscaping design job. She'd gotten it without any help. She'd put in a bid and managed to win based on her own merit and reputation for being hardworking. Every few months, she liked to do the maintenance work herself just to check in and see how well her staff were keeping it. Fortunately, she hired good, reliable staff that held the same high standards she did.

She was about to pack up and take a lunch break before heading to her next job when a loud group of twenty-somethings caught her eye. Their laughter distracted her as they made their way past her car. She smiled politely and locked up her trailer, feeling the slightest hint of hesitation and wariness. A sense of being watched flowed over her skin, setting it alight with nerves.

"Here, boss." Her newest employee, Johnson, snapped her out of her wary state. "I'm all done, do you need a hand?"

She smiled at the young man. He'd proven to be an eager worker in the last few weeks. He was working out well and reminded her of herself when she was younger. He had an actual passion for the job.

"I was about to come and get you. I'm all done and was just going to do a walk-through to see if either of us missed anything."

The tall, lanky twenty-one-year-old joined her, keeping a respectable distance as he checked the garden beds. When Belle bent to pick up a stray piece of grass, he frowned.

"I hope I did okay. I've never worked on a park this big before."

"You'll get the hang of it in no time. No matter how small the garden you're working on, you'll always miss something the first time around," she told him in a reassuring tone. "We're only human, after all."

They reached the spot she'd just been working on, and Belle noticed a dandelion sticking up. "Case in point. How the hell did I miss that?"

He laughed and chatted away as they headed back towards the car park. The feeling of being watched returned to Belle. She looked around without warning Johnson and…

"Fuck."

"What is it?"

Resting a hand on her employee's arm, she smiled at him. "Nothing. Would you mind walking me to my car?"

"Sure thing, boss." They continued on, until they reached her car. "Are you sure you're okay? You look a little pale. Maybe you need to take a break."

She didn't need a break. She needed to get the fuck out of there. Because standing less than ten metres away was fucking Bryce. Dressed in a casual sweater and jeans, very unlike the man who'd always worn a suit or dress pants and button downs when they were dating, but it was definitely him. All six-foot-three of well-muscled man that had beaten the hell out of her just for fun.

"I just saw someone I don't want to see again."

"Oh..." The young man looked around, but clearly didn't see anything untoward.

Trying to play it cool, Belle swallowed past the cyclone of emotions that tore through her. He knew she was here. Why else would he be here? Bryce didn't hang out at parks. He didn't enjoy nature.

"I'll be fine. Go head off for your lunch break," she told Johnson. "I'll see you next week for your review."

The young man gulped and she smiled kindly at him.

"Don't worry, you're doing a great job. This is just to see what you would like done differently. To get a feel for where you're at."

"Oh, okay. Good, because I like this job." He grinned, making him appear even younger than he already did. "You're a great boss."

"Thanks, kid. Go on."

"See ya." He waved as he trotted off towards his own car.

Heart thudding against her ribs, Belle took a moment to breathe before looking back to where Bryce was walking very, very slowly. Phone to his ear, he hadn't appeared to notice her. She was just being paranoid. After all, Perth was a small city. It made sense that she would run into him at some point. Right?

"Shit. Calm down, girl," she told herself as a wave of panic washed over her.

With Johnson gone, she was now alone.

You're in public. You're safe.

But she didn't feel safe. Clutching at the pepper spray she always kept in her pocket, she tried to appear casual as she stepped to the driver's side of her car and opened the door. When she dared to look up, Bryce was walking towards her. He turned down a footpath, placing his hands in his pockets as he took long, leisurely steps towards the car park where she was.

He didn't look at her. Didn't appear to notice her. Fighting the urge to run and hide, Belle stood her ground, still clutching the cannister in her pocket. Bryce continued walking away, disappearing from her sight. Belle jumped in her car and locked the doors, letting go of the pepper spray.

"You're okay," she told herself. "You're safe. You've got this."

Clutching at the steering wheel, she threw the car into gear and drove away carefully, well aware that she could slip into a panic attack at any moment.

Luckily, she didn't.

* * * *

Finishing up a long day at the clinic, Ambrose sat behind his desk and went over the paperwork that had been piling up. Since he'd been seeing Belle each night after work, he'd been neglecting it. He needed to hire an office manager to do these things for him instead.

He had the budget for it. And he was definitely not cutting back his hours with Belle. He'd become addicted to her. She already had him wrapped around her little finger, not that she had realised it yet.

Letting his mind wander to the past weekend, Ambrose couldn't wipe the smile off his face. He'd spent the entire weekend at Belle's house but still hadn't stayed the night again. They'd had sex, played, cooked together, spent most of Sunday at Ayden's with their friends. While she had busied herself with her girlfriends, the other Doms had taken the opportunity to grill him on his intentions towards Belle.

Ambrose understood their need to protect her. Though they were his friends too, they had to make sure he had good intentions. He also felt that deep-seated need to protect Belle. She'd gone her entire life without anyone protecting her. That had been her parents' job and they were severely lacking. This week, he'd been doing research on survivors of abusive relationships, and had asked the counsellors at the women's shelter where he volunteered his time and discovered that journaling helped a lot of women there. It was something the women there were all encouraged to do. So Ambrose had given Belle homework — she had to write in her journal every night, including a page for him to read if she had anything she wanted to bring up with him.

Before he left every night, they would discuss what she'd written, and he'd use it to help her. Last night, they'd discussed her parents. The people who were supposed to love and care for her most in the world had betrayed her trust, time and time again. They'd done a number on her.

While it enraged him, it also saddened him. She'd never grown up with the support he had. At one point, her mother had even gotten drunk and told her she was a mistake. An accidental pregnancy that she'd never wanted. What kind of person did that? A soulless monster. And both of her parents sounded like monsters. High-functioning sociopaths who cared more about their outward appearances than their own child.

The next part of his plan was to teach Belle basic self-defence. He worried about her being alone, especially working at peoples' homes by herself. And with the attempted break-in two weeks ago, she needed to learn how to defend herself just enough to do damage to the bastard who had tried to hurt her. Just enough to be able to run.

Just as he finished up his paperwork, Ambrose received a text from Belle asking what he wanted her to order for dinner. He offered to pick up Chinese for the two of them on his way over. After grabbing dinner, he arrived at her house to find her looking tired and worried, although she tried to hide it behind a brave smile.

"What happened?"

"I'm fine."

Not the answer he wanted. Slipping the Dom tone into his voice, he asked again. "Belle."

She rolled her eyes and let out a small sigh. "I really am fine. I just had a moment today…" She bit on her lip. "While I was at work today, I saw Bryce."

"You what?" He tried to hold back his temper… He really did. But, fuck, it was hard. "Why didn't you call me?"

"I was in public, at Pride Park, just before lunch. One of my workers was with me. While I was getting ready to leave, I happened to look up and see him."

"Did he approach you?"

She shook her head. "I don't think he saw me. I just jumped in my car and headed to my next job. But...I panicked a little on the drive."

"That is exactly why you should have called me." He ran a hand through his hair, frustrated. "Did you at least call one of the girls?"

She avoided his gaze in an instant sign of guilt.

"Fuck, Belle." He sat at the dining table. "How am I supposed to help you if you won't let me?"

"I dealt with it myself," she told him as she stuck her chin out, stubbornly. "I know you're not happy with me, but I coped."

"It's not about making me happy. It's about keeping you safe," he stressed. "What happens if you have a panic attack while driving?" he all but snapped at her. "Do you know how dangerous that could be?"

Tears sprang to her eyes as she avoided his gaze, her bottom lip quivering.

"There is no shame in asking for help. You need to know that."

"I do know that."

"So, why didn't you then?"

Right now, she reminded him far too much of his mum. The stubborn behaviour, the refusal to admit weakness. The incessant need to ignore the help that was being thrown at her because she was a strong, independent woman who could handle things alone. He hadn't dealt with it well when he was seventeen and he wasn't dealing well with it now.

Belle shied away from him, flinching at his raised voice.

"Fuck," he muttered. "I'm sorry. I'm not angry."

"You are." Her voice was so damn faint.

Sucking in a deep breath, he closed his eyes before looking up at her. She'd moved an extra couple of steps away from him. And he didn't blame her.

"I just… Help me understand your thought process. You admitted you started to panic, so why didn't you reach out to me or your friends to help?"

She had no answer for him. She moved and sank into a chair of her own, resting her elbows on the table. "I fucked up, didn't I?"

"You did."

Her bottom lip trembled and she avoided his eyes once again.

"Belle, you have people who love and care for you. You just have to let us help."

She looked at him and blushed, letting him know she'd noticed the fact that he'd just used the L word.

"I know that but…it's hard."

Time to try another point of view. He moved to kneel beside her, placing both hands on her thighs as he softened his expression.

"I know it's hard, but how would you feel if someone you cared about was in trouble and didn't contact you? What if something like this happened to me and I didn't tell you immediately?"

"I'd be hurt." Recognition came over her face. "Oh."

"Exactly."

"I'm sorry. I didn't mean to hurt you."

"I know you didn't." He smiled up at her. "That's why I'm forgiving you, this time. Next time, though, you get spanked for it."

Her cheeks flushed further as her legs quivered beneath his touch.

"Well, then," he said as he took a seat in the chair next to her. "Over my lap, princess."

"What? No."

He narrowed his gaze. "Did you just say no to me?"

"I don't want a spanking." She stuck her chin out and frowned at him as she stood. "I want to eat my dinner before it gets cold."

"And I want a sub who trusts that I will take care of her when she gets scared. But it appears we don't always get what we want, do we?" He pointed to his lap. "On here now or it's ten."

"You know you can't just slip into Dom mode and boss me around whenever you feel like it." A hint of a smile played on her lips, danced in her eyes. The little shit was playing the brat on purpose.

"Fine." He shrugged. "We can wait until later. But now it's fifteen swats."

Her mouth dropped open as she looked at him, absolutely appalled. "You can't do that!"

"Want to make it twenty?"

"You're a real bastard, sometimes, Sir." She said it in such a soft and sweet tone that he couldn't hold back his laugh.

"Fuck, Belle, come here right now or I really will bend you over my knee."

She flopped onto his lap and wrapped her arms around his shoulders, kissing him deeply. He wrapped his arms around her, needing to hold her, to feel that she was safe. To make her understand that her safety was all he cared about.

"I am sorry," she murmured against his lips. "I'll do better next time."

He touched her cheek, cupping her jaw. "I know you will. Now get to your dinner so that I can get to your spanking."

* * * *

Belle's ass burned and ached, but the spanking had finally stopped. A sob escaped her throat, tears running down her cheeks as she struggled to sit, her legs shaky and uncooperative. Master Ambrose pulled her onto his lap, smiling like a sadist when she squirmed as her tender ass hit his thighs.

All the worry and fear from earlier broke free and cascaded down her cheeks in tears of solemn relief. She was safe. She'd seen Bryce, managed to avoid him and stayed safe.

She'd fucked up though—she knew that now. She should have contacted someone she trusted when it had happened, but the thought had never even crossed her mind. The second she had seen him, her mind had shut down. She'd just wanted to get the hell out of there and away from him.

Ambrose was right, though. If the tables were turned and someone she cared about was in a similar situation and hadn't called her, she would have been upset and hurt as well as worried. All the emotions that played over Ambrose's face when she told him what had happened.

Hushing her as she continued to sob, Ambrose ran one gentle hand over her hair in the way she loved. It was amazing how much his touch could calm and centre her. She hadn't even thought of the fact that she was crying in his lap. She sat and enjoyed the comfort he offered. Comfort she wanted to continue. Especially tonight when she still felt vulnerable and unsafe in her own home.

"Master?" She hiccupped a breath, finding the strength to ask the questions she'd wanted to ask all week. "Will you stay with me tonight?"

"Of course I will," he murmured while nuzzling her cheek. One big hand ran up and down her back in a soothing motion. "I will do anything for you. All you have to do is ask."

As Belle looked into those deep green eyes, she realised he was telling her the truth. He really would do anything for her. He cared for her. So why the hell was it so hard for her to ask for his help? Right. Because she was broken, thanks to the arseholes who'd birthed her. The ones who had made her feel weak for admitting when she was struggling.

Wrapping her arms around Ambrose, Belle buried her face into his neck and let go for the first time in months. Hard, painful sobs wracked her entire body as she cried. She'd let him down tonight, made him mad. And she hated that. From now on, she would make a conscious effort to open up to him and ask for assistance the second she needed it. Because she did trust him and every single part of her wanted to please him.

Chapter Fifteen

Two days after talking about trust with Belle, Ambrose felt even closer to her. She had opened up to him more since then, telling him why it was so difficult for her to trust and rely on others. She'd been made to feel weak as a child for admitting when she needed help and support. It had been drilled into her from such a young age that it was now a part of her. But she was trying to change, and he could see that. He appreciated her intent.

Tonight, he planned on staying at her house again because she'd asked him to. Last night, while sleeping alone, she'd had a nightmare and a panic attack that had taken her a while to come out of. It had scared her. But she'd called him right away to tell him and ask for reassurance. He was so proud of her for that.

He enjoyed helping her immensely. It made him feel like he was worth something. That he could make a difference to her life. It filled a part of him that he hadn't realised was empty until now...the caregiver side of his personality. He'd always felt a deep-seated need to help others. It was why he volunteered at the women's shelter and the animal rescue organisation, why he offered to help the new submissives at Haven. But now that need was being filled on a deeply personal level and he loved it.

He'd fallen so hard and fast for Belle, there was no way he could catch himself. Ambrose smiled when his phone rang and he saw it was her.

"How's my princess?"

"Master?" Her voice was small and shaky. "C-can you come over?"

Pulling over to the side of the road, he did a very illegal U-turn and headed towards her house. "What's wrong? Are you okay?"

"I'm fine. I just... Someone broke in."

Fuck. "Have you called the police?"

"They just got here." She was close to panicking — he could hear it in her voice.

"I'm almost there. Don't let them leave you alone."

"Okay." She sounded fucking terrified. He heard her suck in a deep, albeit shaky breath.

"Just hold on, Belle. I'm right around the corner. Hold on for me, okay?"

"Okay," she said with tears evident in her voice.

Ambrose arrived to find Belle huddled on the ground, a female officer beside her with an arm wrapped around her shoulders while Belle fought for breath. Upon seeing him, Belle stood and all but collapsed into his arms. He caught her and scooped her into his arms.

"You're okay. You're safe. Just breathe," he murmured into her hair while stroking her gently.

"I assume you're the boyfriend?" the officer asked.

"I am." He offered her a smile. "Can we get her inside?"

"Of course. She wouldn't go inside until you got here."

Oh, Belle. He squeezed her a little tighter and stepped through the open front door. Settling on the couch, he gestured for the officers to sit beside them and froze when he recognised the second officer.

"Parker?" he asked in a decent amount of shock.

He hadn't seen Parker in almost twenty years, not since he had been a scrawny pre-teen, just before he and his mother had moved away.

"Ambrose." The other man nodded with a small smile. "Good to see you."

"And you."

Both men received a stern look from the senior officer and reined it in.

"What happened?" Ambrose asked.

"We received a call from the security company after Miss Winters didn't answer their call. When we arrived, there was nobody here, but the front door had been pried open and the front window smashed."

Ambrose looked to where the officer gestured to the front lounge room that Belle rarely used. The window had been shattered, glass glittering all over the couch and floor. What a mess.

"What about Bryce?" he asked Belle who was still shaking in his lap.

"We've heard back from his parole officer, who checked in with him quickly. He has an alibi."

"It was him," Belle said in a quiet, shaky voice. "The footage. It was him."

"We'll continue to investigate," the female officer said. "In the meantime, do you have somewhere safe you can stay?"

Belle remained silent, her body tensing.

"She'll stay with me."

The expression on her face just about broke him. Had she thought he'd let her stay anywhere else?

"You'll stay with me as long as you need," he told her gently.

"Thank you, Sir." She smiled a bright little smile that filled him with hope she would be okay.

"Now that she's in good hands, we'd best be off," Parker said and looked at Ambrose. "Can I have a quick chat with you outside?"

He nodded and gave Belle a quick pat on the butt. "Go pack a bag. I'll be right back."

With a little hesitation, she stood and said goodbye to the officers before heading for her bedroom.

Ambrose followed the big cop outside, unsurprised to discover that Parker had ended up in law enforcement. The last time Ambrose had seen him, the other man had been a weedy little twelve-year-old, upset because his mum was moving them over east to escape his abusive father. The mere thought of his father incited a rage inside Ambrose. Men who beat women were a special breed of asshole, but those who beat children were a whole different monster.

"So, you're back," Ambrose commented.

"My father died when I was eighteen. It gave us the chance to move home."

He shifted his weight and looked back at the house.

"Mate, she's terrified," Parker told Ambrose in no uncertain terms. "She's so sure it was her ex on the footage. But you cannot take matters into your own hands."

The warning came from someone who knew Ambrose's past. Knew that he had twice taken matters into his own hands and not only beaten the man who touched his mum in anger, but also Parker's father when he had dared to touch a scared little boy who was simply defending his mother. The man who had seen the aftermath and how much it ate away at Ambrose. But he was no longer a hot-headed seventeen-year-old. He had a good head on his shoulders.

"I'm not going through that again," he assured Parker. "I'll take care of her. Make sure she stays safe."

"I'm happy to see some things change. I was afraid you'd be as hot under the collar as you once were."

Ambrose let out a short laugh. "Like you, I've done a lot of growing up. I can't say I'm surprised to see you're a cop now. You always were the protective type."

Parker pulled out a card and scrawled his number on the back of it. "If anything further happens, give me a call. I live nearby."

"Will do, mate."

"It was good to see you."

"You too." Ambrose shook the other man's hand. "I'll see you around."

"For sure." He smiled and headed to the marked car where his partner was impatiently waiting for him.

* * * *

Sitting on the edge of Ambrose's bed, Belle was numb, out of it. After the police had left her house, she'd lost her shit, sobbing in Ambrose's arms out of pure fear and grief. She wasn't safe in her home. Bryce had come for her, just as she'd feared. Despite the restraining order, he'd come. What if she'd been home? What the hell would he have done to her? The thought terrified her.

Feeling lost and alone, she tightened the fluffy robe around herself and brought her knees up to her chest. What the hell did she do now? Move. She had to move as soon as possible. As soon as her window was fixed, she would put the house on the market and put an offer down on one of the properties she'd decided would suit her. Tears blurred his vision. She had to leave her beloved home all because of some unhinged asshole.

Why the fuck had she ever dated him? How had she not realised what he was earlier? All of this could have been avoided. He'd been too distant throughout their relationship, too unwilling to compromise. Too focussed on his work. He was too much like her fucking parents. But she'd looked past that because he'd liked her. She'd agreed to date him just because he'd shown interest. She'd been so goddamned desperate for love that she had clung to the wrong man. Was she doing it again? Clinging to Ambrose because he showed interest? *No.* He was different. He was unlike any other man she'd dated. So far, anyway.

"Do you think I'm doing the right thing?" she asked Amara over the phone. "Staying with Ambrose?"

"Absolutely," her friend responded without a hint of doubt in her voice. "The man cares so much for you, Belle. He's willing to do anything to keep you safe. And, given his history, he has the ability to keep you safe."

Or hurt me, she thought negatively. He had a history of dealing with an abused woman. But he was also still just a man. And men could change in an instant.

"I just don't want to repeat past mistakes," she said.

"Ambrose is *nothing* like Bryce. You know that."

She sighed. She did know that. It made her angry that she was having doubts about him.

"We would have warned you if we saw any red flags with Ambrose. Agin, Sullivan and Grayson have thoroughly vetted him."

Belle smiled knowing that her male friends had taken him out for a drink during the week to discover his intentions towards her. Ayden had done a little digging further into his past and all he'd discovered was that he'd gotten into a little trouble for beating the man who had hurt his mum. And he had been open about that with Belle. She could understand it. It didn't make him a violent man.

"Sullivan and Grayson are boarding up your window because Ambrose called them to let them know what had happened."

"What?" She didn't know he'd contacted her friends.

"He's a good man, Belle. Better than most. Let him take care of you. Don't let your fears get in the way of that."

After saying goodbye, Belle remained sitting on the edge of the bed, curled up into herself. Amara was right, Ambrose was a good man. He'd taken care of her all night. Cooked for her, run her a bath while she ate then hurried her into the tub where he'd left her to soak and relax. Now, he'd given her the space she'd asked for to gather her thoughts. He hadn't pushed her once.

A sound caught her attention. Ambrose's large frame took up the entire doorway. The silhouette of his body was all she could see. He was intimidatingly large, yet his stance was non-threatening. His hands hung loose at his side as he stepped into the room, the bedside lamp illuminating his handsome face.

He squatted before her, resting his arms on his knees and looked up at her, his damn forehead wrinkling in that way that melted her. His eyes softened further and she realised she'd been a complete arsehole to doubt him.

"Feeling a little better?"

The ice that had formed around her heart cracked and fell away. She smiled and let her legs hang, spreading her thighs for him to settle between as he knelt up.

"I am, thanks to you."

"I think it's time you went to bed. You're exhausted."

On cue, she yawned. She was exhausted.

"If you want your own space, I can sleep in the spare room. You don't have to sleep with me if you're uncomfortable."

"No," she cut him off. "I want to sleep with you. I just… I might panic tonight."

He smiled sweetly and ran his fingers down her cheek. "If you panic, we'll deal with it."

Standing, he undid the belt of her robe. She allowed him to push it off her shoulders.

"Come on, my princess, let's get some rest."

Belle slipped onto the massive bed wearing nothing but a singlet top and underwear — what she usually slept in. She sighed when the silky sheets slid against her skin, causing her to relax as she lay down. Rolling onto her side, she watched Ambrose strip. He was all sleek, lean muscle, his golden skin gleaming in the dim lighting. One day she would ask for permission to lick her way along his body.

Slipping in, he lay on his back, extending one arm beneath her head as he pulled her into his waiting body. She shuddered at the warmth of his embrace and snuggled into him.

"What are you thinking about? You've got the cutest little expression on your face."

"Oh." Her cheeks heated with a blush. "I was just thinking about how I want to lick my way down your body. Master."

"Damn, girl," was all he said before he dipped his head to kiss her.

The soft and sweet kiss was over far too soon. Belle followed, wanting more.

"Not tonight, sweet girl," he said. "You need to rest."

"You're no fun." She pouted.

"Just wait until morning." He wiggled his eyebrows and grinned.

His promise gave her the tingle. She fell asleep sprawled out on his chest, one leg tucked over his, her hand on his chest, head on his shoulder, completely and utterly content. Cared for. Happy.

Chapter Sixteen

Ambrose's dreams that night were filled with scenes of blood and violence, memories he had thought were long buried. Images of his mum on the floor, scurrying away from her own son in fear. The sound of bone and cartilage crunching beneath his fists. His fists pounding on Parker's deadbeat father when he'd found them at the shelter and started beating on an innocent eleven-year-old.

When he woke in a cold sweat, he turned and found the spot beside him empty. Worry filled him as panic rose. Belle wouldn't have left, not without saying something. But the irrational fear was still there, looming over him.

He slipped on his sweatpants and wandered through the house before noticing the back door leading to the patio was wide open. Filled with immediate relief when he laid eyes on Belle, Ambrose took a moment to just watch her. She had a thoughtful expression on her face as she stared over the acreage that was his backyard. With her arms wrapped around herself, she was in a protective stance. She seemed stronger than last night, like she'd gathered more of her resolve.

While his heart broke for her, he didn't feel a single ounce of pity. This woman had gone through her entire life with nobody on her side, nobody in her corner looking out for her. She'd always protected herself. But she didn't have to do that anymore. She had him. He knew he had to walk a fine line, though. If he pushed too hard, she would push back and no doubt recoil from him.

"Your property is beautiful."

Her quiet words startled him. He wasn't aware he'd made a sound.

"I appreciate the quiet," he replied and approached her slowly.

"My grandparents lived on a property like this. Big and open and peaceful. Except theirs was filled with animals."

"Sounds like a great place to grow up."

A sad smile spread across her face as she turned to face him. "It was. I was never allowed to have a pet at home, so my grandparents made sure I had all the animals I asked for at their house."

Fucking bastards. What kind of parents didn't allow their child to have a pet? Children needed pets to look after, to love. Resting his hands on her shoulders, Ambrose focussed on how soft her skin was beneath his calloused palms.

"I just realised you're a vet with no pets." She smirked as she looked up at him.

"I am," he replied sadly. "My last dog died about six months ago. I haven't been quite ready for another one."

He began to massage her neck and shoulders, smiling when she leaned into him and let out a soft moan.

"We can get a rescue dog, when you're ready."

She froze, a sad expression taking over the wistful one. "I had a dog, years ago. She was only three when she died."

"What happened?"

"She had an epileptic fit and never came out of it. I was devastated when it happened. It took me years to get through."

He wrapped his arm around her shoulders from behind and rested his cheek against hers.

"I'm sorry. That must have been awful to go through."

"It was." She sniffed. "I always wanted two little dogs. I was planning to rescue another before she died... But I couldn't after that."

"Losing a pet is hard. Especially under those circumstances."

Belle leaned against him in silence, her hands coming up to hold his forearm.

"I have to clean the house."

"Ashely is on that. I told her to drop by at ten."

She turned in his arms, a look of shock on her pretty face. "Mistress Ashely?"

He nodded. "She owns a cleaning company and says she can get the glass out of the lounge for you."

"Oh. Thank you for organising that. And for getting Sullivan and Grayson to board up my window last night."

"There are plenty of us who want to help you, Belle." He pressed a soft kiss to her waiting lips. "Haven is like a family of its own. Especially the Masters and Mistresses. We look after our own."

"I know that, but I never considered myself part of that group."

He frowned at her sad revelation. "Belle. Three of your closest friends are Masters. Do you think they don't see you as part of their family?"

She didn't respond.

"Do you know how messed up that sounds?"

"It does, doesn't it?" Biting on her lip, she buried her face in his chest. "I don't know why I'm this way."

"Because you grew up feeling alone and unwanted. Some part of you still does, even though you have an entire community who would do anything to help you."

"I'm still not used to relying on others."

"It's a hard habit to break, I know," he said. "But you need to. For your own sanity."

She gave a sad sigh.

"In fact, each time I feel you withdrawing, I'm going to spank you."

She pulled back, her mouth agape as she stared. "You can't do that."

"I'm your Dom. I can do whatever I want." He smirked.

With a small frown, she continued to watch him, understanding slowly hitting her eyes when she gave in. Yes, she understood what he was doing and why he was doing it. *Smart little cookie.*

* * * *

After an exhausting couple of days, Belle decided to skip visiting Haven this weekend, instead having some alone time at Ambrose's while he was doing his dungeon monitor shift. He'd been so incredibly sweet to her since she'd been staying with him, always looking out for her. He'd tried to convince her to have one of the girls over tonight just in case she got scared being alone, but she assured him she would be okay. She had decided to grab some supplies from her house earlier and spend the evening baking cookies and brownies for the friends who had helped her during the week.

She was lucky to be part of a community now. The people at Haven looked out for their own, she'd always known that, but she'd never truly experienced it herself. Even Grayson had helped and that meant a lot to her. Despite him being Sullivan's best mate, she hadn't spent much time with him outside of the club. He'd called last night to check on her. The man was incredibly sweet, no matter how intimidating he could be. And he was bloody intimidating. As was Mistress Ashely. But she'd been so friendly when they'd met at Belle's house two days ago. She'd managed to get all the glass out of the couch and had done it for free, despite Belle's protests.

"We look after our own," she'd told Belle.

Masters — and Mistresses — looked out for each other with no thanks required. Apparently, Ambrose looked after all their pets, requiring them to pay for medications and surgery supplies, never his time. Belle realised there was a lot she didn't know about the secret lives of the Masters of Haven. But now that she was involved with a Master herself, she was getting a peek into that world.

Wiping her hands on her butt, she winced when she touched a sore spot. Two nights ago, she'd woken from an awful dream, a flashback of the incident, and had refused to speak to Ambrose about it. He'd stuck to his word and spanked her until she broke down and opened up to him. And she had felt so much better afterwards. Even if she did still have a sore ass.

Last night, she'd woken from another nightmare and told Ambrose about it straight away. He'd rewarded her with the sweetest love-making session she'd ever experienced. And that was what it was. They didn't fuck anymore. Didn't just have sex. They made love. And, fuck, she loved him. It had hit her over the head this morning when she'd woken to find his mouth on her as he licked her to orgasm. After she'd come, he'd merely stretched out beside her and held her, not allowing her to return the favour. Yes, she did love him.

She'd almost finished decorating the cookies when Ambrose arrived home. The sound of his jingling keys set the small of her back tingling, a smile spreading across her face before she even saw him. He entered the kitchen, all sexy in his fitted jeans and tailored black dress shirt. Wrapping his arms around her from behind, he pressed his hard body against her and nuzzled her neck.

"Mmm, you smell edible." He licked her throat before he bit down gently and growled.

"What got you so excited? See something fun at the club?" she teased when his erection pressed against her butt.

"I saw you," he murmured in her ear, sending a shiver down her spine. "You really don't understand the effect you have on me, do you?"

Turning in his arms, she held him, careful not to touch him with her icing-covered hands. Humming lightly, she leaned up to kiss him.

"You taste like cookies," he mumbled against her lips as his hands wandered to grasp her arse. "Are you nearly finished?"

"I just have a few more cookies to ice."

He looked over her shoulder to admire her handiwork and smiled. "Well, you have been a busy little sub, haven't you?"

"Since nobody would let me pay them for helping, I figure I can pay them in sweet treats."

"And what do I get for helping you?"

She slapped his chest, loving how he teased her. "You do it out of the kindness of your own heart. Not for a reward."

Her face dropped when she saw the white icing sugar handprint she'd left on his shirt. She could actually see the moment he slipped into Dom mode. Her stomach dropped, the floor sinking beneath her feet. She was in trouble.

"This was a clean shirt, Belle."

"Want me to lick it clean?" she offered with a snicker. Her brat side was definitely making a comeback now that she felt safe with Ambrose.

His eyes narrowed. "I haven't given you a proper tour of the house yet."

"What?" He had. He'd even shown her... *Oh shit.*

"Oh shit, indeed, little sub. Wash your hands and meet me in the dungeon."

He left, sauntering out of the kitchen with those long legs she wanted to have wrapped around her as he pinned her to the bed. Another shiver went down her spine as she got moving. They were going to play in the dungeon tonight. She'd never played in a private dungeon before.

Belle met Ambrose—now Master Ambrose—in the romantically decorated dungeon that was his personal wonderland. It was a massive, specially designed room that fit all of his equipment inside of it with room to spare. A virtual playground, it contained a cross, bondage table, spanking bench, bondage horse and even a swing and sling. Two walls were lined with custom shelving to fit all of his toys and implements of pain—and there were a lot of them. Some of the implements still made her shiver with desire yet filled her with dread at the same time.

Her gaze came to rest on the end of the shelving where the harder items were kept. A very harsh-looking flogger made with strands of chain hung beside a specifically heavy cane that she'd quizzed him on earlier in the week. He assured her that he would use them on her once and only when she was ready. Yet a part of her still wondered if he would decide she was ready without discussing it with her first. But no, she knew him better than that. He wasn't that sort of Dom.

The more she played with her Master, the more pain Belle found she could handle. Because it wasn't so much the pain that was the issue anymore—it was the trust. And she trusted him wholeheartedly with her body. She trusted him to stop should she panic. She knew he would help calm her and bring her down from a panic attack—he'd done it enough times now. He would never take her over her limit—she knew that with all her heart and soul.

Master Ambrose stood beneath a chain station that hung from the ceiling, having already removed his shirt, ready for the scene. Her stomach dropped further at the sight of his golden skin twisting as he moved to adjust the chains. His broad shoulders were smooth and toned and straightened when he turned to face her. His chiselled chest was covered with a sprinkling of brown hair, a shade darker than the hair on his head, leading to his flat stomach with a trail that disappeared beneath his pants to the spot she really wanted to see. She adored his cock. Loved looking at it when he was all aroused just for her, wrapping her hands around it when she was allowed to caress him, but she loved nothing more than sucking it into her mouth so she could bring him to completion.

Arousal continued to build when she saw the hungry look in his eyes. All of it was for her. And that knowledge only aroused her further. He was so fucking beautiful to watch when in the zone, in that dominant space that drove her wild. She wanted to sink her teeth into him. Her mouth watered at the thought.

Her eyes widened when she caught his eye and saw the serious look in them. He was well and truly in Master mode. There would be no joking around for her tonight.

"Strip and kneel."

She obeyed eagerly, having wanted this all night. Despite her fatigue, she had been obscenely aroused when he left for Haven and had been thinking about him all night. Kneeling before him, she tilted her head back to look at him. Handing him her wrist, when he held out a hand, she couldn't hide her smile as he placed a lined cuff around it, then did the same with the other arm.

"Stand. Wrists crossed above your head." When she opened her mouth to speak, he shut her down with a stone-cold look. "Not a word, princess."

Oh God, what the tone and look did to her, he would never know. It made everything inside of her melt, had her wanting to drop to her knees before him and beg him to use her as he pleased. It made her submit to him instantly.

Keeping her mouth shut, Belle stood in position and waited, watching him. He looked her up and down, causing her to feel completely vulnerable. Reaching up, he attached her cuffs to a chain each, then moved behind her to winch her arms up, leaving her stretched and standing on her toes.

"Can you hold that position?"

"Yes, Master." Her voice was small and hushed. She was in the zone already.

"Very nice," he murmured as he came to stand behind her, his body heat wrapping around her.

Belle sucked in a breath when his naked chest pressed against her bare back. She let out a low moan of pure desire when his skin caressed hers. God, she loved the feeling of him against her. She wanted to rub up against him like a kitten.

Palming her breasts, he ran his hands up and down her torso, waking her skin. Her arousal was already dripping down her inner thigh. She'd never thought it was possible to be so turned on from a few words and touches.

"I was going to go easy on you tonight." His lips grazed her ear as he spoke. "But I think you need to let go."

Oh, she did. She really did. She wanted to feel nothing but his hands on her, inside of her, his cock thrusting in her while he made hard love to her. When he reached around to her cunt, he dipped a finger between her folds and swore under his breath.

"Jesus, Belle. How are you this aroused already?"

"It's you, Master," she whispered. "I'm always aroused around you."

Her honesty earned her a deep, hard kiss that stole her breath. Her stomach dropped and she clenched her thighs together. She had the feeling she was in for quite the ride tonight.

* * * *

Restrained on his cross, hair a dark curtain surrounding her face, Belle looked an absolute treat, on display just for him. Ambrose had flogged her into subspace and drawn her back out several times. Each time, she'd looked at him with those glazed eyes and that dreamy little smile that told him she was having a great time. He'd given her countless orgasms, but he'd yet to make love to her. He was waiting—he wanted her to beg for it. The problem was that he was torturing himself in the meantime.

His cock strained against the zipper of his pants, begging to be freed. Looking at her just made things worse. She was intensely beautiful when lost in a scene. Her lids hooded, lips red and swollen from his kisses, breasts pinkened by his flogger and cane, Belle looked at him through her lashes, silently begging.

Good enough.

Releasing himself from his pants, he wrapped one firm hand around his cock, pleased when her gaze immediately fell to watch him stroke himself. He gripped it harder, pumping one, twice, then looked as she licked her lips.

"Master," she all but whimpered, her voice lost from her screaming orgasms. "Please."

Finally. He could never resist when she called him Master. He gave in, fisting himself as he kissed her, enjoying the way she whined into his mouth. Reaching up to cup her breasts, he pinched her nipples a little harder than he'd done before. Belle pulled away and gasped, fighting against her restraints. But there was no fear in sight. There was nothing but pure, unadulterated passion in her eyes.

Arching her back a little, she pushed her breasts against his hands. He repeated the movement, pinching harder until her head fell back on a moan and she slipped further into the zone he'd been chasing. The one where all her worries were forgotten and she was forced to do nothing but feel.

Ambrose dipped his head and pulled a nipple into his mouth, biting down gently, heart swelling with pride when she moaned, completely uninhibited. The sound drove him further into Domspace. He bit again, sucking hard, finding the sweet spot that had her hips thrusting, straining to reach his cock. Repeating his movements on the neglected peak, he nuzzled her neck when she began to tremble.

"Please," she whispered. "Master, I need…"

He saw tears in her eyes. *Yes, she needed.* She needed more.

Thrusting two fingers inside of her, he moved hard and fast until a sob escaped her mouth. Belle fought against the restraints, her hips writhing in sweet agony as he drove her closer to the edge. Tears fell down her cheeks as her head dropped forward, almost clashing with his.

His sweet little princess cried and cried like he'd never seen, all the while fighting against both sets of restraints. Cradling her face in his hands, he rested his forehead against hers and pressed his lips to her mouth.

"Shh. You're okay, princess," he whispered as he ran a gentle hand over her hair. "I'll get you down."

"No," she sobbed. "I need you. Please." A louder sob. "Fuck me, please, Master."

She broke his heart. "I won't fuck you, Belle." He kissed her tear-stained cheeks, rubbing his nose against hers. "But I will make love to you."

Without moving his face from hers, not wanting to break their connection, he positioned his cock right at her soaking wet entrance and slipped inside, her cunt grasping at him like a vice. He let out an involuntary groan as he thrust home. On a loud sigh, she dropped her head back and closed her eyes. Fuck, she was absolutely stunning.

Finding a rhythm, Ambrose stuck to it, knowing he wouldn't last long. He reached up and released her wrist restraints, pleased when her hands came down on his shoulders, fingers digging into his flesh.

She came on a cry not a second later, sobbing as she struggled for breath and dragged him down with her. Her inner muscles milked him dry as he continued to thrust his cock, drawing out his orgasm as long as he could, coming so hard he couldn't feel his legs.

"Fuck, Belle," he said breathlessly. "I love you."

The words had slipped out by accident. But he meant them. And he wanted to say them again.

Chapter Seventeen

Belle froze.

"Let me down," she said quietly.

Ambrose looked at her as he withdrew, the spell broken, the moment gone.

"Let me down," she repeated with a sense of urgency.

Wondering what the fuck had gone wrong, he bent and undid her ankle cuffs, removing them for her. He'd just bared his soul to her, told her he loved her. He hadn't expected her to say it back—he knew she wasn't ready for that—but he'd expected something positive. Never in a million years would he have expected her to be on the verge of a panic attack upon hearing three simple words.

Helping her off the cross, he went to move her to the bondage table to rest but she straightened and shrugged out of his hold, even as she struggled to stand on her wobbling legs.

"Sit down," he said as he touched her with steady hands.

Avoiding his gaze, Belle stepped out of his reach and shook her head. Ambrose looked at her, eyes wide, breath speeding up, lips paling. She was panicking.

"You need to sit before you fall."

She snatched her arms away when he reached for her, taking a slow step backwards, appearing to be afraid of him. It was a punch in the gut. His lungs emptied at the unexpected blow.

"What's going on? What I said — "

"Don't," she snapped, her voice wet, before she stalked out of the room.

He followed as she made her way straight to the master bedroom. He blocked her attempt to slam the door behind her and swept in to wrap a blanket around her as she curled up on the bed. No matter what was going on in her mind, she needed aftercare and would damned well receive it, even if he had to fight her. He would not leave her alone, no matter what she said or did to him.

Curling into a ball, she buried her face in her knees and sobbed. Heart-wrenching, body-shaking sobs. Body trembling in response to her visceral reaction to him, he wrapped an arm around her to comfort her, even as she shook him off.

"You can't," she cried, the sound muffled by her legs.

"Can't what?" Silence.

"Princess, please. Tell me what's going on."

More silence.

"I can't help if you won't talk to me."

She remained silent, continuing to cry in awful-sounding, harsh sobs that broke his heart. But she leaned into him, seeking comfort. His heart twisting in agony, he pulled her onto his lap and wrapped both arms around her. In a sea of confusion, Ambrose tried to comprehend why telling her he loved her had triggered such a visceral response. Did she not love him back? No, she did, he knew that. So, what the fuck had he done wrong?

Belle eventually stopped crying and moved to wrap her arms so tightly around Ambrose's neck, he was afraid she would hurt herself. He continued to hold her, murmuring words of love and affection and support all the while worrying out of his mind.

"You… You said you l-love me," she said, her voice thick with unshed tears.

"I did," he whispered gently. "I do."

"You can't…" A hiccupped sob. "Please, don't… Don't leave me."

All of a sudden, it hit him like a tonne of bricks. Belle didn't just have trust issues… She had abandonment issues. She saw herself as unlovable and undesirable. She thought she was an easy person to leave.

"Belle," he said, keeping his tone firm yet gentle. "I am not going to leave you."

"Every…" A hiccupped breath. "Everyone who loves me…leaves…" She cried again.

The admission shattered his heart into a million tiny pieces. He held her even tighter, pressing a kiss to her temple as he began to rock her soothingly. Listening to her quiet whimpers, he would have given anything to be able to read her mind. She wasn't being rational at all. If she were, she would realise her friends loved her and hadn't left her. But her rational mind wasn't in charge right now, that was evident. Her primitive mind was. The part that told her she was unworthy of love and easy to abandon. That she was all alone in the world.

Ambrose made a promise to them both, right then, that he would do everything within his power to get Belle to recognise and believe she had him now and he was never, ever going to abandon her.

Belle had never been more embarrassed in her life. Who the hell would have thought that hearing those three little words would have caused her to have a total breakdown? She'd been yearning to hear them from him, needed to hear them. Yet when she had, everything had just stopped. Her heart had frozen and dropped to her gut. Feelings of abandonment rushed through her with each panicked breath. Because only two people had ever said those words to her and they'd both left her so suddenly it had traumatised her.

Ambrose continued to soothe her, rocking her like a child while she wept silent tears, beyond drained. She felt safe in his arms, loved. But he suddenly shifted and left her filled with total doubt. He moved her from his lap, placing her on the bed before pulling the blanket around her.

He placed an achingly gentle kiss to her forehead and said, "I'll be right back."

Returning with a bottle of sports drink and three cookies, he stripped off his pants and moved to sit at the end of the bed, pulling her onto his lap again.

"Drink and eat." It was an order from her Master, no doubt about it.

When it became evident he wasn't going to push her to talk, a wave of relief washed over her. As she took a sip of the sports drink, her mind came back from the pile of mush it had been. She was not firing on all cylinders right now. Yet she couldn't make sense of the thoughts rushing around her head.

After she ate the cookies, the sugar rush hit and her mind stopped racing. Her thoughts were more collected now. Ambrose continued to stroke her skin, her hair, while murmuring sweet nothings into her ear. He was being so patient with her.

She really didn't deserve him.

"I'm sorry," she all but whispered as she snuggled further into him. "I don't know why I reacted that way."

"Who was the last person to tell you they loved you?"

"Nanna."

Belle remembered the day so clearly. Nanna's smiling face as she kissed her through the open window of the car after dropping her home. There was still sadness in her eyes from losing Grandad, but she always appeared happy for Belle. They had spent the day going through Grandad's things. She'd given her one of Grandad's prized gerbera daisies to take home so she could care for it herself. She'd also given Belle a handwritten copy of her recipe book just in case anything should happen to her. Then she'd driven away, leaving Belle forever.

"Nobody has said it to you since?"

"No," she admitted.

Wasn't that just a little sad to admit out loud? It was no wonder she always felt unlovable. No men had ever said it to her. Not even her friends had said those words.

"Sweet girl," he murmured into her hair and began to rock her again.

She felt so, so safe in his arms. She wanted to burrow further into him. Tried to.

"I love you, Belle. And I am not going anywhere."

Fresh tears burned her eyes and she moved to wrap her arms around his shoulders, burying her face in his neck, inhaling his scent, letting it calm her.

"Please don't leave me," she whispered pathetically.

* * * *

In a world of pain, Belle leaned over with her hands on her knees, sweat dripping down her temples. Her muscles ached, arms crying out in pain as she lifted them to push her damp hair from her face.

"Why are you doing this to me?" she asked between panted breaths.

"You agreed to be mine," Ambrose said with that evil grin of his. "I take care of what's mine."

As she straightened, a trickle of sweat dripped down the dip of her lower back and she shuddered. She'd never felt as unsexy as she did right now.

"This is not fun," she told him in no uncertain terms.

Exercising sucked. She hated getting all hot and sweaty like this. All she wanted was to jump in the shower and wash off the gross feeling.

"I'm not sure if you've noticed, but I'm a little fragile right now."

"All the more reason for you to work out. It will help clear your mind."

He was right, of course. Her emotions were still all over the place this morning, but her mind was no longer racing as it had been last night. It had cleared now that she had one thing to focus on. Physical pain caused by her damned Master.

Ambrose moved towards the weight bench and Belle cringed. She was done. Absolutely done. There would be no more exercise for her today. He'd already put her through a rigorous self-defence lesson then made her complete a horrible weights routine.

"How are you feeling?" he asked as he tossed her a small towel.

She wiped at her face and muttered an obscenity at him.

"I know you're not happy about it, but you need to build up muscle so you can defend yourself."

"I'm not going to be able to defend myself when I'm so fucking sore I can't lift my arms above my head," she grumbled and sat on the bench.

Laughing, he moved to rest a hand on her shoulder, bending to kiss her quickly.

"Don't," she whined. "I'm all gross and sweaty."

"You may be sweaty, but you're definitely not gross," he murmured as he licked her throat and nuzzled her ear. "Come on, if you finish the workout, you'll get a reward at the end of it."

Her reward was getting bent over the bench and taken from behind. And what a reward it was. She came so hard, her legs gave out beneath her. Then Ambrose pushed her down on the bench and massaged her to help relieve her aches and pains. The massage threatened to turn her into a puddle. The man then drew her an Epsom salt bath and ordered her to stay in it for at least ten minutes while he showered and dressed.

Belle had always thought she'd hate it when a man slipped into Dom mode outside of the bedroom, but with Ambrose, she loved it. She looked forward to it. Craved it, even. It was one thing she loved about staying with him. She was so used to being alone and independent, but it was nice to have someone take care of her. And she needed it right now. She hadn't realised how vulnerable she'd felt until last night.

Now, she sat curled up on the couch writing in her journal while Ambrose was at his parents' house. He'd invited her to go with him, but she'd been hit by a wave of anxiety. It was too much, too soon. Yet he hadn't pushed, just comforted her then left her to her own devices.

"Write it out and we'll discuss it tonight," he'd said. "I'm not letting you run from your emotions, Belle. No more hiding."

As she continued to write, she found herself very tempted to shut down, but fought through it. Shutting down was her automatic response to experiencing strong emotions. Life was easier that way. But Ambrose had been working on her ability to accept and experience her emotions and to communicate as well as trust. He really had gone above and beyond for her. It made her feel treasured. Loved.

Oh, how she loved him. So, why couldn't she say it back to him? She definitely sensed it. Looking down as she turned to the specific page for Ambrose, she wrote the words, 'I love you, Master' and smiled. Now, she just had to work on saying the words out loud.

* * * *

When Ambrose arrived home with three large dishes in his arms, Belle shot him a questioning glance and got up to meet him in the kitchen where he placed the items down on the bench.

"What's all this?"

"Mum made us some dinner."

"Some? That looks like a smorgasbord to me."

His face lit up with that gorgeous grin. "She does tend to go overboard. She made us a roast dinner for tonight, since we're not joining them, then there's a lasagne and potato bake for tomorrow. Since neither of us are great at cooking, I accepted it all."

"Oh…" She'd forgotten he had dinner with his parents once a month, since the concept was so foreign to her. And now she was keeping Ambrose from seeing his parents. "You can still go tonight. I'm not going to keep you from your parents."

He shook his head. "We have things to discuss tonight," he said firmly. "We can see them next Sunday instead."

Guilt turned to nerves at the thought of meeting his mum. What would she be like? Would she judge Belle? Would she hate her like her own mother did? Would she think Belle was trying to steal her son away from her?

"Hey, relax." He rested his hands on her upper arms, squeezing gently. "Don't worry about it. They're both going to love you."

Tears burned her eyes as she forced herself to look up at him. "You don't know that."

"But I do. I love you and you make me happy. That's all that matters to them."

Oh, how she wished she could believe him.

"Belle. I was stuck in a bad marriage for years. I was unhappy almost the entire time."

"And you mum didn't say anything to you about it?"

He laughed. "Oh, she most certainly did. Almost every time I saw her towards the end, she'd point out how unhappy I was. I was just too stubborn to listen."

Two strong arms wrapped around her waist as he pulled her body into his.

"I can tell you honestly" — he pressed a small kiss to her lips — "I've never been happier than I am with you, Belle. They'll see that and that is all that will matter to them."

"I hope so."

"You love me for me. You respect me. You take me as I am and won't try to change me. And you're not after my money. You are the exact opposite of my ex."

The more she heard about his ex-wife, the more Belle hated her. It also made her wonder what redeeming qualities the other woman'd had. Ambrose had assured her he had just been young and stupid and thought he was in love when he married her. Wrapping her arms around him, Belle smiled despite the tears blurring her vision. She loved that she made him happy... She just couldn't fight the feeling that their relationship was a little lopsided. So far, he'd come to her rescue several times. He was her emotional support system. It had happened so quickly that Belle didn't even recognise the moment it had happened.

Pressing his body against her, Ambrose rubbed his erection against her stomach and she grinned, filled with a raw, sexual heat that his touch always brought on. She knew she pleased him sexually — there was never any doubting that. What she wanted was to be an emotional support for him as well. She just needed to figure out how exactly to do that.

"You trust me, don't you?"

"Of course," she answered with a little too much shock and offence in her voice.

"Then trust me to always be honest with you." He made it sound so simple. "If I'm ever unhappy, I will tell you."

"I love you."

The words slipped out naturally as she continued to smile up at him. A weight lifted off her shoulders when she realised what she'd said. The smile he gave her in return was all the reward she needed. It brightened her from the inside out.

"You have no idea how that makes me feel, princess." He cupped her face in his hands and planted a gentle kiss to her lips. "Now, how about you show me just how much you love me?"

He wiggled his eyebrows in the way that always made her giggle. She loved when he got silly with her. Crooking a finger, she gestured for him to get closer.

"I have something else to tell you," she murmured against his ear. Then she whispered, "I'm not wearing any underwear."

Ambrose growled and dipped his hand beneath her jeans, straight into her wetness. She sucked in a gasp and went up on her toes as he slipped a finger inside of her.

"Always so ready for me," he said against her lips. "That's my good girl."

Chapter Eighteen

Dressed in a gown of cerulean blue that kissed the ground, Belle turned in front of the full-length mirror to check the back of the dress, or lack thereof. The dress was open to the small of her back, revealing her muscular physique, while the front dipped just low enough to reveal a little cleavage, while still remaining tasteful. She smiled at her reflection, remembering the look on Ambrose's face when she'd tried on the dress for him last week. His eyes had widened, his mouth spreading into an amused grin as he had said, "That's the one," before pushing her into the change room to claim her mouth in a kiss so hungry it had taken all her strength not to climb him like a tree in the store.

Tonight, they were attending a charity fundraiser for the animal rescue organisation he was on the board of. Belle didn't often attend charity events, preferring to just donate money silently rather than dress up and rub shoulders with people she had nothing in common with. The stuffy, often false, rich people who attended those events reminded her of her parents. All too often, they attended charity functions to be seen as doing the right thing, supporting the less fortunate. When Belle had been in her late teens, Mother had dragged her to balls and galas where she had paraded her around and introduced her to all her socialite friends. And Belle loathed every second of it.

"Straighten your shoulders," Mother would say in that snippy, cold tone of hers. *"Don't push your breasts out like that, you're not a whore."*

Belle's all-time favourite had been when she was eighteen and her mother had said, *"It's amazing how even when you're trying, you still remain a bitter disappointment."*

That had been the last time Belle had attended a public function with her mother. She'd been so hurt by the words, she'd retreated immediately and had gone home to cry, refusing to answer her mother's calls for days.

Wiping those thoughts from her mind, Belle focussed on the task at hand, putting the final touches on her hair. She was excited for tonight, to see what Ambrose had been spending his time and energy on in recent months. He lit up every time he talked about the organisation, just like a kid on Christmas morning.

That was when Belle had decided to donate the funds required to build the new rescue facility. Earlier in the day, she'd discussed it with Gianna, another board member, and had the funds transferred earlier that afternoon. She would tell Ambrose about the donation tonight after it had been announced. She wanted to see the look on his face when he realised the organisation had accomplished their goal.

After slipping in her favourite pair of tanzanite and diamond earrings, Belle fiddled with the strands of hair that framed her face and gave herself a nod of approval.

"What are you thinking so hard about?" Ambrose asked as he entered the bedroom.

Mouth agape, she couldn't help but stare at him when she turned.

All her words disappeared when she laid eyes on Ambrose, wearing a goddamned tuxedo. She'd never seen him look so sexy before. The tux was tailored to his body, hugging him in all the right places, accentuating his broad shoulders, his slender waist and muscular thighs. The man was beautiful — there was no doubting it — but in a tux, he was something else entirely.

"Hot damn," she said in a low, sultry voice when her brain caught up.

"You can say that again," he said with a grin. "That dress looks like it's been painted on."

"Can I tell you a secret?" she flirted, knowing the answer would leave him hot and bothered. "I can't wear underwear with this dress."

With a glimmer in his eyes, he ran his hands down her bare back to her butt, feeling around, the heat from his skin radiating through the thin material to sear her flesh.

"Fuck, Belle. Do you have any idea what that's going to do to me all night?"

She stuck her tongue between her teeth and flashed him a teasing grin. "I'll be feeling the same, having to look at you in that tux all night and knowing I can't grope you in public."

"Just think of it as extended foreplay, princess," he said before he took her lips in a sweet kiss. "Because I'm going to fuck you senseless when we get home."

Belle actually giggled in response as her body heated and moistened.

"Come on, the car will be here any minute."

Grabbing her clutch, Belle followed him out of the house to find a limousine pulling into the driveway. Smiling as Ambrose slid in the car behind her, she rested a hand on his inner thigh and received a light growl in response.

"You're playing a very dangerous game, sweet girl," he murmured in her ear before kissing her gently.

Feeling naughty, Belle continued to tease him with her hand, squeezing his inner thigh, running her hand up and down his leg without ever reaching the one spot she really wanted to touch.

"I'll be a good girl when we get out of the car, I promise."

His heated gaze burned as he covered her hand with his. "Don't make promises you can't keep."

Oh yeah, tonight was going to be a fun night.

* * * *

Belle felt out of place in the extravagant ballroom of the swanky hotel they wandered through. Luckily for her, so did Ambrose, something he'd verbalised twice already. She hugged his arm as they received glances from several people as they made their way around the room, heading for his fellow board members who had gathered on the far side.

After being introduced to several women and a man, Belle settled into a conversation with Gianna, the woman she'd spoken to earlier about her donation. An older woman, appearing in her early fifties, she was almost regal in appearance and immaculately dressed in an age-appropriate gown that had been tailored to fit her.

"Have you told Ambrose about your donation yet?"

Belle shook her head and smiled. "I was going to mention it after it's announced tonight."

"You've done a great thing here, Belle."

"It couldn't be for a better cause," she responded. "Plus, it's so close to Ambrose's heart, how could I not help?"

Ambrose joined the two of them, slipping his arm around Belle's waist to rest his hand on her hip in a subtle sign of possession that he often did while they were around others.

"Has Gianna told you the good news?" he asked, a beaming smile on his face. "An anonymous donor gave us enough funds to get the facility built. The project is now fully funded."

Belle grinned at the excitement in his tone, the brilliant smile on his face, the way his eyes lit up in pure happiness. It really was special to him.

"Actually..." She trailed off as a woman joined him. A woman she *definitely* hadn't expected to see tonight.

"Well, this is quite the surprise," the older woman said with a saccharine-sweet tone that hid the layer of poison beneath her words.

With hair of a deep brown threaded with gold, icy blue eyes that reflected the chill in her soul and skin a shade darker than Belle's, hinting towards their African descent, there was no mistaking her beauty. But what lay inside was a complete contrast to her outer beauty. Mother's face held that same false smile that fooled most into believing she was a nice person. But Belle saw through it, saw the cold reflection in her eyes. Eyes that looked at Belle with nothing but judgement.

"I didn't expect to see you here tonight," she said with that false sweetness again.

"Nor I you," Belle responded coolly while everything inside of her raged with a fiery heat that threatened to shatter her into pieces.

"You know each other?"

"Of course." Mother glanced at him with that flirtatious smile before glancing back at Belle. "This is my darling daughter."

Belle stiffened at the false term of endearment. All her life, she'd been called 'darling daughter' by both her parents. But never once had they meant it, despite her most sincere efforts to please them. But tonight would be different. She wouldn't cower to Mother. She was no longer the broken woman she'd been when they'd last seen each other two years ago.

"A pleasure to see you as always, Doctor Ambrose." Mother leaned in to kiss Ambrose's cheek, her lips lingering a little too long for Belle's liking.

It was an all-too-painful reminder that Mother had hit on every single one of Belle's boyfriends she'd ever met. Mother had a reputation for hitting on younger men — boy toys. She had even tried to pick up Bryce the one time they'd met, and he had punished Belle for her mother's actions.

"A pleasure, Amaretta," Ambrose responded with far more steel in his voice than Belle had ever heard.

He took a step back and tightened his arm around Belle in a show of silent support. No, he wouldn't have fallen for Mother's act. He was far too smart a man for that. He was a Dom. He was not some young, desperate fool, out for the attention and affections of a predator.

"I'm surprised to see you here," Belle said when she found her voice again. "Considering you hate animals."

Mother didn't skip a beat, laughing in that shrill, false tone that haunted Belle's nightmares. "Oh, don't be so melodramatic. Just because I never allowed you to have a pet doesn't mean I hate animals."

She leaned a little closer, to speak only for Belle's ears.

"Go ahead and act the bitch. See how much that impresses your new man. He will tire of you soon enough and you'll be all alone in life again, just like you deserve."

The drunk's words went straight to Belle's heart, an icy dagger that cut deep. But she was right. Belle did deserve to be alone. She didn't deserve Ambrose. She didn't deserve love.

Without a word, Belle shook out of Ambrose's hold and left, fleeing for the bathroom where she could lock herself in a stall and pretend the world outside didn't exist.

Ambrose felt the exact moment he lost Belle. Whatever Amaretta had said had cut Belle to the core. Her entire body stiffened and she removed herself from his hold before fleeing.

"Always so dramatic," Amaretta said with a roll of her eyes and Ambrose now saw her for the ice queen she was. "She loves to be the centre of attention."

Pot, kettle.

Barely able to conceal the rage he felt, Ambrose turned to face the other woman with a cold expression on his face. The one he reserved for submissives who had really misbehaved.

"That woman is one of the strongest, most caring, generous people I have ever met. You could learn a lot from her." He all but sneered down at the woman who dared call herself Belle's mother.

She offered a cool smile as she ran her hand along his arm, sending a chill down his spine. Was she always on? Always prepared to make a move on a man?

"Oh, Doctor Ambrose," she purred. "Don't be like that."

Stepping away from her touch, he clenched his jaw against the choice words he wanted to spit at her. He'd always thought her cold and calculating, but now that he knew who she was, the stories Belle had told him all made sense. Amaretta was a sociopath.

"Enjoy your night, Amaretta." He dismissed her with a wave of his hand and left to find Belle.

When he tracked her down in a bathroom, he stopped and watched as she stood and stared at her reflection, looking like a broken doll. Gone was the strong, independent woman he knew and loved. She'd been replaced by the innocent, sensitive child she must have been. A child who was always desperate for approval and love from a mother who simply wasn't capable of giving it.

After making sure they were alone, he locked the door behind him and stood a few feet from her. "Princess."

Belle turned to face him, tears in her beautiful eyes, an expression of pure vulnerable sadness on her face. "Why do I still let her get to me like this?"

The tone of her quiet voice just about broke him. He had no answer for her. He stepped forward and wrapped his arms around her shoulders, holding her close to his body to comfort her in the one way he knew how. She didn't cry, though, didn't sob, just exhaled heavily and wrapped her arms around his waist.

"I had no idea she was your mother, but it makes sense now," he said, trying to keep his tone light. "I always knew there was something I didn't like about her. She always rubbed me the wrong way."

Belle pulled back, naked vulnerability on her face as she looked directly into his eyes, unblinking. "Did she ever make a pass at you?"

He considered sparing her feelings, sure she would be embarrassed by his admission, but he couldn't lie to her.

"She did once. I rejected her immediately. I do not sleep with ice queens."

Something he couldn't name flashed through her eyes before she broke the gaze.

"I prefer warm, sweet princesses." He brought one hand to cup her cheek. "Come on, let's head home."

Belle shook her head. "We have to wait for the announcements."

Ambrose smiled. "I already know we hit the goal, thanks to you."

She frowned, adorably.

"Gianna let it slip earlier, by accident." He shifted his thumb to caress her bottom lip. "Thank you, Belle. It means the world to me."

"I wanted to do something nice for you."

He laughed and noted the way her eyes glazed over as she began to shut off her emotions. "Come on, I don't want you to shut down on me and be fake happy for the rest of the night. I want you cuddled up against me in bed where you can talk to me."

Belle let out a small sigh. "I don't want to talk about it."

"Too bad." He moved and took her hand in his. "Even if we fight, we're discussing this tonight."

Because he would not have her be closed off to him. Not again.

Chapter Nineteen

Belle arrived at Ambrose's early on Wednesday afternoon after her final two clients for the day had cancelled on her. It had been an exhausting week. After the charity ball, she'd tried to shut down but he hadn't allowed it. Instead, he had forced her to strip naked both physically and emotionally. She'd cried, yelled and sobbed. But she'd done it all with Ambrose wrapped around her, holding her so that she felt safe and secure. Mother was wrong—she did deserve love. She deserved Ambrose.

There was a strange car parked in the driveway and Belle automatically reached for the pepper spray in her shorts pocket. Belle exited the car, cautiously stepping towards the front door. Making her way through the house, she heard sounds coming from the kitchen and stepped in to find a woman standing behind the island bench, humming to herself.

Belle recognised Ambrose's mother immediately. She'd known the other woman was short, but she was tiny. At probably five foot four with a slender and petite build, she reminded Belle of Larissa, right down to the natural blonde hair.

"Oh," she said, startled as she looked up to Belle's sudden appearance.

"Sorry, I didn't mean to scare you," Belle said, suddenly feeling like a scary giant around the much smaller woman.

"No, you didn't. I was in a world of my own," she said with a laugh. "I should be the one apologising. After all, I'm a strange woman in your home."

"I wouldn't exactly call you a strange woman," Belle teased, feeling oddly at ease with the other woman. "I'm Belle." Belle let go of her pepper spray and smiled.

"Veronica. Ambrose's mother. But you already knew that."

"He does have a lot of photos around the place."

Belle stuck her hand out as she approached, but Veronica gently slapped it away.

"None of that," she said and reached up to wrap her arms around Belle's shoulders, pulling her in for a tight hug. "You should know I'm a very affectionate person."

Belle stood in stunned silence, too busy experiencing the single most maternal hug she'd ever received in her entire life. Warm and firm, yet gentle and filled with a feeling that Belle couldn't explain, it reminded her of Nanna's hugs.

A mother's hug. That was what it was.

Belle's phone buzzed in her pocket.

Just a warning, Mum might still be at the house when you get home. She needed the dishes she gave us the other night.

I told her to let herself in while we were both out, Ambrose texted.

"Ambrose is just telling me you're here. A little late." Belle texted back.

Thanks for the late notice. I just scared her!

"I meant to come over earlier but got side-tracked. At least this way we got to meet."

Belle smiled, still unsure if it was a good thing or not. "Can I get you a drink?"

"Oh no, I should get going. I don't want to impose."

"Oh." Belle couldn't hide the disappointment from her voice.

While she hadn't planned on meeting Ambrose's mum so soon, now that she was here, she was looking forward to getting to know her a little, to make a good impression while she had the chance.

"You know what? I will stay for a bit. Since I'm here already, I can grill you for a while."

Belle made them each a cup of tea and handed Veronica her mug before they settled at the dining table. Looking down at her clothing, Belle winced when she realised she was covered in dirt from today's maintenance jobs.

"I must apologise for the state of my dress," she said politely. "I had a full day of maintenance work today."

"Oh please, I used to spend my days cleaning houses. I'm the last person to judge someone."

Already, Veronica was the absolute antithesis of her own mother. Mother had always judged people based on their appearance. She'd had a talent for tearing others down.

"You don't need to feel nervous around me, Belle," the other woman assured her. "While I hadn't planned on meeting you today, I'm very glad I did."

"I admit I'm a little nervous. I've never met a boyfriend's parents before."

"Boyfriend, hmmm?" She smirked and took a well-planned sip of her tea. "I get the feeling it's far more serious than that. For Ambrose anyway."

"It is. I just feel awkward telling you that." Belle's cheeks heated with a blush. "I'm not exactly sure what to call him."

"I assumed you'd call him Master or Sir."

Belle choked on her drink and smacked her chest to clear her throat.

Holy shit. She hadn't expected that response.

"I know all about his dominant activities. He tells me almost everything, even when I wish he wouldn't," she said with a smirk. "But like I said, I'm not judging you for it. I'm no hypocrite."

Belle eyed the other woman. Did that mean…?

"Yes. My husband and I are in the lifestyle as well."

Rather than feeling awkward, Belle was far more comfortable with Veronica now.

"So, now that the awkwardness is gone, let's get to know each other a little, shall we?"

Belle sat back and chatted with Veronica, amazed at how at ease she felt with her so soon. She got a glimpse into what kind of mum she must have been to a young Ambrose. It appeared she chose her words carefully, much like Ambrose, and meant everything she said. She appeared strict yet gentle and caring. And she had a wicked sense of humour, filled with a healthy dose of Aussie sarcasm.

After spending half an hour with her, Belle had already opened up her heart to her, telling her things she probably shouldn't have, including how scared she was of moving too fast with Ambrose.

"My son inherited his honest attitude from me, Belle. You can trust that everything I tell you is the truth, even when it's uncomfortable to hear. I think you're good for my son and I like you. But if that changes at any stage, I will be telling you."

Belle couldn't help but smile, even as her heart ached. This was what a parent was meant to be. Someone who protected their child's heart. Who was there for them and loved them with ferocity. Not once would Ambrose have ever felt like a burden with this woman for a mother. He would have experienced nothing but absolute love and support.

"I'm sorry if that upsets you," she said.

"No, no, it's not that." Belle blinked away the tears. "I don't know if Ambrose told you, but I grew up with really shitty parents. I just realised what a great mum you must be. Ambrose is lucky to have you."

"Oh, sweetie." Veronica's tone was gentle as she reached over the table to gather Belle's hand in hers.

Such a simple touch went directly to Belle's soul.

Ambrose arrived at that moment, just in time for Belle to snap out of her sad mood. Greeting her with a quick kiss before he greeted his mum in a similar fashion, he moved to stand beside Belle, running a hand over her hair.

"How are my girls getting on?"

"Splendidly," Veronica answered with a genuine smile. "I was just about to invite Belle to family dinner on Sunday."

"Oh." Belle couldn't hide her surprise. "I'd love to come. Thank you."

"Wonderful." The other woman stood and excused herself before heading to the front door. "We'll be home all day. If you feel like coming over earlier, you're more than welcome."

She said goodbye to each of them with a kiss on the cheek. Belle felt an instant warmth as the woman smiled up at her, showing genuine approval.

"I like this one, my boy." She patted her son's cheek.

"I do too," he agreed as she grinned at Belle.

Belle loved the other woman already. Was that even possible? Ambrose turned to wrap his arms around her waist and looked down at her.

"I'm sorry I didn't warn you sooner. I hope it wasn't too awkward meeting her."

"Not at all. After the initial shock, we had a lovely chat. In fact, I think I might love her more than I love you," she teased.

"Careful, little sub. Words like that will get you punished."

"Ooh, I'm so scared." She taunted him a little, enjoying the stern expression that came over his face. "The big, bad Dom can't handle a little teasing."

Without warning, his hand came down on her ass, sending a thrill through her veins even as she squeaked in surprise. Grinning up at him, she wrapped her arms around his neck and leaned against him.

"Just so you know, I told your mum I want to see all your baby photos when I visit. I heard there's an embarrassing one of you trying to ride your dog while naked when you were three."

He squeezed her arse roughly and frowned. "I have a feeling I'm going to regret letting the two of you get to know each other."

"Well, it's too late now, isn't it?" She went to tease him some more but was shut up by his mouth crashing down on hers in a rough, wet kiss.

"You're lucky I love you, even when you're being a smartass," he said as he brought his hands up to cup her face. "Seriously though, I hope you're okay with meeting her."

"I don't lie, Ambrose. I was nervous when I first saw her, but she's amazing." A hint of sadness that she couldn't hide came across in her voice. "You're lucky to have her. She seems like an incredible mum."

"She's the best." Fingers running through her hair sent a shiver down her spine. "And now that you're mine, she'll start treating you as her own, too. I hope you realise that."

"She did say that. I thought she was just being polite."

Ambrose shook his head. "My ex's betrayal hit her hard because she treated her like a daughter. But I know that will never happen with you."

She raised her brows in a questioning glance.

"You're different, Belle. Different than any other woman I've been with. Better than any other woman I've met. And I trust you, implicitly. I know you'll never betray me."

"No, Master," she said sternly. "I never will."

She would cut off her own arm before even thinking about betraying Ambrose's trust. He was a man to be treasured. The greatest gift she'd ever received.

* * * *

It had been quite a week, Ambrose thought as he got himself dressed to attend Haven. Each night this week, he and Belle had sat down to work through her issues, specifically putting time aside to talk. And he loved their chats and getting to know her on an even deeper emotional level. He loved that she allowed him to help her through the emotional turmoil she was feeling after seeing her mother. And she'd grown to trust him intrinsically.

Last night, when she'd returned from picking up some more clothing from her house, she'd made a point of telling him how unsafe she felt at home. She hadn't danced around the issue. She'd just come right out and said, "I felt scared," without hesitation. Because she now understood that he would never judge her. He was always going to be on her side.

Belle had put her house on the market this week and was now looking for a new home in the same area. She'd enlisted the help of his friend and fellow Master, Harvey, to help her find something suitable. Despite his protests, she insisted she needed to find a home of her own. That she wouldn't move in with him permanently when they'd just started their relationship. He understood, of course, but he also knew that she had made his house a true home.

Her laughter and giggling as she teased him filled his home with love and light. Now, she often teased him, playing with him constantly, even giggling when she made him mad. And he loved every second of it. Which was why he was gifting her with a play collar tonight. Fuck, he hoped she accepted it. It would break him if she took a step back from him now. He'd grown so damn attached to her that he couldn't imagine his life without her in it every day. If she ever decided to leave him, he would never be the same man.

Butterflies thudded around his gut when the shower turned off.

Fuck, yes, he was nervous.

He hadn't been so nervous when he'd proposed to his ex-wife. That alone proved how much more Belle meant to him.

Exiting the ensuite with a towel wrapped around her, Belle looked at the bandage dress he'd laid out for her to wear tonight. It was a short, strapless number, the perfect dress to show off her new cuffs and collar.

"You want me to wear that tonight?"

"You *are* wearing that tonight," he told her firmly.

While he had no interest in having control over her everyday life and clothing, Ambrose insisted on choosing what she wore to Haven now that they were in a relationship. And tonight, he was in the mood to see some flesh.

"I might as well be naked," she muttered.

"That can be arranged," he offered with a smirk.

Quite often, submissives ended up wandering around Haven completely naked. While he hadn't done that to Belle yet, perhaps tonight would be the night. The thought of her bare save for his collar and cuffs made him hard. Oh yeah, she would definitely be spending the night naked now.

Slipping into the dress, she adjusted the fabric so it covered her private areas and looked at herself in the mirror, fiddling with her hair.

"Now I know why I've never worn this before," she mumbled to her reflection. "I feel like I'm wearing nothing at all."

"Your outfit isn't complete yet." He handed her a small box that she accepted eagerly.

"Ooh, you got me a present?" Her face lit up as she grinned.

Fuck, she was beautiful.

She slipped into submissive mode the second she opened the box and saw the cuffs. Eyes shimmering with tears, she ran her fingers along the engraving on the outside of them. His initials. So everyone would know who she belonged to.

"Master?" Her voice wavered as she looked at him.

So damn vulnerable.

Nobody had ever claimed her in this way. While he was glad she had remained available for him to snatch up, it also angered him that no other man had seen her for the true treasure she was.

"These are the only cuffs you are to wear from now on." He attached one. "Whether we're playing at home or in the club, I want everyone to know who you belong to."

"You didn't have to..."

"I wanted to." He kissed her as he attached the other then reached into his back pocket. "But there's one more thing."

Nerves coursing through his veins, he brought his hand out and displayed the collar to her, inside up so she could see the words engraved on the lining.

Master Ambrose's Princess.

Her face crumpled when she saw it, hands flying to cover her mouth as she sucked in a gasp.

"You're mine, princess," he told her in a gentle voice. "I promise to always take care of you. To protect you. I promise to love you always and forever. Will you do me the honour of wearing my collar?"

The look of vulnerable hope in her eyes told him she understood the magnitude of what he was asking. He wanted her to be his. For always.

"Of course I will," she whispered.

Unsure his body could hold this amount of happiness, he swallowed past his constricting throat and moved to stand behind her, placing the collar around her neck. It was a symbol of his love for her. Of how far they'd come in their relationship. It would be a symbol to every other Dom that she was officially off the market, for good. She was his. And he was never letting her go.

Chapter Twenty

Seated beside Master Ambrose, Belle sank further into the lounge as she listened to her dominant friends chat away, filled with a complete and utter happiness she never thought she would experience. She touched her collar for probably the hundredth time tonight and smiled. Her Master looked down and caught her expression, grinning at her as he ran one strong hand along her bare shoulder before bending to press a sweet kiss to her lips.

"You look beautiful in my collar," he murmured in her ear and nuzzled against her. "I love you, sweet girl."

Unable to speak, she smiled at him like a giddy idiot and placed a hand on his inner thigh, leaning into him. He had claimed her, publicly. He owned her, body, heart and soul, and she couldn't have been happier about it. Filled with so many different emotions, she couldn't identify them all. She chose to focus on the pure, unabashed joy that kept rising to the surface.

Even now as he touched her, she felt nothing but happiness. With one arm draped over her shoulder, he cupped and played with her breast beneath her dress. The other grazed her inner thigh over and over, getting a little higher with each pass, yet never touching her where she wanted it.

They hadn't played yet. Tonight, they'd just socialised with their friends. Even Mistress Ashely had joined them with her submissive for the evening, Clint. Belle didn't know the man very well but enjoyed talking to him when they encountered each other. He currently knelt at the Mistress' feet, his head resting on her thigh while she stroked his head in a loving manner. The Mistress was a very good Domme. The one time Belle had scened with her, she'd ended up having a full-blown panic attack right in the scene area. Mistress Ashely had been amazing about it, sitting with Belle while she had calmed herself. She had held Belle until she had relaxed enough to be handed off to Agin, the only man she had trusted at the time.

Belle smiled when she realised just how far she'd come in recent weeks. All because of her Master. A Master who was currently watching her with intense eyes.

"You doing okay?"

Snuggling further into him, she gripped at his thigh and smiled. "I'm great, Master."

Across from her, Agin laughed at something Sullivan had said, all the while casually playing with his wife's breasts while she knelt between his legs. Amara was propped on Sullivan's lap, naked and cuddled into him, still lost in the aftermath of an intense scene they'd just finished.

For once, Belle didn't feel a single pang of envy. Because she had her own Master now. She belonged to someone. And she was in love. For the first time in her life, she was in love.

"So much thinking," Master Ambrose murmured in her ear. "Anything I should know about?"

"Just that I'm in love with you and have never been happier."

He ran a finger along her slit, smiling when he found her nice and wet for him. "Now that's something that deserves a reward, don't you think?"

"What if I'm not in the mood?" she teased.

As she hoped, he thrust a finger inside of her pussy, pulling a gasp from her as she squirmed a little, a rush of heat flowing through her veins.

"Oh, you're definitely in the mood," he all but growled. "But since you're clearly feeling a little bratty, I'll add a little punishment as well."

He stood, pulling him with her, excusing them by saying, "I have an arse to spank," then picked her up, throwing her over his shoulder in a fireman's carry. Squealing, Belle hit her fists against his back and kicked her legs. He responded by smacking her hard on the arse, while laughing.

* * * *

Sitting with his happy little submissive in his lap, Ambrose couldn't have been happier. After delivering a "funishment" she'd thoroughly enjoyed, he'd taken Belle in a public space, something he hadn't done yet. It appeared his princess had a healthy exhibitionist streak in her that he hadn't discovered yet. She'd come long and hard while he thrust into her.

After taking a little while to recover, she'd begun mouthing off to him again, vying for another spanking, which he had gladly delivered. Ambrose loved seeing the brat in her come out to play. He had never thought he would be attracted to bratty behaviour again, but it was different with Belle. He realised she had spent her entire life behaving, had never been allowed to rebel against her parents, so she was getting it out of her system now, with him. All because she felt safe enough. She knew he wouldn't leave her just because she acted out a little. Instead, he rewarded her bratty behaviour, encouraged it, even.

"I'm thirsty, princess. Why don't you go get us a couple of drinks?"

"Yes, Sir," she responded and bounced to her feet.

Completely naked, except for her collar and cuffs, Belle didn't seem to mind one bit. He loved the way her ass jiggled with each step she took, the way her breasts shook as she moved towards him with a drink in each hand.

A loud bang sounded from one of the private rooms upstairs and Ambrose spotted Grayson rushing inside. Jumping to his feet, Ambrose stood on alert.

"Don't move."

Belle nodded in response and he rushed for the stairs, coming face to face with a Dom who had just lashed out at Grayson, elbowing the owner in the face. The man took a swing at Ambrose. Ducking out of the way, Ambrose moved quickly and punched the other man in the solar plexus, knocking the wind out of him. Grayson joined him at the bottom of the steps after Ambrose had restrained the man.

"Get him outside," the owner growled as he wiped blood from his bottom lip.

Without hesitation, Ambrose pushed the struggling man through the main club room, heading for the entrance. The other man suddenly fought back, slipping from Ambrose's grasp. Responding without thinking, he subdued him with one single punch to the nose. Cartilage crunched beneath Ambrose's fist and the other man dropped like a sack of potatoes.

"Get up, you prick," Grayson snapped and dragged him to his feet.

Grabbing the other arm, Ambrose helped Grayson push the man outside and let him go with a shove.

"You're done here." Grayson stood over the furious man. "If you ever try to step foot in here again, you'll be leaving in a body bag."

The man cursed and held his nose but turned and left without argument.

"What the fuck was that about?" Ambrose asked when Grayson had calmed a little.

"The fucking arsehole ignored a safe word. Lucky for the sub, I happened to be checking on them at the time. He was caning her and continued, even after she screamed the safe word."

"Jesus."

"No matter how hard I try, these assholes keep getting through the background checks." He thrust a hand into his dark blond hair and swore. "I don't know what to do about it."

"You do everything right, you know that. You know as well as I do that arseholes like that are very good at disguising their true colours." He slapped the other man on the shoulder. "Come and get a drink and rest a bit."

Grayson shook his head. "I need to deal with this mess and make sure Ellie's okay."

"It was Ellie? Shit."

"Exactly."

The new submissive was still in the process of exploring and finding her boundaries. She was close with Grayson and Sullivan, the other men seeing her as a little sister. Because of that, all the Masters knew her and had been helping her explore different kinks. Now that she'd encountered an asshole, it would no doubt set her back in her exploration and confidence.

"Thanks for your help taking out the trash."

"Any time, mate."

Ambrose headed towards Belle and discovered she'd left their spot. As had Larissa and Amara. It took a second for him to realise the mistake he'd made. He'd just gotten violent in front of Belle.

"Fuck."

He rushed to where he'd left her and found Ayden heading for him, a look of sincere worry on his face.

"Where is she?"

"The girls took her to the bathroom. It was pretty bad, mate. She just began to panic."

Fury and guilt were a fist in his gut. He went to step around Ayden, but was stopped by a firm hand in the centre of his chest.

"You need to calm yourself. The last thing she needs to see is you in a fury."

"Don't tell me how to deal with my own sub."

Ayden gave him a firm Dom look. "You're going to scare her."

"Fuck." He blew out a breath. The other man was right.

Sucking in a few long, deep breaths, Ambrose forced himself to calm before Ayden let him go. He made a beeline for the bathroom at the far end near the recovery corner and knocked on the door, unsurprised when Amara opened it a mere crack.

"Have you got a handle on it?" the gutsy little sub asked as she looked him up and down.

"I have."

After one more narrowed look, she opened the door farther and stepped aside. Everything inside of him crumbled when he saw Belle huddled on the settee, struggling to breathe as Larissa stroked her hair.

"Belle," he said softly and knelt at her feet.

Looking up, she reached for him. Relief poured through his veins as he held her, wrapping his arms around her waist. He knelt to press his body against hers.

"You're okay, princess," he whispered as he ran a gentle hand up and down her back. "Just breathe."

Larissa and Amara hovered for a few moments until Belle had calmed enough to sit on her own. Her hand suddenly flew to her throat.

"My collar," she rasped.

Larissa handed it to her. "I took it off so you could breathe easier."

"Thank you." Belle accepted it and clutched her hand around the item.

"Can you give us a minute?" he asked the women, pleased when they both nodded and left without a word. "Belle, I'm sorry you had to see that."

She shook her head. "It's okay. It wasn't that bad, I just... I had a flashback."

"Of course you did," he murmured and kissed her forehead. "I'm sorry. I didn't think how it would affect you—I just reacted. I'll do better next time."

"I know you're capable of violence. But I haven't seen it... I just... I know you'd never hurt me..."

"But it still scared you," he finished her thought. "It won't happen again."

He would beat himself up for reacting without thinking for a long time. He'd just decked a guy in front of her and caused her to have a traumatic flashback. He felt like a real asshole.

Belle held up her collar and looked at him through her lashes. "Will you put it back on, please?"

"Of course." He did so, pleased when she continued to smile at him. "Are you sure you're okay?"

A firm nod. "I just had a moment."

"You can have all the moments you need, as long as you lean on me."

"Always, Master."

* * * *

Ambrose lay awake in bed that night, with Belle snuggled into him, fast asleep. He'd fucked up tonight. He hadn't even considered how him manhandling someone might affect her. He'd just reacted without thinking and caused her to have a panic attack.

Although she had reassured him that she was okay, had immediately cuddled into him and refused to let him leave her all night, he still felt guilty. He'd known she wasn't completely calm — he could see it in her eyes, the way the small muscles around her mouth tensed when she wasn't speaking.

It had been so long since he'd been in an altercation like that, Ambrose had forgotten the effect it had on him. Adrenaline still rushed through his veins. He hated that there were so many assholes in the world. But the fact that the man had chosen to prey on an inexperienced submissive made Ambrose furious.

"I can hear you thinking," Belle murmured, but she didn't move. "Go to sleep."

"Sorry, princess." He kissed her forehead.

After another few minutes, she shifted to straddle him, propping herself above him on her hands, her wet centre precariously close to his hardening cock.

"What's wrong?"

"Nothing," he lied.

"Ambrose," she warned as she looked down at him with those eyes he got lost in. "I know when you're lying, you know. Now tell me what's bothering you."

"It's nothing important. You need to get some rest."

"Well, I'm up now." She wiggled her hips and caught his erection, slipping the tip inside her hot, wet cunt. "I might as well have some fun."

He hissed in a breath as she sat back a little, lowering herself onto him completely.

"Belle. You know I don't tolerate topping from the bottom," he warned in his Dom tone.

"And I don't tolerate lying, but you still did it." She sat up straight, pulling him balls deep inside of her.

Fuck, she was incredible. She pushed her hair over her shoulder and ran her fingers along her plump breasts, teasing him.

"I'm sorry about tonight."

She moved her hips slightly, up and down.

"I told you, I forgive you. I understand why you reacted the way you did."

"I shouldn't have, though. I should have stopped to think about how my actions would affect you."

"I'm a big girl, Ambrose." She rocked her hips back and forth. "I can handle myself. It wasn't that bad."

"Still…"

"I said it's fine. Let it go," she snapped as she dropped forward on her hands. "I'm not dwelling on it and neither should you. I love you, that's what matters."

His heart swelled at her saying the L word to him. She'd said it twice now and each time he felt like he was going to burst with happiness. He didn't deserve her.

"I love you, Belle." He brought his hands to rest on her hips, ceasing her movements. "And if you try to top me again, I'm going to tie you down on the spanking bench and cane you until you cry."

She grinned and clenched her inner muscles around his cock. "Don't give me a reason to do it, then."

Sucking in a breath, he lifted her off him and slammed her back down on his cock, enjoying the way her eyes rolled back as he impaled her. So responsive, so beautiful and all his.

"Since you're already here," he murmured as he pulled her down for a kiss, "you might as well finish what you started."

He crossed his arms behind his head and settled in for a ride.

"Really?" She beamed. "I get to play?"

"Just this once," he agreed. "So, you'd better enjoy yourself."

And she did. She rode him until she came twice, bringing him down with her on the last orgasm. He gathered her on top of him, running his hands up and down her bare back beneath the blanket and pressed kisses to her forehead, cheeks and temple. She fell asleep sprawled across him. He eventually followed her, drifting into a restless sleep.

Chapter Twenty-One

On Sunday evening, Belle sat back and enjoyed the company of Ambrose's parents after having a nice home-cooked meal. It reminded her of the Sunday evenings she used to spend with Nanna and Grandad. Each week in the winter months, Nanna would cook a massive roast dinner and they'd have a formal meal at the dining table while enjoying each other's company.

Watching Ambrose interact with his mum and stepdad brought a hint of sadness and envy to Belle's heart. It must have been great for him to grow up in such a supportive environment. He and his mum reminisced about the days when it had just been the two of them, how they had spent their time together.

Belle loved hearing of their exploits. Like the time Ambrose almost gave his mum a heart attack by climbing a tree in their backyard and hiding there when he was six, all because she had told him it was time to get a haircut. He'd fallen out of the tree and broken his arm. But, as Ambrose proudly pointed out, he had avoided getting a haircut for another couple of weeks.

Rob, his stepdad, was an interesting man. Over six feet tall, though shorter than Ambrose, he was a large, burly man, the very definition of a gentle giant. He was softly spoken, a far cry from Veronica, who was outspoken and made her opinion known. Yet the two of them appeared to have a great relationship. Rob worshipped the ground Veronica walked on.

He'd set the table for her, brought in the food she'd made and was now washing the dishes with Ambrose while Belle set out the dessert she'd made for them, her favourite triple-choc layer cake. It had taken hours to make this afternoon, which was why she didn't do it very often. But she wanted to impress her partner's parents.

"Let's get started while they're still occupied, shall we?" Veronica said sneakily as she sliced into the cake. "Sometimes it's the only way I can get my fair share with these two around. It's no wonder they're the sizes they are with the amount they eat."

"I had noticed that." Belle laughed. Ambrose ate twice what she did. "He must have eaten you out of house and home growing up."

"Oh, you wouldn't believe it. He ate so much I was going to the grocery store every second day to restock. I had no idea where he put it all until he had a growth spurt at fifteen. He shot up to six feet tall without warning. And my baby boy suddenly became a man."

Belle smiled at the term of endearment. Veronica called Ambrose her baby boy quite often and it was sweet to hear. Belle's parents had never had a pet name for her. Although her grandparents always called her their "special girl."

"You're good for him," Veronica said plainly, as she served Belle a slice of cake. "Even Rob can see that and he's not the most observant man when it comes to emotions."

"I hope I'm good for him," Belle replied. "I come with a lot of baggage."

"Sweetie." The other woman laid a gentle hand on Belle's arm. "We all come with baggage. It's a part of being human. From what Ambrose has told me, it's not all that bad. It's how you work through it that counts."

Belle let those words sink in for a moment. "Any advice on getting him to open up to me?"

"Has something happened?"

She gave Veronica a basic rundown of what had happened on Friday night.

"He hasn't been sleeping well since, but he won't talk about it. He feels guilty about causing me panic. No matter how many times I tell him I'm okay — and I really am — he doesn't seem to believe me."

"There are two things that have never changed about my son. His need to protect women and his inability to forgive himself for hurting those he cares for. The fact that he caused you pain must be eating him up from the inside."

"I know. But he won't talk about it with me. No matter how hard I try, he just shuts down and pretends he's okay."

At least now Belle knew how much it hurt to have someone she loved shut down on her. She owed her friends a well overdue apology for all the times she'd done it to them.

"Perhaps you should suggest he join you for a psychology session," Veronica offered. "That helped him after the incident with my ex and Parker's father. He didn't sleep properly for weeks after those two nights. I sent him to a psychologist and speaking about it with an unbiased party seemed to make a big difference."

"That's a good idea."

"He's a very stubborn and private man, my son. As much as I love him, he's not as in touch with his own emotions as he'd like everyone to think."

"So I've noticed," Belle muttered. "Yet he expects me to tell him everything."

"That's the problem with dominant men, Belle. They quite often live by a code of 'do as I say, not as I do.'"

"You're right." Belle sliced her fork through the piece of cake and scooped some into her mouth, allowing the instant sugar rush to calm her.

"Just don't give up on him. He's worth fighting for."

"I will never give up on that man," Belle told her firmly. "I love him with all my heart and soul. He's not getting rid of me without a fight."

Veronica grinned from ear to ear. "That's what I like to hear. I knew I liked you."

* * * *

"You what?" Ambrose barely managed to keep the growl out of his voice.

"I think it would be a good idea to stay at my house for a night or two," Belle told him. "One night apart would do us some good."

"Have I done something?" He knew it had been a tough couple of days with him not sleeping and refusing to talk about what had happened on Friday night, but it wasn't enough for her to leave him.

She cupped his face in her gentle hands. "It's nothing you've done. I just need some alone time and I think you do, too."

"You can have your alone time here. If you want me gone, I'll stay with Ayden or my parents. But you are not going back there."

There was no way in hell she was spending the night at her house alone. Not with that psychopathic ex of hers out there. After speaking with Parker during the week, he had found out that Bryce had skipped out on his most recent court-appointed counselling session. That wasn't a good sign.

"I'm not kicking you out of your own home, Ambrose," she said sternly as she dropped her hands.

"It's our home now, Belle. You belong here as much as I do." He meant those words with everything he had in him. This was her home now. She had made it a home.

She smiled and moved to sit on his lap. "It's been a great couple of weeks, but you have to admit it's been a lot in a short period of time," she said. "I love you. I just need a night alone to gather my thoughts."

He couldn't help but be hurt by that sentence. She was right—it had been a lot in a very short period of time, but it felt natural. To him anyway.

"How about a compromise?"

"I'm listening."

"You can stay at your house as long as you have one of your friends stay with you."

"Ambrose." She let out a huff of exasperation. "That completely defeats the purpose of me having alone time."

"You understand why I don't want you there alone, don't you? I'm genuinely concerned for your safety."

She reached up to cup his face so tenderly it hit him right in the soul.

"I understand. And I promise to call you the instant I feel unsafe or scared."

He sighed. He knew why she wanted to be alone. But just because he understood didn't mean he liked or agreed with it.

"If you promise to call me, I'll agree to it. Even if it's the middle of the night and you get woken by a sound. I expect that phone call."

"You know I will." She smiled, her beautiful eyes twinkling with gratitude. "Thank you."

She kissed him. "I promise I'll come running straight back to you afterwards."

"I love you, Belle."

"I love you, Ambrose."

* * * *

With a heavy heart, Ambrose watched Belle drive away the next evening to spend the night away from him. As a show of trust, she'd given him the log-in details to her security camera system which allowed him to receive alerts when someone approached the property. The app sounded an alert as she arrived. He watched her blow a kiss to the front door camera as she unlocked the door and headed inside.

Cute.

He texted her and received a smiley face emoji in response. Now he had to figure out what to do with the rest of his evening. After a workout, he showered and found himself sitting on the patio lounge alone. Lonely. He'd gotten so used to having Belle's presence in his home that he'd forgotten how big his house was. Far too big for a single man. Belle had made his house feel like a home. And it wouldn't be a home without her in it.

* * * *

The first thing Belle did when she got home was have a long, relaxing soak in a bubble bath. After reading a couple of chapters of a book on her Kindle, she got out and greeted her friends when they arrived right on time for an impromptu girls' night. While Belle was looking forward to having some true alone time, Amara had called to say she had the night off from looking after her mum and wanted to catch up to get all the gossip from Belle's dinner with Ambrose's family.

The three of them settled in the lounge room, dishing out some Indian food to share family style. While the other two dug in, Belle served herself a small plate, not feeling particularly hungry with the sense of nervousness that flew around her gut.

"So, how does it feel to be back home?" Amara asked around a mouthful of dahl.

"It's strange. I don't feel safe here, but I also don't feel comfortable. It's like something's missing."

"Or someone," her friend teased.

"You miss Ambrose already," Larissa chimed in.

Much to Belle's dismay, her cheeks heated with a blush and she nodded quickly, while avoiding their prying gazes.

"Oh, girl, you've got it bad."

"I love him so much it hurts to be away from him."

"Then why are you? Why aren't you with him right now?" Amara asked with a hint of worry in her tone that said she could sense something more was going on.

"He needed a night away from me, although he would never admit it. He still feels guilty about Friday night and hasn't been sleeping properly. I hope that if

I'm not there to remind him what happened, he'll take the time to do some thinking himself."

"And?"

"I kind of need to know that it's real," she tried to explain. "It's all happened so fast, I need to know if I'm clinging to him because I love him or because he's safe."

"That's a tough one," Larissa admitted. "I did something similar with Agin when we were dating. I didn't see him for an entire week because I got scared that we were moving too fast."

"I remember that," Amara said and rolled her eyes. "You called us crying because you were worried that you'd ruined the relationship by taking that break."

"I ended up crawling back to him with my tail between my legs because I missed him so much. We haven't spent a day apart since."

"I don't know if I can function that way. Living in each other's pockets. It's been great so far, but I don't want to completely lose my independence."

"That's understandable," Amara agreed. "I felt the same way. I enjoyed my freedom and didn't want to lose it, but I'll tell you this—I still have my freedom even though I live with Sullivan. If I need alone time at home, he leaves. He spends the evening with Grayson and does whatever manly things they do together. And I do the same. But when he comes home at the end of the night to share the bed with me, it makes it all worthwhile. I usually end up missing him so much when we're apart that I jump all over him as soon as he returns."

Belle smiled, now knowing what her friend meant. It had only been a couple of hours since she'd seen Ambrose and she was already dreading the thought of spending the night without him.

"Is it bad that I miss him so much already?"

Her friends shook their heads.

"Not at all," Larissa said. "You've just never been in love before. This is what love is. It's all consuming, terrifying, freeing and utterly wonderful."

"I just don't want to get stuck in another unhealthy relationship."

"We can't comment on what happens behind closed doors, but whenever we see you together, you're always happy," Amara said, offering her a kind smile. "You weren't like that with Bryce. You were always on edge around him, waiting for him to criticise you, trying to please him to no end but he never pleased you."

"It really is different with Ambrose," Belle said wistfully. "He takes care of me. I just... I love him so much it scares me."

"Love is scary," Amara told her. "If you're not scared, you're doing it wrong. I definitely did it right. Giving myself over to Sullivan was fucking terrifying. But I would do it all over again because he's my person. And Belle, I think Ambrose is your person."

Belle agreed. He was it for her. If things didn't work out between the two of them, she would embrace spinsterhood.

Now that she was convinced she was doing the right thing with Ambrose, she didn't want to stay alone tonight. She wanted to go right back to him and sleep wrapped in his arms all night, in her safety net.

* * * *

Belle woke during the night to the sound of her security camera app screeching in the silence. The high-pitched noise grated on her nerves. She opened her phone to find nothing on any of the cameras. *Strange.* A quiet scraping on the front door had her on high alert in an instant. That was something.

Jumping out of bed, she slipped on a pair of leggings and grabbed her pepper spray then made her way to the front door to check the monitor. It was completely black.

Against her better judgement, she opened the wooden front door and found herself standing face to face with a nightmare.

Fuck.

Bryce stood on the other side of the door, watching her through the security screen. His hands resting on either side of the doorframe, he leaned forward menacingly.

"Hello, Belle," he said in that low, threatening tone she recognised all too well.

It was the very same tone he'd used the night he'd broken into her house.

"Aren't you going to invite me in?"

A wave of nausea churned her stomach as she clung to her phone, trying to unlock it blindly. Ambrose would have gotten the alert. Right? Unless he'd slept through it.

"You need to leave," she said when she found her voice.

"Aw, don't be like that. I just came to say hi." He pushed off the wall and stood up straight, his large frame as threatening as ever as he towered over her. "You at least need to hear me out. You owe me that much."

"I owe you nothing," she snarled. "I have nothing to say to you."

From the corner of her eye, Belle saw her phone unlock and fumbled with the touch screen to call Ambrose.

"Oh, but I have a lot to say to you, baby." He swayed on his feet and she realised he was under the influence of something. The darkness of his hooded eyes, the very slight slur in his speech. "I gave you everything. I would have given you a great life. And you threw it all away."

Finally dialling Ambrose, she felt slight relief. Hopefully he would answer and hear her speaking and call the police.

"You cheated on me."

He rolled his eyes. "One time."

"That's bullshit and you know it," she snapped, feeling anger tear through her. "You cheated on me the entire time we were together. You were just too much of a coward to admit it."

Thatta girl, poke the inebriated and threatening bear. She was being an idiot, but she couldn't hold back. For two years she'd been holding on to her anger towards him. Now it was finally going to come out.

"I did everything you asked. I obeyed your every stupid order. I was the ultimate submissive for you. And *you* decided to throw it all away. Not me."

"You have no idea how much I regret my actions. To this day, all I think about is winning you back."

"Too bad you decided to beat the shit out of me instead."

Something inside of him snapped. His calm demeanour changed in a flash, his face contorting into a horrid sneer as he slammed his fists against the door. "You ruined my life!"

Right now, her anger far outweighed her fear. Limbs trembling with rage, she clutched at her phone and pepper spray.

"You sent me to the hospital for a week. You broke my bones. You knocked me unconscious over and over, waiting for me to wake before laying into me again. Then you had the audacity to pretend you didn't remember doing it. But you do, don't you? You remember the entire thing."

A slow, sinister smile spread across his handsome face. "I remember every single second. And I'd do it again if it meant you'd learn your lesson. You are mine. You will always be mine."

"I'll never be yours," she spat back at him. "I've found a real man now. Someone who actually knows how to please a woman. And he's better than you'll ever be."

"You bitch!"

What happened next happened so fast, Belle barely had time to register it. Bryce pulled the security door open and slammed his hands against the wooden door as she tried to slam it in his face. He stepped inside, grabbing her by the throat, and slammed her head against the wall.

Belle saw stars as she found herself on the floor with no memory of falling. Bryce leered over her, his hand gripping painfully at her hair, the other tightening around the throat, squeezing hard enough to cut off her air as he dragged her to her feet. She began to panic, her vision blurring.

"You ruined my life, you dumb cunt," he sneered at her. "I lost my job, my friends, my reputation. I lost everything because of you."

Belle kicked out, aiming for his groin, but got his hip instead when he shifted. He roared his anger and backhanded her, knocking her to the ground again. She made it to her feet, trying to keep her wits about her, to remember the lessons Ambrose had taught her. Fisting one hand, she punched him square in the groin but didn't have time to enjoy landing the blow. He latched onto her throat again, lifting her up and bashing her head against the wall as his other fist connected with her jaw.

Blood filled her mouth and she looked at the monster she'd once thought she'd been in love with. Now she knew better. Now, she had a real man. One who had taught her to defend herself against a large opponent. Holding the pepper spray cannister, Belle flicked the lid open and pushed down, bringing it up to get him right in the eyes.

"Fucking bitch," he yelled as his grip around her throat slipped.

Bryce scrambled, reaching for her legs as she tried to run. He pulled her down, her face hitting the floorboards before she could catch herself. Running on pure adrenaline, she kicked out at him, only just missing his face. He crawled on top of her, his eyes red and swollen, his movements sloppier now. Scratching at his face, Belle kicked and screamed, making it harder for him to get a hold of her. She managed to get him again with the pepper spray before he knocked it out of her hand.

Her foot connected with his groin as she scratched at his face and throat, finally managing to squirm out from beneath him. Scrambling to her feet, she ran for the ensuite.

"Fucking cunt!" He chased her down. "I'll kill you for that!"

Belle barely managed to lock the door behind her before his body slammed against it. After a few bangs, Bryce began smashing his body against the wood. Huddling in the tub, Belle curled into herself, silently begging for the police to show up. She knew that if he got his hands on her now, she would be dead. That was a certainty. There was no way he would let her get away, this time. She'd seen it in his eyes.

The banging stopped. Bryce's shouting ceased. With blood roaring in her ears, she stayed in the tub, not daring to move just in case it was a trap. Wailing sirens got closer by the second and relief swept through her. Help had arrived.

Sometime later, still trembling, Belle tried and failed to catch her breath. Her vision began to go black at the edges. Why was it so quiet outside? Why hadn't the police come to get her yet? Had Bryce gotten away? God, she hoped not. She couldn't handle that.

There was a quiet knock on the door.

"Belle, it's me. Open the door, princess."

The voice made it through the haze. "Master?"

"Yes, it's me. Please open the door, I need to know you're okay."

"Is it… Is he gone?"

"The police have him," he told her firmly.

Managing to stand despite her shaking legs, Belle staggered out of the tub and reached for the door. Leaning against the bench, she sagged and slid to the floor in a heap. Ambrose crouched in front of her, his hands roaming over her body. He checked her face, touched her hair, gently caressed her arms and legs, before he finally kissed her. She took a moment to look at him. Blood dripped down his face from a gash on his forehead, his lip was swollen and split and there was a purpling bruise on his jaw and cheekbone.

"What happened to you?"

"Are you okay?"

She nodded. She was okay, despite the pain tearing throughout her body. Because she was with Ambrose. And she trusted him wholeheartedly to take care of her. Now that she was with him, everything was right in the world.

Chapter Twenty-Two

Sitting beside Belle's hospital bed, Ambrose held her free hand a little too tight while the nurse took photographs of her injuries as evidence. Parker stood over her, supervising while asking questions about the attack. Belle had a bruised cheek from where the prick had backhanded her, swelling on her rapidly darkening jaw where he had punched her. Add to that a gash on the back of her head, a sprained and swollen wrist and ankle and Ambrose was barely able to keep a hold on his anger. This had all happened because he hadn't been there for her. He hadn't gotten to her soon enough. He should never have let her go home alone.

But she was safe now. As Parker had said, it could have been a lot worse. Still, Ambrose would never forget the look of fear and relief on her face when she had opened that door. The way she'd crumbled immediately. He would never forgive himself for not being there to protect her.

Belle winced as the doctor injected a local anaesthetic into her scalp to give her stitches on the swollen wound. Bryce, the piece of shit, had smashed her head into the wall several times. Blood smeared the entry wall as a result. Ambrose would have to get Ashely to clean up the house before Belle entered it again. She didn't need to see her own blood all over the floor.

Ambrose felt physically ill as he watched her hurt. Her eyes glazed over as the painkillers began to sink into her bloodstream. Her hand softened in his, her tense muscles relaxing. He'd been amazed that she hadn't passed out from the head trauma, especially considering she had a concussion. Instead, she'd stayed awake and spoken to him the entire drive to the hospital, even telling him she loved him. His resilient little submissive.

"I should have killed him when I had the chance," Ambrose muttered after the doctor and nurse left the room.

"You damn near did," Parker said. "You're lucky he isn't pressing charges."

"He wouldn't have a leg to stand on."

The other man's lips twitched. "No, he wouldn't. I think you may have beaten some fear into him."

Good.

"Is he here?" Belle asked in a timid voice that he'd never heard before.

"He's under police guard and unconscious. He's being transferred to RPH soon. You don't have anything to worry about."

It pleased Ambrose to hear that pathetic excuse for a man was unconscious. While he'd pulled several of his punches, it had been damned hard to do. He'd ended up choking him out to subdue him. Bryce had been high as a kite and apparently hadn't been feeling any pain, despite the constant blows. He kept coming back for more.

"Now that I've gotten your recount, I'll let you get some rest. We'll be in touch in due course." Parker lowered his voice and spoke only for Ambrose to hear. "You did a good job, my friend. I owe you a drink for taking him down."

Ambrose nodded solemnly at his old friend. While it gave him no joy to beat another man, he'd done what he needed to, to protect his love.

"Can we go home?"

"Lie back, I'll go check on the discharge paperwork," he said and placed a small kiss to her knuckles.

Once discharged, Belle allowed Ambrose to push her out of the hospital in the supplied wheelchair then carry her to Ayden's waiting car. Their friend had come to give them a lift home.

"Fuck, sweetness, he did a number on you, didn't he?" Ayden said as he checked her over.

Belle shrugged and winced at the same time. "It's nothing compared to last time."

The mere thought of it made Ambrose's blood boil. Once home, he tucked Belle into bed—his bed—right where she belonged.

"I'll let you rest tonight, but tomorrow we have some things to discuss."

She looked up at him, tears in her eyes. "We do?"

"I want you to move in with me, permanently."

"Oh." Her bottom lip quivered. "I thought you were mad at me."

"Sweet girl, no." He stroked her cheek and sat on the bed beside her. "Why on earth would I be mad at you?"

"Because I wanted alone time. If I hadn't been at my house, this wouldn't have happened. I wouldn't have scared you."

"Belle." He continued to caress her, wiping away the tears that fell across the bridge of her nose and down her temple. "I'm not mad at you. I understand why you wanted to be alone."

"I don't want to be alone anymore."

Her words made his heart soar. Smiling down at her, Ambrose noted the look of relief in her eyes. She had thought he'd be mad.

"I really love you," she all but whispered.

"I really love you." He pressed a soft kiss to her forehead. "Get some sleep."

"Where are you going?" Her hand clung to his arm when he made a move to leave.

"I just need to shower, then I'll be right here, in bed with you."

He desperately needed to rinse off the blood staining his body and get rid of the reminder of what he'd done. Then, he would curl his body around the love of his life and stave off nightmares for them both.

* * * *

Belle woke with a scream stuck in her throat. Barely managing to swallow it, she opened her eyes and found herself looking into the beautiful, intense green eyes that she loved so much. Her handsome man looked at her, one strong hand touching her face.

"You're okay. You're safe at home."

Struggling to sit up, she groaned as her aching muscles reminded her of what had happened last night. Her head throbbed in time with her rapid heartbeat, adding to the ache she felt.

"Ow." Her voice croaked as she shuffled to sit against the head of the bed.

"I'll get you some painkillers." Ambrose pushed off the bed and returned with a glass of water and two tablets for her. "Here, it'll help you get back to sleep."

"But it's already morning." The early morning rays shone through the cracks in the blinds, taunting her, telling her to get out of bed.

"You've only had two hours of sleep," he told her in that stern tone that left no room for argument. "Now lie down and get some more sleep."

She followed his order, turning to lie on her right side to face him. Ambrose moved one arm beneath her neck, pulling her body into his. In the arms of the person who loved her most, Belle, safe and secure, drifted off into a dreamless sleep.

When Belle woke next, she was in the same position, wrapped up in Ambrose's arms. Trying to ignore the pain in her head, the stabbing in her ankle and wrist, the overall stress and throbbing of her muscles, she instead focussed on the hard, warm body pressed against her, on the man who was murmuring sweet words in her ear to keep her calm. With a small sigh and a little too much effort, Belle rolled over. Ambrose was watching her. God, he was so beautiful, it hurt to look at him and not touch. Those gorgeous green eyes darkened as he continued to look at her, his gaze pinning her.

The small of her back tingled with arousal and she brought her uninjured hand up to caress his cheek. She offered him a smile and leaned forward to kiss him. Ambrose didn't move. He lay there and kissed her back slowly, thoroughly, pouring his heart into her. Every part of her body was set alight by his lips on hers, but he stopped her from moving.

"Just stay here and enjoy the moment," he whispered against her lips.

He kissed her again, so soft and sweet that her heart ached. They lay there making out gently for what felt like hours. When they came up for air, Belle saw so much emotion in Ambrose's face it made her heart ache.

"I love you so much." A stray tear trickled down her cheek. "I'm never leaving you again."

His smile was so bright, it lit up her soul. "Good."

* * * *

Belle managed to shower and dress with Ambrose's help. He even washed her hair very carefully for her, managing not to touch the sore spot of her skull once. Each muscle in her body ached. She soon discovered she couldn't open her jaw enough to eat properly. Although the doctor had assured her nothing was broken, it sure felt like the last time she'd been punched in the face.

It was mid-afternoon when visitors began arriving. Ayden and Grayson showed up first, bringing an array of chocolate and ice cream for her, knowing she would want some comfort food.

Grayson wrapped her up in the warmest, most careful hug she'd ever received from him. Though he had only been involved on the periphery, she always knew he cared about her and her safety.

"You did us proud, girl," he murmured into her hair as he continued to hold her. "I'm very happy you're safe."

"Thank you, Sir." She looked up at his gorgeous face and smiled as best she could.

"Just don't do it again."

She winced as she laughed. "Don't worry, I don't plan on going near that house alone ever again."

It was true. What had once been her home, her safe haven, was now just a reminder of some very bad memories. The only reason she had to return to it was to move out her belongings.

Ashely rocked up not long after the men, showering her in more gifts of chocolate. Amara and Sullivan arrived, bringing her proper meals with them plus a bottle of very expensive scotch for Ambrose. Larissa and Agin followed with even more meals. The group of them hung out for a while until fatigue took over and Belle needed to excuse herself to take a nap.

When she woke, she found Veronica and Rob sitting on the lounge chatting with their son.

"Sweetie," was all Veronica said before she stood and enveloped Belle in the sweetest, most comforting maternal hug she'd ever received.

Belle held on tight and began to cry while the other woman stroked her hand up and down her back, soothing her.

"I'm so glad you're safe," she murmured into her shoulder.

Rob joined them and laid a kiss on the top of Belle's head.

"You did good, girl," he said while resting a firm hand on her shoulder.

This is what a family should be, Belle thought.

Supportive, caring, loving. And she finally felt all of that. All because of Ambrose.

When Veronica let her go, Belle settled on the couch, resting against her love with her leg stretched out, injured ankle elevated.

"Did you bring us more food? My friends went a little overboard with the amount they brought us."

"Yes, but Veronica's is made with a mother's love," Rob commented with a broad smile. "It's extra special."

Belle grinned at the man. She loved him already. Though he was a man of few words, those words all meant something.

"Ambrose mentioned you were having trouble eating so I made you some soups and custard for dessert."

"You're the absolute best," Belle said, fighting tears. "Thank you so much for coming. It really means a lot."

"We'll always be here for you, sweetie," Veronica said with a genuine smile.

"Have you told your parents what happened?" Rob asked.

Belle shook her head carefully. The thought hadn't even crossed her mind. "They wouldn't care."

"They might surprise you."

Belle scoffed. "The last time this happened, my mother blamed me for it. Said it was my own fault for choosing the wrong man."

Ambrose's parents looked absolutely appalled and disgusted at the same time. Ambrose just looked furious. He'd heard the story before, but it didn't impact him any less. He tightened his arm around her and pressed a gentle kiss to her forehead as she leaned further into him.

"At least you have a real family now," he murmured.

She never had to worry about her parents again. They were out of her life for good. She had a new family now. One who loved and supported her wholeheartedly.

* * * *

Ambrose sat at home nervously awaiting Belle's arrival. After two weeks off, she'd felt well enough to return to work today. She'd called him once after having a mild episode and he couldn't have been prouder. She had come to trust him, that he would always be there for her, no matter what.

When she arrived home, she frowned when she saw Parker sitting at the dining table with him.

She visibly paled as she sat beside Ambrose. "What's going on?"

"You know that Bryce made bail last week," Parker stated.

The son of a bitch had enough powerful contacts that he had been out of custody before he'd even been discharged from the hospital. His parents had paid the significant bail on the condition that he not leave their house.

"He was rushed to the hospital this morning after hanging himself. He didn't make it."

Ambrose sat back, absolutely stunned. The fucking coward couldn't handle having to pay for his actions and had killed himself. He really was a piece of shit. Relief flooded through him when he realised Belle no longer had anything to worry about. She was free.

"He killed himself?" she asked in a small voice.

Parker excused himself soon after, giving Ambrose a few words of advice as he walked him out.

"Don't let her shut down. She'll be in shock right now. It happens often. Just keep the line of communication open. Take her to her therapist." He clapped a hand on Ambrose's shoulder. "Look after her."

"Always."

Ambrose waved the other man off and headed inside to find Belle sitting in the exact same position. She didn't even look up when he sat beside her.

"I don't feel anything," she said before looking at him, her face still pale, eyes wide. "Why don't I feel anything?"

"You're in shock. Let's get you into the tub and I'll give you a nice massage to relax, hey?"

With a small nod, she stood and allowed him to lead her through to the ensuite. He ran her a bath, sitting on the edge beside her while she lay there and soaked. She skipped the offer of a massage to sit outside alone to gather her thoughts.

Ambrose left her to her own devices, only interrupting to feed her. She returned to the backyard, sitting on her favourite ornate seat in the middle of the garden, staring off into space, a blank expression on her face.

He joined her, scooping her into his lap.

"It's okay to be happy, you know," he murmured as he wrapped his arms around her waist. "It doesn't make you a bad person."

"That's just it." She rested her hands on his arm. "I don't feel anything. I'm numb."

"That's not entirely surprising. You've been through a lot and now it's all over." He kissed her sweater-covered shoulder. "It may take a few days to comprehend everything."

She didn't respond, just continued staring into the trees.

"Maybe you should speak to your psychologist."

"I made an appointment for tomorrow evening," she said before turning to face him. "Will you come with me?"

He smiled. "Of course."

She'd asked for help without prompting. She had come a long way since he'd met her.

"I just don't know how to feel. I know that he's dead and he can't hurt me anymore, but I don't feel it. I can't comprehend it."

"You have spent the last two years living in fear, whether you want to admit it or not. But you don't have to now. I would imagine it's going to take you a while to feel relief. But we'll discuss it tomorrow and figure out how to handle it in a healthy way."

Turning, she wrapped her arms around his shoulders and buried her face in his neck. She let out a long, slow sigh and squeezed tight. She relaxed into him. Yes, she would be okay eventually. Because she had support.

Chapter Twenty-Three

"That was exhausting," Belle said as she entered the house behind Ambrose.

After one hell of a draining counselling session, she had finally broken down and begun to cry. But she was still incapable of identifying the different emotions she felt. They all melded into one giant ball. There was a lot of relief, though, because she no longer had to look over her shoulder at every turn. She could live at home alone if she wanted to. Not that she did. She couldn't imagine not waking up in the same bed as Ambrose each morning.

There was also a little grief in her tears. Not for Bryce—fuck that asshole. But grief for the girl she had once been. And anger that she'd allowed herself to be put in that situation in the first place. All of this boiled down to her trust issues. And those had all been caused by her parents. It was her parents' fault she had ended up with Bryce. That she had never felt like she belonged and had sought acceptance in the worst possible place.

"Are you going to give some thought to what the psychologist said?" Ambrose asked as he sat on the couch beside her.

"I can't even think about that right now. I don't think I could handle it."

"It might be good for you to get some closure," he offered. "But you know that I'll support you no matter what decision you make."

The psychologist had suggested Belle meet with her parents to discuss her trust issues. That it might give her some closure to speak her mind to both of them, rather than just moving on. To tell them how her upbringing had affected her.

Seeking comfort, she curled into Ambrose and rested her head on his shoulder. "I see where she's coming from, but I don't think I want to see them again. I gave them so much power for so long. They would probably get satisfaction out of knowing how they affected my life."

"I understand," he said and held her. "If you change your mind, just know you won't be seeing them alone. I will be coming with you, even if I have to fight you on it."

"Thank you." She tilted her head and gave him a small kiss. "I appreciate you coming today. Having you there helped."

"I'm glad I could do something to help you."

Hearing a sense of disappointment in his voice, she looked up at him, finding a small frown on his handsome face.

"You have no idea how much you have helped me already." She brought one hand up to cup his face, angling it so he was forced to look at her. "You helped me trust. I never thought I would be in a relationship again. Not after that."

A small smile. "Neither did I. You bring out the best in me."

That filled her with such joy she thought she might burst out of her skin. Kissing him, she poured all her happiness into it, sweeping her tongue into his mouth. She sat up and moved to straddle him, cradling his face in her hands. His arms came around her, his hands holding her possessively as he took control of the kiss. Letting out a low moan, Belle sank down onto him, feeling his erection press against her centre.

One hand slipped beneath her shirt, leaving a searing trail on her skin. She pushed herself impossible close to him, smiling into the kiss when he gave a low groan and bit on her bottom lip. They stayed that way, caressing and kissing without moving further. Because he understood that it wasn't about sex right now. She just needed to feel close to him.

* * * *

A couple of days later, after many long talks with Ambrose and her friends, Belle was beginning to feel better, almost like her old self again. The fog in her brain had receded, and she had begun functioning again. She headed to her favourite bakery to pick up some pastries for the girls' night she was having with Larissa and Amara tonight.

The bakery had been a favourite of her grandad's. He'd often brought her here as a child and bought her a blueberry danish, her favourite, after they'd been at work in the garden. When she stepped inside, a young couple looked at her and stared for a few long moments. Though healing, she was still covered in bruises, her black eye evident even as it was yellowing.

Feeling a little self-conscious, she ordered her pastries and headed out, coming face to face with the last person she wanted to see right now.

"Mother," she said, trying to keep her voice steady.

"Belle." Mother's voice was as icy as ever as she looked her up and down in a gaze of pure judgement...harsh judgement.

Rather than unsettled, Belle found herself realising she no longer cared what her parents thought of her. If they were going to judge her because she wore jeans and a sweater and got dirty each day at her job, that was on them. She loved her life.

"What happened to you?"

It almost sounded like she gave a shit.

"Bryce happened again."

With not a single sign of worry on her youthful face, Mother asked, "Are you still with Ambrose?"

Belle held back a scoff. "I am and he's amazing. He even beat the shit out of Bryce after the attack."

Clearly appalled, Mother clutched at her throat and gasped. "He wouldn't. He's not that kind of man. That is not the sort of man you should be with."

"He loves me and has shown me how to trust again. What better man for me to be with? His family have taken me in as their own."

Mother's cold smile was a reminder of the lack of compassion Belle had received as an adolescent.

"Still a brat, I see."

Belle looked down at the mild shake in her mother's hand. The shake she had developed when Belle was fifteen because of her alcoholism.

"Still a drunk, I see."

Belle realised she couldn't find the energy to play dirty with her mother. She wouldn't play her games anymore.

"Ambrose taught me I'm worthy of love. Something you and Father made sure I never felt."

"Now —"

"No," Belle cut her off. "I spent my entire life trying to please the two of you, to win your love and approval. But I don't need or want it anymore. Your opinion means less than nothing to me."

Mother pressed her lips into a thin line, but she didn't say a word.

"I have a new family now. One who accepts me for me. One who loves me for the person I am. The person Nanna and Grandad helped me become. The person I became despite the two of you constantly telling me I was worthless."

A small smile played on the older woman's lips. "Still as disrespectful as ever."

At one point in time, that would have cut Belle deep. Now, she just let out a harsh laugh. "Your words mean nothing to me. I wish you no ill will, but I no longer want anything to do with you or Father. As far as I'm concerned, we are no longer family."

A flicker of something flashed in her eyes. Hurt? Disdain? It didn't matter.

"Take care."

And with that, Belle walked away with her head held high. Pleased to find that her mother's words had made absolutely zero impact, she got into her car and drove away with a smile on her face.

She found Ambrose working in the shed, where he'd been building a new piece of BDSM furniture for his — their — dungeon. When he'd first told her he'd built all the furniture in the dungeon, she'd been shocked and amazed at his talent. Then she'd seen Rob working on his own furniture and put two and two together. The two of them had bonded over building together when

Ambrose was a young man. The thought of the two of them together made her heart swell. It must have been sweet to witness.

"What are you working on?" she asked.

"A hanging stockade," he said without looking up. "I figure since you enjoy the one at Haven, I'd make a more refined version to play with here."

Hanging stockade. The very thought of it made her shiver.

He stood and winced as he straightened his back. Hair fell over his forehead, shadowing the remnants of the black eye he'd received from the fight. Lips pursed, he moved to stand beside her.

"What happened?"

"I saw my mother."

"Belle."

She raised a hand at the sign of sympathy on his face. "No, I'm fine. I kind of told her off. Told her I didn't want to see her or Father again."

"Is that the truth?"

A month ago, it wouldn't have been. But so much had changed since then. She'd truly come into her own. And now that she'd met Veronica and Rob, she knew what real parents were, how they were supposed to act towards their children.

"I have a new family now," she said with a simple nod. "One who is actually supportive. I don't need my parents weighing me down any longer."

He moved to rest his hands on her hips. "You do have a new family. But they are still your parents."

She knew what he was getting at. He didn't want her to regret cutting them out of her life. But she never would. She was better off without them.

"I've already been estranged from them for years," she explained. "Cutting them off completely just means

I have closure. I'm better off without their toxicity in my life."

Wrapping his arms around her shoulders, he rested his chin on her head and just held her.

"You have to do what's best for you. I will support you."

"Thank you," she murmured into his chest.

She was so goddamned lucky to have him.

* * * *

The following weekend Ambrose finished his dungeon monitor shift and handed his vest over to Ayden. With Belle fully healed, she was ready to go to Haven. And he had quite a scene planned for her tonight. She'd been asking for it all week. He was going to push her, deliver more pain than he had previously.

"Are you going ahead with it?" Ayden asked as he slipped on the silver-trimmed vest.

Ambrose nodded. "She thinks it's going to be a basic scene."

"Then she's in for quite a surprise, isn't she?"

He laughed. Of course, he would tell her what he had planned, but only once they stepped into the area. "She has no idea. Just keep an extra close eye on her for me."

Earlier in the evening, he'd asked Grayson, Sullivan, Agin and Ashely to keep an eye on them just in case he overloaded Belle and she began to panic, and he required help to get her down. Because he really did plan to push her limits. She'd told him all about the level of erotic pain she used to enjoy and while they'd been working up to it, tonight was the night he would dish it out.

"Always, mate." Ayden gave him a slap on the back and walked away. "Have fun."

* * * *

Belle stood in the centre of a scene area, her arms held up in a wide V, wrists hooked up to chains that hung from boltholes in the ceiling beam. With her legs held apart by a wide spreader bar, she was completely naked except for her precious collar. And beneath Ambrose's heated gaze, she felt vulnerable.

He'd already warmed her up, giving her a light flogging and attaching a butterfly to her, the constant low thrumming vibrations on her clit just enough to keep her aroused but not anywhere near enough to get her off. He was going to torture her tonight. He'd said as much. She turned her head to look at the toys he had spread out on the table but she couldn't see.

Giving a low whine, she pulled at the chains and watched as Master Ambrose appeared in front of her. He had that look in his eyes, the one that said he wanted to devour her. Fuck, it made her hot. Made her feel unbelievably desired.

With a small smile, he pulled something from the table. A fucking cane. Whacking it against his palm, he tilted his head to assess her before approaching. He gripped a fist in her hair, tilting her head back. She gasped and looked up at him, melting into his hold.

"I'm going to push you, princess. I'm going to give you what you've been asking for," he murmured against her lips. "And you're going to take it because you're my good girl."

"Yes, Master," she whispered, arousal building further inside of her.

"I'm going to blindfold you, so you just focus on the sensations." His voice was silky smooth as he spoke only for her ears. "I expect to hear yellow the second you feel overwhelmed."

"Yes, Sir," she whispered and tilted her face up in a silent request for a kiss.

He obliged, kissing her so sweetly that tears blurred her vision when she looked up at him. He smiled and placed the blindfold over her eyes, tying it behind her head, then running a finger beneath the straps to check it.

"How we doing, my sweet girl?"

"I'm good, Master," she told him with confidence. "I'm ready."

"Of course you are." He gave her one more gentle kiss before he slipped into full Master mode, his voice gaining that firm tone that made her go weak at the knees. "No more speaking unless it's a safe word."

"Yes, Sir."

She heard him move away and pull something from the table, a scrape of leather against wood. Thin tendrils dragged along her breasts, down her stomach, along her thighs and back up. He was going to flog her first. Excitement built as she wiggled her body in preparation, flexed her fingers and let out a small sigh. She was ready for the pain. *You got this, girl.*

Yes, she did.

Ambrose watched, transfixed, as Belle rose up on her toes when the cane struck her ass. When he removed it, her hips arched, seeking more. He upped the ante in careful increments, bringing the cane down on her ass hard enough for it to welt. She cried out, her body going slack as she slipped into subspace. He moved to check on her, slipping the blindfold to her forehead. Glassy chocolate eyes looked at him, beautiful and unfocussed.

"How are we doing, princess?"

"Good." Her smile told him she was doing well.

He slipped his free hand to her pussy, finding her appallingly wet and deliciously swollen. Running one finger alongside her clit, he smiled as she whimpered and arched into his touch. He found a rhythm. Up and down, on either side of her clit, then over the top. She let out another whimper as he applied barely any pressure directly over it. Thrusting one finger inside, he used his other hand to grasp her swollen, tender ass, smiling with pride as she cried out and looked at him, her eyes never leaving his.

The atmosphere was palpable, their connection deep. With two fingers buried deep inside of her, he curled them and pumped over and over until she teetered on the edge. Then he brought his hand down on her abused flesh in one hard smack.

"Fuck!" she cried as her entire body started to tremble. "Please, Master," she whimpered. "Please."

He gave her what she needed, rubbing his thumb over her clit in firm and steady strokes until she came hard. He kissed his way along her shoulder and up her neck until she lifted her head. Cupping her face, he rested his forehead against hers.

"I'm so proud of you, Belle. You've done amazingly well tonight." A soft kiss. "Just a little more."

Just a little more? What else could he do? He pulled the blindfold back down, surrounding her in darkness. Every inch of her skin was hot and so taut she felt like she might burst. Her arse burned where he'd spanked her. But she could handle more. She would take everything he dished out to her.

Something cool grazed her skin, running down her thighs, over her ass and up her back. Another flogger. She closed her eyes and rested her head against her arm, just waiting for him to continue. With one hard whack, the flogger connected with her back. Heat and pain radiated through her entire body, shooting straight to her throbbing clit. Again. She cried out, almost losing herself. One more hard whack and she was thrown over the edge into absolute and pure bliss. Subspace.

She vaguely heard Master Ambrose say, "Almost there," and nodded. He hit her again and again, the pain immediately converting to pleasure, heat pulsing through her veins as she was taken higher and higher. He pressed himself against her back, her skin searing as his clothing scratched against the sensitive flesh. One warm hand cupped her mound, a finger grazing her clit. She rocketed into the clouds, her entire body disappearing.

Barely aware of hands on her, she was lifted and moved. Voices swirled around her, but it was her Master's that she focussed on. He murmured sweet words as he held her.

* * * *

She'd done so well tonight, he thought as he cradled Belle in his arms, remaining careful of her sensitive skin. All snuggled into him, she came back to herself.

"Did I do good?"

He smiled at the vulnerable quality of her voice that always showed up when she was in subspace.

"You were amazing, princess," he told her. "Thank you for taking it for me."

"Mmm, I'd do anything for you, Master."

He tilted her chin and gave her a soft, sweet kiss that lasted several long minutes until she began to giggle.

"And what is so funny?"

"Nothing." She shook her head even as she continued to make the adorable and lovely sound. "I don't know why I'm laughing."

It was the endorphins, obviously. And he wouldn't stop her because he loved seeing her laugh.

"I love you, sweet girl," he said with a big smile on his face and pure joy in his heart.

"I love you."

Epilogue

One month later

Belle prepared herself for a night at Haven, their first in two weeks. They'd both been so busy with work in recent weeks that they hadn't felt up to attending the club. But tonight, Ambrose had dungeon monitor duty. And Belle was excited to be scening at Haven again. Apparently, he had something planned for them but wouldn't tell her about it at all. That just built further anticipation as Belle got dressed.

Ambrose had set out an outfit for her. She should never have agreed to let him have control over what she wore at Haven. Tonight, he had chosen a tiny dress that barely covered anything. Strangely, he'd set out some underwear for her. With a smile, she picked them up and noted they were crotchless panties.

Sneaky, Sir.

Slipping on the stockings and garter belt, she dressed and assessed herself in the mirror, pulling the hem of the deep red dress down so it would cover her butt. As soon as she took a step, it rode up again. Looked like she'd be flashing everyone tonight.

Ambrose appeared in the bedroom, already dressed and ready to go. Tonight, he wore a dark-blue button-down and dark-blue jeans. He was drop-dead sexy, as always. He approached then wrapped his arms around her waist from behind.

"You look delectable," he murmured in her ear and nuzzled her.

"I was surprised to find you've given me underwear until I saw what they were."

"You should never have given me the idea of crotchless panties, princess." He chuckled.

"I've created a monster, haven't I?"

His laugh was low and deep and filled with amusement. It ran over her skin, bathing her in happiness and comfort. Leaning back in his hold, she looked at the two of them in the mirror and sighed.

"We look good together."

"We look perfect together," he corrected.

They really did.

And she had never been happier in her life. Everything had come together. They were living together. She'd sold her house quickly and was happy to be free of the bad memories that stained her once beloved home. Moving in with Ambrose was her chance at a fresh start, to be surrounded by only positive memories. Like the one they'd created last week when she'd injured herself at work and he'd carefully wrapped her sprained ankle and carried her throughout the house whenever she wanted to move so that she wouldn't have to walk. They'd both laughed and teased each other. It was silly. And she'd loved every second of him caring for her.

"Belle, do you love me?"

"Of course," she said with a small frown.

"Do you enjoy living with me?"

"You know I do."

"Will you wear my collar?"

She scoffed. "I already do."

Belle turned to face him, to scold him for being stupid, and found him on one knee in front of her. In his hand was an open box displaying the most beautiful diamond and tanzanite necklace she'd ever seen. Embedded in white gold, the stones shimmered, leading down to a small lock that dangled in the centre of the necklace. It was the single most beautiful necklace she'd ever seen.

"Ambrose, what is this?"

"Wear my collar. Be mine forever."

She reached out to touch her fingertips to the jewellery, not quite believing it was happening. Her gaze fell to the lock at the front. A true collar. She would be his and everyone would know it.

"Princess, you're making me a little nervous here..."

"Of course I'll wear it, you idiot." She launched into his arms, placing a series of kisses all over his face. "I can't believe you got me a collar."

"I can't believe you called me an idiot." He chuckled. "If you wear this, I will have the key. It will only come off when you wear your play collar."

He would own her. He'd claimed her. Asked her to be his forever. With tears in her eyes, she took a step back, her eyes never leaving his.

"Put it on me."

He complied, snicking the lock shut, then put the small key in his pocket, moving so his hands sat on either side of her throat.

"You're mine, Belle. Don't ever forget that I love you with all my heart and soul."

"Me too." Her throat was thick with emotion. "I love you so much it hurts. Thank you for claiming me."

"Ditto." He smiled before his lips came down on hers in a kiss that left her breathless.

Want to see more from this author? Here's a taster for you to enjoy!

Masters of Haven: Never Again
Liia Ann White

Coming February 2024

Excerpt

Standing on her friend's front porch, Ellie inhaled a deep breath, sucking in the floral scent that accompanied the beautiful gardens. She put a smile on her face, hoping it appeared real. It was fake, of course, but none of her girlfriends would notice. She was the master of masking. Over the last couple of months, all of Ellie's smiles had been fake and, so far, not a single person had commented. Not even Sam, who was a psychologist and good at reading people.

Ellie's eyes widened when the door suddenly swung open, the fresh floral scent becoming stronger when Sam threw her arms around her, enveloping her in a hug.

"Girls' night!" Sam exclaimed, a wide grin spread across her pretty face.

Ellie wished she could emulate the other woman's enthusiasm. Sam was always so happy, whereas Ellie often lived by the rule "fake it 'til you make it". She'd been running on empty for weeks. Whether it was an ADHD burnout, or an end-of-year burnout, she wasn't sure. Either way, it sucked and Ellie was tired of being tired. She wanted to go to bed and sleep for a week.

Ellie had been scattered and unfocussed all day, again, despite the stimulant medication she took for her disorder. It was a shame because she'd been looking forward to spending the night with her girlfriends. After weeks of non-stop work, she was finally having a proper catch-up with them. She hadn't had girl time in weeks and had missed quality time with her friends.

Sam led Ellie through the immaculately kept house to where the other girls — Amara, Belle and Larissa — were already congregated in the expansive lounge room. She gestured for Ellie to take a seat on the soft, comfortable couch.

After greeting her friends with quick hugs, she settled onto the couch with an audible *humph* sound. Ellie sank into the couch, enjoying the way it hugged her on all sides. With a sigh, she closed her eyes and enjoyed the feeling of being relaxed for the first time in weeks. She hadn't had a night off in far too long. But all her hard work was about to pay off. The gym she ran — and now was a fifty-percent owner in with Sullivan, her friend and former boss — was opening in a month in new, larger premises.

With rooms for healthcare professionals to work from, including a chiropractor, nutritionist, psychologist and massage therapist, it was going to be a proverbial one-stop health shop. Because staying fit and healthy wasn't just about eating right and exercising. There was also a room for Sullivan to run his physiotherapy business from a couple of days of week, which he was already utilising.

After coming up with the plan twelve months ago, Ellie had gone to Sullivan with it, nervous that she was overstepping because she was simply his head coach and trainer. He had announced that he not only thought it was a great idea, but had offered her a fifty-percent stake in the gym she'd worked so hard on. The gym she had helped start from the ground up was now half hers. She couldn't have been happier about it. Her professional life was heading exactly where she'd wanted it to. Her personal life was another story.

Now that the gym was almost complete, the health and lifestyle app she'd been working on was out of the planning stage and ready to hit the practical trials, such as filming exercise and stretches as well as meal prep videos and other videos she'd planned for it. It would take a while and be a hard slog, but it would be worth it for Ellie to realise her dreams.

"I haven't seen you for so long, I was beginning to forget what you looked like," Amara said with a teasing smile.

Reaching forward for a hunk of cheese and a cracker, Ellie nodded and sighed. She'd been burning the candle at both ends for too long. And once the gym was open, the app was going to be her priority in life.

One thing at a time, she had to keep telling herself.

She had a bad habit of piling too much on her proverbial plate, then burning out. She still had to remember that having ADHD made things more difficult for her. There was a finite number of hours in the day where she was medicated and her brain worked properly. Other than that, she was an unfocussed, inattentive mess. It had been six years since her diagnosis, but she was still getting used to the idea that she wasn't "neurotypical". She had a disorder, a learning disability. It was a lot to take in.

"It has been a while. I've been so wrapped up in work, I haven't had a chance to breathe in recent weeks."

"How have you been?" Sam asked, her recently dyed red and green hair—for Christmas—shiny and glossy as it spilled over her shoulders.

"My life has literally been all about the gym," Ellie said.

"As long as you're not running yourself into the ground," Sam replied, her voice filled with concern.

"Ever the psychologist, aren't you?" Ellie teased.

Sam shot her a knowing look that Ellie had dubbed her psychologist look. It said she saw right through Ellie's cheerful bravado to the raw stump that was her mushed psyche.

"How are you feeling, honestly? I can't help but notice you still haven't been to Haven."

Ellie slumped. Of course that would come up tonight. Three months ago, she'd had an incident at Haven—the BDSM club they all frequented—where she'd essentially been assaulted by a so-called Dom who had taken advantage of her. She'd been naïve and had paid more attention to his stellar reputation at the club rather than the gut feeling she got about him. Never again would she ignore her gut instinct.

After that, she had decided to take a few weeks off to deal with her emotions regarding the incident. Then she'd buckled down with work and hadn't had a chance to head back to Haven. It had been three long months and she'd missed the place. Well, she missed seeing her friends each week more than anything. She hadn't had much of a sex drive recently.

"I will always put on my psychologist hat when it comes to my friends burning out," Sam said sternly.

It wasn't the first time Sam had raised concerns for Ellie's mental health, it probably would be the last, either.

The others joined in, shooting looks of concern Ellie's way. She hated being judged. It felt extra harsh and made her feel self-conscious when it was her girlfriends. Like she couldn't take proper care of herself, even though she was an adult.

"I'm okay, really. I'm just tired," Ellie said, expressing what she hoped was convincing self-confidence. "I've just been working hard, but I'm coming out the other end. You'll be seeing me more now."

"What have you been up to, other than gym work?" Belle asked, the raven-haired amazon resting back on the couch with a glass of wine in one elegant hand.

"Nothing. Honestly, I've been so focussed on getting everything ready for the new Better Health premises, I haven't done much else, other than my usual jobs." Ellie rested against the back of the couch, allowing her head to drop back. "The new facility is finally finished and looks great. Sullivan is working out of there, as is the chiropractor. I've been organising the equipment this week."

"Sullivan has been running himself ragged with the gym, too," Amara said of her fiancé and Dom. "I think you've both earned a month off after working too hard on it."

"It'll be worth it," Ellie said, reminding herself as much as the others. "It'll be a one-stop shop for the body and mind once it's up and running."

"It might even get me to join now that you're doing open gym hours during the day," Larissa said, then tipped her glass of wine up to empty it.

"Considering none of you girls have been to my gym, maybe that was my plan all along," Ellie teased.

The others laughed. Ellie ran a CrossFit gym and while CrossFit wasn't for everyone, she had always hoped her girlfriends would give it a shot. The men all had. By adding open gym hours, Ellie was hoping to attract more people like her friends—people who didn't want to participate in a class but still wanted to exercise. Ellie herself was like that. She preferred to work out alone where nobody could see her face when it became beet purple from overheating.

"Did Sullivan tell you guys we have a massage therapist joining three days a week?" Ellie exclaimed with genuine excitement. "I used to see her before she had her kid. She's just started working again and has the strongest hands. She really gets in there and finds all the knots and tension."

"Now you're talking." Belle rubbed her hands together. "I love a good deep tissue massage."

"She's the best." Ellie forced a grin. "Anyway, enough about my boring work life, what have you guys been up to?"

Listening to her friends chat about their lives, Ellie took a moment to appreciate just how great a group of close girlfriends she had now. She'd never experienced it before. That was a little sad for a twenty-six-year-old woman to admit, but the truth was she'd always struggled to make and maintain friendships.

She'd been a tomboy as a kid, with all her friends being boys until she hit puberty. They hadn't known how to treat her after that. High school had been just one shitty blur where she'd been in survival mode the entire time. Then university had happened and she had been too busy studying to achieve two degrees to be fussed with making lasting friendships. Instead, she'd had dozens of acquaintances, but nobody ever got close. Not until now.

But over the past year, Ellie had scored in the friend department. She now had a great group of people to socialise with. It just happened her female friends were all submissives as well, although Sam was technically a switch.

And she had her job to thank for finding friends. At first, she'd become close with Sullivan, then his best mate, Grayson. Then she'd met Amara through Sullivan a little over a year ago. She and Amara had quickly bonded over caring for ill parents before realising they had more in common than a shared trauma. Amara had taken Ellie under her wing and introduced her to her own girlfriends. Ellie had discovered that Haven existed, and the rest was history.

"Are you still planning on working on the app once the gym is open?"

Ellie nodded in response to Amara's question. "I can't wait. I've got so many ideas prepared for it. Once the gym is completed, I'm going head-first into getting the app sorted. By the way, the gym officially opens on the eighth of January, but the Sunday before, we're having an open-day celebration for everyone to check out the premises. There'll be food trucks, face painting, a bouncy castle for kids, plus one for adults…"

"I'm definitely going to that," Belle said with a little laugh. "Even though I plan on never doing a CrossFit class in my life, I'll be there for support."

Ellie snorted. "It can actually be fun, you know. You might enjoy yourself."

Belle rolled her eyes. "We have very different definitions of fun, girl."

"Speaking of," Larissa chimed in, "when are you returning to Haven?"

"I'm actually hoping to go tomorrow night."

The four other women literally cheered in response. Ellie felt uplifted by the response. It was nice to know she'd been missed. She had been so sure nobody would have noticed her sudden disappearance from the club.

"That's great," Sam exclaimed. "I've missed having a single friend to troll the Doms with."

The other three women were partnered up—with Masters of Haven no less. Masters and Mistresses of Haven were a group of experienced dominants who had been voted in by the members to be in charge of and help run the club. Only the most experienced, competent and respected dominants were voted in. It was an honour to be made Master. It also happened that Ellie's closest male friends were all Masters.

"Before I forget," Amara piped up. "Have you three got next Sunday marked off in your calendars for the dress fittings?"

Belle, Larissa and Ellie all nodded in response. Ellie had been shocked when Amara had asked her to be a bridesmaid for her upcoming wedding. In the time since they'd met, the two of them had grown close—Ellie honestly saw Amara as a big sister. She viewed Belle in a similar fashion, the two of them hitting it off immediately when they had met. But being asked to be a bridesmaid for Amara's wedding had been a shock as much as it had been an honour for Ellie.

"Sooo, Miss Ellie," Amara said in a teasing tone. "Are you going to scene with anyone tomorrow night? There are a lot of single Doms at the moment."

Ellie shook her head. "I'm not allowed to, remember? Grayson has that rule about submissives returning after a traumatic event. He laid down the law last night, telling me tomorrow I am to socialise only, then next week—if he feels I am coping well enough—I may be allowed to play. But he has to clear it first."

Amara rolled her eyes. "I forgot about that rule."

"We can still make trouble, though," Sam said. "Even if you aren't playing, we can torment some of the Doms we already know. Have some fun."

Ellie and Sam had made a name for themselves as brats who enjoyed tormenting their dominant friends and other Masters. Often, it resulted in small punishments for them, but the Doms were in on the joke. Ellie only ever acted the brat with people she knew and trusted. A few Doms she'd played with in the past had expected her to be a brat with them, but she couldn't. She withdrew with strangers. With friends, she was her true self.

"Too many submissive girls are focussed on being good girls now," Sam said with faux-disgust. "There's nobody for me to get into trouble with. They think the Doms don't like brats so they refuse to join me in escapades."

"Most Doms don't like brats," Ellie pointed out. "At least not in my experience."

"Ooh, you know who does like brats?" Belle leaned forward with a wiggle of her brows. "Parker."

That snagged Ellie's attention. "How do you know that?"

"I overheard him and Ambrose talking during the week. Parker asked where all the brats were and said he enjoyed brat taming but hadn't found one at Haven."

Parker was the latest addition to their circle of friends. Ambrose, Belle's partner and Dom, had known Parker when they were kids and they'd recently reconnected. When Belle had had an incident with her abusive stalker ex-boyfriend a few months ago, Parker had been a police officer on her case and had been socialising with them since.

Ellie bit her lip at the thought of Parker. She'd been immediately drawn to him. Within seconds, she'd known he was a Dom—the man exuded confidence and power as well as dominance. Often her submissive side came out around him, unlike when she was with her other dominant friends. Parker in the vanilla world was enticing and attractive to Ellie... She had to imagine Parker in Dom mode would be even more appealing. She might have developed a little crush on him in the short time they'd spent together. Not that she would do anything about it. Ellie didn't date. She didn't have time for a relationship. But if anyone could get her to begin, it would be her tall, dark and handsome new friend.

"There's another tick in the Parker box for Ellie," Sam teased.

Ellie rolled her eyes and tried to play off her interest. She'd made the mistake of telling her girlfriends she found Parker attractive months earlier and they'd been teasing her about it since. "I think the guy's hot. Don't the rest of you?"

They nodded. "Thank you. It's not a bloody crush. I'm not twelve."

It so *was* a crush, though. She hadn't seen him in weeks and had missed him.

"Look at her cheeks!" Larissa teased. "That's so stinking cute."

Ellie threw a cushion at the other blonde. "Quiet, you."

"I'm sorry," Amara interrupted. "Are we going to just ignore what she said about Grayson laying down the law?"

Belle nodded. "You know how serious he is about club rules. He even made me abide by that one, even though I already had Ambrose as a Dom."

Upon returning from an incident, whether in or outside of the club, Grayson ruled that all submissives needed the help of a Master to negotiate their first couple of scenes. Grayson, as the owner of Haven, was allowed to enforce those rules. As were the Masters and Mistresses. And they were already stifling Ellie. She might be considered new to the lifestyle still, with only a few months of experience under her belt, but she hadn't needed help negotiating since her first month attending Haven.

Grayson, however, saw Ellie as a little sister and had a seriously protective streak when it came to her. Since the incident, he'd become unbearable. He had forced her to speak to Sam in a professional context a few times to deal with the fall-out of the incident. He'd tried convincing her to stay away from Haven. She still hadn't figured out why he and Sullivan were against her joining Haven in the first place.

"He has the same rules for all submissives," Sam said.

As the receptionist of Haven, she was privy to more information than the rest of the submissives. She'd been doing the job for a couple of years and had seen it all.

"It's stifling," Ellie muttered. "He's overprotective as it is. But the incident just made him paranoid, too. If he thinks I'm letting him help negotiate scenes for me, he's got another thing coming."

Having not grown up with protective energy around her — her brother and father hadn't cared about her dating life, or lack thereof — she struggled when it came to her friends being protective and intrusive. At first, it had been comforting, but now it made little sense. They tended to treat her more like a kid sister than a grown woman capable of making her own decisions.

"Don't think of it as him being overprotective," Sam said. "It's simply club protocol."

"I hate being babied." Ellie sighed. "I may be new to the lifestyle but I'm not some young naïve girl. I've done years of reading and research about BDSM. I feel like the incident was just another excuse for him to hover."

The other woman disagreed, but Ellie couldn't help how she felt. Sometimes she thought she came across as ungrateful and petulant.

"We won't let him hover," Amara promised. "If he oversteps, I'll talk to him about it."

Ellie received sympathetic looks from her friends in response to her admission. She hated those looks. She'd been seeing them most of her life and it had grown tiresome.

"It could be worse. They could not care at all," Amara said.

That was true.

Ellie had to put on her big-girl pants and get used to being around Doms in Dom mode again. No matter how much she wanted to, she couldn't assume that every new man she met was a dirtbag or out to get her vulnerable to take advantage of her. She needed to be reminded that there were still good men out there. Maybe she'd even find one for herself.

About the Author

A born and bred Aussie, Liia hails from Perth, Western Australia. After spending her childhood years dreaming of far-off lands, she eventually discovered her love of romance and hasn't looked back since.

A self-proclaimed geek, she loves all things Disney and Star Wars. Being a bisexual, bipolar and ADHD battler, she is passionate about mental health and LGBTQIA+ rights, as well as advocating for animal rights.

When not writing, she can be found curled up with a good book, with her two dogs by her side.

Liia loves to hear from readers. You can find her contact information, website details and author profile page at https://www.totallybound.com

Home of Erotic Romance

Sign up for our newsletter and find out about all our
romance book releases, eBook sales and promotions,
sneak peeks and FREE romance books!

www.ingramcontent.com/pod-product-compliance
Lightning Source LLC
Chambersburg PA
CBHW021953010726
47494CB00003B/723